MAFIA KING'S BRIDE

A DARK BRATVA ARRANGED MARRIAGE ROMANCE

A J SUMMERS

Copyright © 2024 by A J Summers

All rights reserved.

No part of this book may be reproduced in any form or by any electronic or mechanical means, including information storage and retrieval systems, without written permission from the author, except for the use of brief quotations in a book review.

FOREWORD

Be sure to subscribe to my newsletter where you'll receive up to date information about my latest releases and special offers.

ONE

ANA

"Dochka."

The familiar word slices through the heavy air, pulling me from my thoughts. I turn, seeing my father standing in the doorway. He's dressed in a perfectly tailored suit, holding a small bouquet that feels like a cruel joke. His eyes are haunted as they meet mine. He's trying to smile, trying to be strong. For me.

I walk toward him without a word, stepping into his arms as they open, and the second his warmth wraps around me, something inside me breaks. A tear slips free, hot and fast, but I wipe it away quickly, as if it never existed. He can't know. He's carrying enough guilt without my pain adding to it.

"How are you holding up?" His voice is rougher than usual as he hands me the bouquet—small, delicate, like me. Like the old me. "Do you want me to stay? I can wait with you until it's time."

I force a smile so tight it hurts. "I'm fine, Papa. It's my wedding day, right? I'm happy."

The lie tastes bitter on my tongue. He sees through it,

his jaw tightening as he reaches out and cups my cheek, his touch too soft for this moment, for the nightmare this day has become. "You don't have to do this. I can find another way. We can delay—"

"No," I cut him off, my voice sharper than I intended. The bouquet slips from my hand, landing on the floor with a dull thud. "We both know there's no other way."

His face crumples, the weight of the world pressing down on him. He's been my rock, my protector, my everything since the day my mother died. He was the one who held me through every scraped knee, every disappointment, every victory. And now I have to save him.

Tears fill his eyes, and for the first time in my life, I see him break. My father—the man who never flinched when his men were gunned down, the man who stood tall even as his empire burned—is crying. I swallow down the scream clawing its way up my throat.

"Papa," I whisper, grabbing a handkerchief from the dresser and dabbing at his eyes. The sight of his tears shreds me to pieces, but I can't fall apart. Not now. Not yet.

"You were always dreaming about your wedding when you were little," he says, his voice cracking with nostalgia. "Your dolls, the dress, the big church. It was all you ever talked about."

I smile bitterly, the ache in my chest spreading. "That was before I knew what the world is like."

He shakes his head, pulling me closer. "The world may be ugly, *dochka*, but your dreams are still yours. I was supposed to protect you from all of this. Not," his voice breaks, and it feels like my heart is being ripped from my chest, "make you pay for my mistakes."

I can't hold it back anymore. The tears spill over, hot and unchecked, running down my face in streaks. "I'll be fine," I manage to say, even though it's a lie. A lie I've been telling myself since the day this nightmare began. I've learned from him how to put on a mask, how to make the world believe you're unbreakable when you're already shattered.

His hand drops to his side, but the look in his eyes is killing me.

"I know you will," he whispers, his voice filled with both pride and sorrow. "You're my daughter."

We stand in silence, the weight of what's coming pressing down on us both. This room feels like a tomb—cold, suffocating, the exact opposite of what a wedding should be. I always imagined a day filled with light, love, and laughter. I dreamed of a beautiful dress, walking down the aisle toward a man who looked at me as if I was his entire world.

Instead, I'm walking toward a man I despise.

No expenses have been spared, but there's no amount of luxury that can mask the truth. In a few short minutes, I'll be promising myself to a stranger—a man I'm marrying not for love, but for survival. Twelve-year-old me would have run screaming from this moment. She would have refused.

But I don't have that luxury. If I don't marry him, my father will lose everything. His empire, his men, maybe even his life.

What a sick, twisted fairytale.

My father steps back, clearing his throat. "I should check on things," he says, though his voice wavers with uncertainty.

I shake my head, cutting him off before he can offer to stay again. "I'll be fine. I'm Nikolas Petrov's daughter, after all." The words are meant to comfort him, but the pride in my voice feels hollow. Still, it makes him smile, a flicker of hope in his tired eyes.

He pulls me into one last hug, and I cling to him, holding on tighter than I ever have . "I'll see you at the chapel, *dochka*," he whispers.

I kiss his cheek, fighting the urge to beg him not to leave. Helplessly, I watch as the door closes behind him. The moment he's gone, my legs give out, and I collapse into the chair, burying my face in my hands.

My tears continue to fall freely, and I pray for a miracle. For the ground to swallow me whole and spit me out somewhere far, far away from here. Somewhere I can forget this day ever happened.

But I'm not a child anymore. I don't get to run and hide. This is my duty, my fate, and I'll walk down that aisle and marry the man I loathe to save the one person I love most in this world.

There's no other choice.

An hour later, I sit in front of the mirror, my hair twisted into a blooming low bun, my face smoothed and sculpted by layers of makeup. The woman staring back at me is a stranger—her lips too perfect, her eyes too bright, her expression too composed. It's as if I'm looking at a mask, rather than a person.

The makeup artist gently dabs beneath my eye with a small brush, her movements practiced and gentle. My eyelids flutter closed, grateful for the brief reprieve from staring at the stranger I've become.

"Do you have allergies?" she asks, her voice laced with concern.

"No. Why?" I reply, even though I already know the answer.

"You're teary," she explains, frowning a little as she

inspects her work.

I raise a hand instinctively to touch my face but catch myself just in time, letting my arm drop back to my lap. "I'm sorry."

She gives me a reassuring smile in the mirror. "It's okay. Brides cry all the time. It's an emotional day." She pauses, applying more powder under my eyes. "Don't worry, the mascara is waterproof. It won't run when you see your husband."

I don't correct her or tell her I'm not a typical emotional bride. It's the dread pressing down on me like a stone, threatening to crack me open.

I just want this wedding to be over.

She brushes the last bit of powder away. "He's quite the catch, you know. Your fiancé." She leans in, her voice dropping to a conspiratorial whisper. "He was on the cover of *Most Wanted Bachelors* last month. And now he's getting married to you."

Her eyes gleam with something—envy, maybe admiration. Either way, it twists in my gut like a knife. If only I could hand him over to her, let her take my place.

"Thank you," I murmur, unsure of what else to say.

She hesitates, biting her lip before asking, "Was it love at first sight?"

Love. The word tastes like ash in my mouth.

I almost laugh—an empty, bitter sound—but I hold it in. How could anyone think love had anything to do with this? Why would I love a man who is marrying me only to punish my father?

Dmitri Orlov. Heir to the Orlov empire. To the outside world, he's a businessman, the golden boy gracing magazine covers, his every move followed by cameras and admirers. But to those of us who know him—truly know him—he's the *pakhan*. A man feared for his ruthlessness, a man who crushes his enemies without blinking.

The makeup artist doesn't understand. She could never.

I let the silence stretch, and she takes my pause for confirmation, a dreamy smile spreading across her face. "I knew it," she says, nodding as if she's solved some great mystery. "With men like that, it's impossible not to fall in love with them. The way they look at you, it gives you butterflies."

If only she knew. There are no butterflies, only terror.

I sigh, glancing back at the mirror. She's still waiting for an answer, her expression expectant. "Yes," I lie, forcing a smile. "It was... love at first sight. We met at an event, and when I saw him across the room, I just knew."

Her smile widens, and she nods, satisfied. I feel the weight of my lie settle like a stone in my chest.

THE ORGAN'S DEEP, resonant chords fill the air as the chapel doors swing open. I take a deep breath, the veil pressing lightly against my face, my wedding gown heavy around me like chains. My father's arm slips through mine, his grip steadying me.

"*Dochka*," he whispers, his voice thick with emotion. "I'm proud of you."

I swallow the lump in my throat, my lips trembling as I force a smile. "Thank you, Papa."

We walk down the aisle together, each step a deliberate effort to keep my body from betraying the panic bubbling just beneath the surface. Faces blur in my peripheral vision —familiar faces, dangerous faces. Friends and enemies alike are watching, waiting.

I keep my gaze forward, locked on the man standing at the altar.

Dmitri Orlov.

He towers over the priest, his expression unreadable, his broad shoulders rigid beneath the perfectly tailored suit. His features are sharp, striking—handsome, yes, but in a way that feels dangerous, predatory. The kind of beauty that warns you not to get too close.

My heart stutters as our eyes meet through the thin veil. There's a cold intensity in his gaze, like he's stripping me bare, seeing parts of me I've never shown to anyone. I look away, focusing on the priest's voice, though the words slip past me like fog.

The vows come and go, my voice sounding distant and hollow as I recite the lines I've memorized. Dmitri's response is short and clipped. He barely looks at me, yet I can feel the weight of his presence, the power he exudes.

"And now," the priest announces, "you may kiss the bride."

The words hang in the air, heavy with finality. I stand frozen, my body stiff, waiting for him to move. For a moment, nothing happens. Then, slowly, Dmitri reaches out, lifting my veil.

I hold my breath as his fingers graze my skin, his touch unexpectedly gentle. He steps closer, and I can feel the warmth of his body, the clean, masculine scent filling the space between us.

He leans in, his breath ghosting over my lips, and for a fleeting second, I wonder if he's going to stop. If he'll pull away and leave this moment unfinished.

But he doesn't.

His lips brush against mine—a soft, barely-there touch, yet it ignites something strange and unwelcome inside me.

It's a simple kiss, brief and restrained, but my heart is pounding in my chest, my pulse thrumming loudly in my ears. A flicker of heat surges through me, confusing and unwanted.

He pulls away before I can process the feeling, and the room erupts in applause. My hands are trembling as I clasp them together, trying to hold on to something, anything, that makes sense. I glance at my father, watching him wipe a tear from his cheek, but all I can think about is the ghost of Dmitri's lips on mine.

As we step outside the chapel, Dmitri's hand slips from mine.

"I'll see you at the reception," he says, his voice detached. "There are things I need to attend to."

Without waiting for my response, he turns and walks away, his broad back disappearing into the crowd.

I stand there, watching him go, swallowing down the knot of anger and hurt that rises in my throat. The applause still rings in my ears, but all I feel is emptiness. The tears burn behind my eyes, but I force them back, smiling for the crowd as they spill out of the church.

Married.

To a man who couldn't even stay by my side after the ceremony.

TWO
DMITRI

"Mr. Pavlov is waiting in your office," Jakob, my secretary, says as I stride in.

I nod, not breaking pace, and push open the door.

Igor Pavlov, the *pakhan* of one of the New Jersey Bratvas, stands as soon as he sees me. His massive hand stretches out, and I grasp it firmly. "Orlov," he greets me with a smirk. "You could've scheduled this for another time."

"Why would I?" I drop his hand and move behind my desk, letting my briefcase hit the floor with a thud.

He shrugs, watching me with sharp, calculating eyes. "You just got married. Figured you'd be on your honeymoon. Or are the rumors true?"

I arch an eyebrow, leaning back in my chair. "Rumors?"

Before he can answer, there's a knock. The door swings open, and Alexey steps in, another *pakhan*, with a reputation as unpredictable as his temper. He doesn't bother with formalities, taking a seat next to Igor like he owns the place.

"Roman won't be joining us," Alexey informs us, lighting a cigar with a flick of his lighter. "He's dealing with some . . . unpleasantness."

I loosen my tie, ignoring the blatant disrespect. This meeting is delicate. Patience is key. For now.

"I trust you will relay my message to him," I say coldly. "Let's get this started."

Alexey takes a slow drag from his cigar, blowing the smoke in a deliberate circle. I could snap his neck for the sheer insolence, but today's not the day. No, today requires tact. We're here to talk about power. Mine, to be exact.

I reach into my drawer, pull out a document, and slap it onto the desk. "Here's a list of the territories our organizations control. It's extensive, as you both know. But I'm here to propose an alliance."

Igor's frown deepens and Alexey's eyes narrow.

"An alliance?" Igor leans forward, disbelief etched on his face. "Why would *you* want that?"

Alexey nods, puffing on his cigar, his expression skeptical. "You've got more than all of us combined. More money. More connections. Hell, you came to this country later than we did and still outran us. Why do you need us?"

I let the silence hang, their doubt filling the room like the stench of Alexey's cigar. Only then do I speak. "I've heard whispers. Some gangs think the Bratva doesn't belong here. They plan to run us into the ground, starting with the largest groups. I don't take threats lightly, and we've all seen our power challenged before. We may have our differences but we're brothers. We should solidify our dominance before they make their move."

Alexey takes another slow puff, his eyes calculating. "If you're really doing this for the Bratva, why not involve the other *pakhans*? Like your father-in-law." He sneers at the words, pushing a clear button. "Nikolai Petrov might be disgraced, but he still commands respect on his side of the city. You gonna work with him?"

I feel my jaw tighten, the muscle twitching with the effort it takes to remain composed. My hands clench under the desk as his words slice through the air.

Nikolai Petrov. The traitor.

"Never," I hiss, the word cutting the air like a blade. "He's a disgrace to the Bratva, and I don't work with men who break our code."

Alexey blows another smoke ring, his eyes gleaming with amusement. "The code? If I recall, Orlov, when someone tries to steal what's yours, you cut off his arms, his legs, and ensure he never tries again. But you didn't do that, did you? Instead, you married his daughter. To the rest of the world, you're partners with the Petrovs now."

He's poking at an open wound, and he knows it. The truth is, in the Bratva, a marriage between two families is seen as a strengthening of bonds. A sign of unity.

But that's not what this is. Not for me.

I lean forward, locking eyes with Alexey, my voice low and dangerous. "I didn't marry Anastasia to strengthen anything. I married her to destroy him. I took the one thing that matters to Nikolai Petrov. His daughter is mine now, and when he dies, there'll be no one left to inherit his empire."

I SEE the flicker of understanding in their eyes as the truth settles in.

This isn't about partnership. This is about annihilation.

Igor chuckles, shaking his head in admiration. "I have to admit, I didn't see that coming. Taking the one thing he cares about? That's cold, even for you, Orlov."

Alexey leans back, taking a final drag of his cigar before stubbing it out on the edge of my desk. "Clever. Ruthless."

He pauses, a smile tugging at his lips. "And here I thought you'd gone soft after marriage. But I'm in. It'd be stupid to say no, considering your new... influence."

I let a slow, predatory smile creep across my face. I've won them over. I've got them right where I want them.

Before the wedding, Alexey would have fought me tooth and nail, and Igor would've stayed on the sidelines, waiting to see which way the wind blew. But now? Now that I have Anastasia Petrov under my thumb, now that the world believes I'm in league with her father?

I hold all the cards.

They think they're aligning with me for power. They don't realize they're just pawns in my game. And once Nikolai Petrov is gone, every last piece of his empire will fall to me. No one will dare challenge me.

The game isn't over. It's only just begun.

HOURS LATER, with the sun already sunk beneath the clouds, I pull into the driveway of my mansion on Long Island, the weight of the day pressing heavily on my shoulders. The headlights sweep across the pristine lawn as I park the car near the house, killing the engine with a press of my finger. My valet is already there, stepping forward to take the fob from my hand without a word. I nod in acknowledgment and head inside.

The door swings open before I even reach it, and Janet, my housekeeper, greets me with a polite nod, her posture rigid and professional as always.

"Welcome, sir."

"Thank you, Janet," I reply, shrugging out of my coat. She takes it from me with a practiced motion.

I move swiftly through the foyer, my footsteps echoing through the expansive hallway, heading past the grand double staircase. My room is on the third floor, and Ana's is located on the second. A deliberate arrangement. I wanted distance between us. Enough privacy to avoid unnecessary run-ins because there's no reason for us to interact more than necessary. She's my wife only in name, nothing more.

"Your dinner is ready in the dining room, sir," Janet says as I reach the base of the stairs.

I shake my head, not even slowing my pace. "Not tonight. Just bring me water."

"Yes, sir."

My foot touches the first step, but something stops me cold. A thought that sneaks in, unwelcome and persistent. I turn my head slightly, the words leaving my mouth before I can stop them.

"Janet."

She pauses, looking up. "Yes, sir?"

"My... wife." The word feels foreign, uncomfortable. "Did she eat?"

Janet's expression shifts, a slight crease forming between her brows. "Mrs. Orlov hasn't left her room all day, sir. I tried taking her meals up, but she refused them."

My frown deepens. "She hasn't eaten since I left?"

"Not since last night," she clarifies gently.

That's almost twenty-four hours. What is she playing at? Is this some kind of childish rebellion? Starving herself to make it look like I'm some monster who locks his wife away without food? I rub my temples, trying to shake the irritation bubbling beneath my skin.

"Take a plate to her room."

Janet hesitates, her lips parting as if to protest. "I've tried, sir. She wouldn't answer the door."

"Try again," I snap, my patience wearing thin. "Do as I say."

Without waiting for her response, I continue up the stairs, my steps heavy with frustration. This ends now. If she thinks she can pull some stunt to make me look like a villain, she's sorely mistaken. She's lucky I don't demand more from her—she could be working for me, earning her keep, but instead, she does nothing but sit around all day.

I stop in front of her door and make a fist, knocking firmly.

No answer.

I knock again, harder this time. "Ana. I need to talk to you."

Silence.

Panic flickers in the back of my mind, unwelcome and ridiculous. Has she fainted? Is she lying unconscious behind that door? I press my ear to the wood, listening for any sound, any indication that she's in there. My heart picks up its pace.

"Ana, answer me." My voice is sharper now, tinged with an edge I rarely show. "Ana!"

Still nothing.

Without thinking, I brace myself, ready to kick the door in if necessary. My foot is poised when the door suddenly creaks open. I stumble slightly, surprised, and straighten, clearing my throat to mask the moment of weakness.

She stands in the doorway, her appearance disheveled and raw. Her dark hair falls in tangled curls around her face, her eyes rimmed with smudged black makeup, and her lower lip is swollen like she's been biting it all day. For a split second, I'm hit with an image I shouldn't be thinking of —a post-coital haze that lingers after a night of passion. The thought catches me off guard, and I shake it off.

"What?" she asks, her voice flat, emotionless.

I stare at her, trying to remember why I'm here. Her appearance has thrown me off, but I quickly recover. I narrow my eyes, my voice cold and clipped. "Janet told me you haven't eaten all day."

She shrugs, a flicker of defiance in her eyes. "Is that a problem?"

A problem? The sheer audacity of her words leaves me momentarily speechless. Is this a game to her?

"If you don't eat, you'll get sick," I say, my tone hardening. "I won't have you playing these tricks."

She cuts me off before I can finish. "Tricks? You think I'm doing this to get back at you for threatening to kill my father?"

The bluntness of her words knocks the air out of me. For a second, I don't respond. She knows exactly what I'm capable of, and she's daring to challenge me.

I step closer, and when I see the flicker of fear cross her face, I stop short. "Would you rather I expose your father's betrayal to the world? Do you know what happens to traitors in our world, *kotyonok*?" My voice drops, laced with danger.

Her chin lifts defiantly, her eyes burning with hatred. "First off, I'm not your kitten," she snaps. "And yes, I know what happens. But you act like you're any better. You're feared, Dmitri, but not respected. You don't inspire loyalty—you inspire terror. And there's a difference."

Her words are sharp. Alexey's taunts from earlier echo in my mind: *What other choice do I have?*

I close the distance between us in one swift motion, my hand shooting out to grab her chin. My fingers grip her jaw, forcing her to look at me. "Don't push me, Ana," I say quietly, my voice dark and dangerous. "Your father betrayed mine—betrayed my family. He tried to take what was mine before my father's body was even cold. Be thankful I didn't end him right there."

Her eyes widen, and I see another flicker of fear flash across her face. For a moment, I think I've broken through her defiance. But then she composes herself, forcing her features into a mask of calm.

"And what guarantee do I have that you won't betray me?" Her voice is low, almost a whisper. "You're not a man to trust, Dmitri. You're a man to fear."

I release her, letting my hand fall away. She stumbles back, but there's something almost proud in the way she recovers, in the way she stands there, facing me with her chin held high. Almost admirable.

Almost.

I turn my head as Janet's footsteps echo up the stairs, and she appears with a tray of food in hand.

"Janet went through the trouble of making you dinner," I say, my voice flat and final. "Don't let it go to waste." Without another word, I turn on my heel and leave, heading toward my own room.

As I climb the stairs, I flex my hand, trying to release the tension coiled in my fingers. I didn't expect her to get under my skin like this. It usually takes more for someone to rile me up.

But Ana managed to do it effortlessly.

Still, I've made my point clear. If she tries anything else, I'll show her exactly who she's dealing with.

Because when I exact revenge, I leave no one standing.

THREE
ANA

The house feels too quiet as I step out of my room; an oppressive silence seems to press against my ears, making the vastness of this mansion even more suffocating. It's been less than two weeks since I married Dmitri Orlov, yet it feels like a lifetime, each day stretching endlessly in this cavernous prison. I walk down the long hallway, my footsteps echoing unnaturally loud in the empty space, a reminder that despite the grandness of this house, there's nothing for me here.

I head downstairs, desperate for a small moment of normalcy—a cup of coffee to start my day. But even that feels hollow, a ritual that no longer brings comfort. As I enter the kitchen, I find Janet busy at the stove. She notices me immediately, turning with a polite nod.

"Good morning, ma'am. What would you like for breakfast?" she asks, her voice as warm as ever, but I can see the concern flickering behind her eyes.

It's the same concern she's shown every morning since I moved in, every time I've turned down a meal. "Nothing, thank you, Janet. I'll just make myself some coffee."

Her lips press into a thin line, but she doesn't push. She never does, and I feel a pang of guilt. She's only doing her job, and yet here I am, punishing her with my cold indifference because I'm trapped in this house—this life—against my will.

"Okay," she says softly, turning back to the stove.

I brew the coffee in silence, focusing on the task as if it's the only thing tethering me to reality. The machine is state-of-the-art, of course. Dmitri doesn't do anything halfway. It's the one thing I can stand in this place—the only semblance of control I have left. I take a sip, letting the bitterness roll over my tongue, but even that can't shake the heaviness sitting in my chest.

After finishing the cup, I drop it in the sink and make my way back upstairs, eager to retreat to the one space that feels remotely safe: my room. As I climb the stairs, I hear the faint creak of a door opening on the third floor. My heartbeat spikes, my legs moving faster without conscious thought. Dmitri. I don't even need to look to know it's him.

I quicken my pace, hurrying back to my room and closing the door behind me with a soft click. My pulse is still racing, and I press my back against the wood, forcing myself to breathe. I shouldn't be afraid of him. Dmitri Orlov might be a monster to others, but to me, he's just... indifferent. Cold. And yet, I find myself avoiding him at every turn, not out of fear, but out of sheer revulsion for the man I'm now tied to.

Every interaction with him feels like standing on the edge of a cliff, staring into a dark abyss. It's not fear that makes me retreat—it's the weight of knowing I married him not for love, but because one man's hatred for my father outmatched even his thirst for revenge.

I sigh heavily, peeling myself away from the door and

heading to the bathroom. Today, at least, I have work to keep me occupied. It's the only thing I have left to cling to, the one thing that reminds me I had a life before all of this. A purpose.

"MRS. ORLOV."

The sound of the name stops me in my tracks. I turn, realizing with a jolt that the senior partner calling out is addressing me.

Mrs. Orlov.

The name feels like sandpaper in my mouth, rough and unwelcome.

Anastasia Orlov. I mentally repeat it, trying to make sense of the new identity forced upon me. The more I say it, the more it feels like a bad joke. But the man walking toward me doesn't know the truth. He sees me as Dmitri's wife, and that means I have to play the part.

"Good morning, sir," I say, forcing a smile that barely touches my eyes.

He catches up to me, his expression warm. "For a moment, I thought I had the wrong person. Welcome back!" He extends his hand, and I shake it mechanically. "How was your honeymoon?"

Honeymoon.

I almost laugh. The week I spent locked in my room, pretending that none of this was happening? I raise an eyebrow, but he continues, oblivious.

"I didn't expect you to be back so soon," he adds as we walk toward the elevator. "But I'm glad you are. We have some cases that are right up your alley. Of course, take your time easing back in. I'm sure you'll want to leave early these first few months to enjoy married life."

Married life. Another bitter laugh sits on the edge of my tongue, but I swallow it down, keeping my voice neutral. "Don't worry about me. Work comes first."

He gives me a curious look, no doubt wondering why I'm choosing to immerse myself in work instead of spending time with my husband. But I don't explain. I don't owe him —or anyone—an explanation.

The elevator doors open, and I step inside, pressing the button for the tenth floor. "I'll have Steve bring you an urgent case," the partner says as the doors begin to close. "Welcome back, Anastasia."

The elevator ride is silent, and as soon as I reach my floor, I exhale, stepping out into the familiar space of my office. It looks exactly as I left it, everything in its place as if nothing in my life has changed. But it has.

I walk to my desk, running my fingers over the smooth wood before sitting down. This is where I belong—where I've always belonged. Not in Dmitri's mansion. Not playing the role of a dutiful wife. Here, surrounded by folders and paperwork, with nothing but my cases to occupy my mind.

A soft knock at the door pulls me from my thoughts. Steve walks in, holding a thick folder and a bouquet of roses. I suppress the urge to roll my eyes.

"Congratulations, Mrs. Orlov," he says, placing the flowers and the folder on my desk and sitting down in front of me. "How does it feel to be married?"

Like my life is over. Like I'm trapped in a cage I can't escape. Like I've lost every part of myself that ever mattered.

I force another smile, my jaw tight with tension. "It's... amazing," I lie, the words tasting like ash.

Steve grins, oblivious. "I have to admit, I didn't believe it when I heard you were getting married. You never mentioned a boyfriend, and now you're Mrs. Orlov? Wow. And why wasn't I invited to the wedding?"

I laugh lightly, keeping up the charade. "It was a surprise," I say, the lie slipping out easily. "We wanted to keep it small."

He nods, buying it without question, but his eyes linger on me, as if searching for something beneath the surface. "Well, I'm happy for you. But you know, if you ever get tired of the married life, I'm still available." He winks, and I roll my eyes.

"That ship has sailed, Steve," I say lightly. "Now tell me about the case."

He hands me the folder, and I flip it open, skimming the details. Money laundering and fraud. It's a typical case for me—defending someone whose hands are dirty but not as dirty as the people they stole from. It's the kind of work I've grown numb to.

As I read through the file, I can feel the familiar pull of focus returning. Work is my refuge. It's the only thing that keeps me from drowning in the reality of my life.

Steve stands to leave, and I nod, already diving into the case.

The door closes behind him, and I exhale a long, deep sigh.

Despite my new name, I don't feel like Mrs. Orlov here. I'm still Anastasia Petrov. And in this office, I can almost pretend that nothing has changed. But the moment I step outside these walls, I'll be reminded of the truth: that my life is no longer my own.

MY PHONE BEEPS as I pull into the garage, breaking the silence. It's a reminder about the case I've been assigned to, but the glowing screen also shows the time. Ten-thirty p.m. I had no idea it was so late, but then again, time has lost all meaning lately. The office is the only place that feels like it hasn't shifted into something unrecognizable. The only reason I'm here at all is because the bed in this mansion is softer than my chair at work, and that's hardly a selling point.

I grab my bag and step out of the car, moving toward the front door. When the handle doesn't budge, I knock, and within seconds, Janet opens the door, still in her apron, her rubber gloves covered in soap suds.

"Welcome, ma'am," she says politely, her voice calm and predictable.

Does this woman ever sleep?

I nod, feeling an unexpected wave of exhaustion hit me.

"Would you like some dinner?" Janet offers, pausing with the hesitancy of someone who already knows the answer. "There's still some risotto left. I made it for Mr. Orlov."

Risotto. The idea of it might have been appealing if it hadn't come with the added detail of being "for Mr. Orlov." The very thought of eating what he was meant to enjoy makes my stomach churn.

"No, thank you," I say, trying to sound polite despite the gnawing hunger making itself known. My stomach growls in protest, a reminder that the only thing I've eaten all day is a half-stale sandwich at lunch.

Janet doesn't press further, and I'm grateful for it. "I'll go to my room. Goodnight."

I yank my bag higher on my shoulder and head for the stairs, hoping to make it to my room before—

Shit.

Dmitri.

He appears at the top of the stairs, stepping out of the shadows of the second floor. The gray T-shirt he's wearing stretches across his chest, showing off the hard muscles beneath, and the black sweatpants hang just low enough to hint at the strong lines of his body. It should be illegal for a man like him to look this good. It's almost comical, really, how the universe saw fit to give him both power and the body of a Greek god.

"Ana," his deep voice cuts through my thoughts as he approaches, and I freeze on the stairs.

I take my time replying, dreading what this encounter will bring. "Yes?"

He's standing just a few steps away, too close for comfort, and I can't help but notice how the air seems heavier when he's nearby. "Do you have a moment?"

It is a question, but it's more of a command, really.

And what could we possibly have to talk about?

I shake my head. "No. And I doubt there's anything we need to discuss unless it involves making my life more miserable."

Without waiting for his response, I move around him and head up the stairs, trying to escape. I hear his footsteps behind me. I bolt to my room, slamming the door shut behind me.

"Good riddance to bad rubbish," I mutter, flopping onto my bed. My body feels like dead weight, drained from the day, from *this*—all of this. The migraine that's been brewing at the edge of my skull throbs, and I rub my temples, trying to push away the exhaustion and frustration.

How the hell have I created this shit in my life? And how do I uncreate it?

There's a knock on my door.

Seriously?

"Ana?" Dmitri's voice is on the other side of the door. "I waited for you all evening. Why didn't you call and tell me you'd be late?"

What now?

I sit up, frowning, disbelief etching across my face. He waited for me? That can't be right. But before I can process the thought, he keeps talking.

"You should know better than to stay out late like that."

I storm across the room and throw the door open, glaring up at him. "Why are you butting into my business?"

Dmitri's eyes darken with annoyance. "Your business? Your safety *is* my business. There are people out there who wouldn't hesitate to use you to get to me."

"And whose fault is that?" I snap, taking a step forward, fury bubbling inside me. "I didn't ask to be included in your life, Dmitri. Before you, I never had to worry about being snatched up on the way home. So, don't put that on me. If you think I'm at risk, find a way to protect me. *Without me noticing.*"

I turn to walk away, but his hand closes around my wrist, and before I can pull free, he yanks me into the hallway. His other hand presses against the wall beside my head, caging me in, his body towering over mine.

His eyes meet mine, and they burn with something intense, something I can't name but feel in the pit of my stomach. It makes my pulse race.

"You like to play games, don't you, *kotyonok*?" His voice is a rumble, washing over my skin like a warm shower at the end of a long day.

"Don't call me that," I spit, lifting my chin in defiance.

"I'm not your kitten. I'm nothing to you but the girl you bullied into taking your last name."

He lets out a dark laugh, the sound causing goosebumps to pop over my arms. His hand, large and warm, brushes over my cheek, and I hate that my body reacts, a flutter of something unwelcome blooming in my chest.

"Bullied?" he murmurs, his thumb tracing the edge of my lip. "I gave your father a choice. Marriage or death. He chose to give you to me rather than pay the price himself."

The rage that fills me is sudden and blinding. How dare he speak about my father like that?

"So, what's in it for you?" I hiss, glaring up at him. "What do *you* get out of this?"

"Influence. Power. Revenge." His smirk is cold, his eyes glinting with satisfaction.

"My father is a better man than you'll ever be."

His smirk only deepens. "Is that why you bend the law for him?"

"None of *your* business."

"But it is," he says, voice soft but menacing. "You're mine now, Ana, and everything you do reflects on me. That's why I want you to stop working."

The words slam into me like a punch, and I blink, not sure I heard him right. "You *what?*"

"You heard me. Quit your job."

I laugh bitterly, stepping away from him, folding my arms. "You have some nerve. What's next? Are you going to lock me in this mansion and parade me around like a trophy at your parties?"

He doesn't flinch. "I might."

I could burn a hole through his head with the look I give him. "I'm not quitting my job, Dmitri. Do your worst."

"You will," he says, his voice lowering, "or you'll work for me. Exclusively."

I stare at him, incredulous. His arrogance is truly astounding. He actually believes the world revolves around him.

Mirthless laughter bubbles out of me, and I shake my head. "You're delusional, Dmitri. I'm Anastasia Petrov, and I don't give a damn what you want. Go ahead and try to make me quit. I dare you."

For a moment, he just stands there, staring at me like he's assessing whether or not I'm serious. Then, without a word, he steps back. I take the opportunity to wrench open the door and slip back inside, slamming it behind me.

As I press my back against the door, the adrenaline starts to fade, and my heart pounds like I've just run a marathon.

"Holy mackerel," I breathe, trying to steady myself.

I'm not usually one for confrontation, but there's something about Dmitri that makes my blood boil. The words I hurled at him felt good. They weren't rehearsed, they weren't planned—they just came out, and in that moment, I felt powerful.

I smile to myself as I head for the bathroom. The image of Dmitri's face when I stormed off is burned into my mind, and I know it'll be a long time before he forgets it.

Feeling victorious, I soak in the bath, letting the tension drain from my body. But as I finally crawl into bed, Dmitri's words from our first argument creep into my mind. His threat. His promise to make my father pay if I cross him.

If he ever touches my father, I'll never forgive him.

And I'll make sure Dmitri pays for it in ways he never sees coming.

FOUR
DMITRI

I head down the hallway from the conference room, just having concluded a meeting with other members of the Bratva who've come to pledge their allegiance and support to the Orlov enterprise.

Some of them, like Alexey, didn't seem so willing, but I could tell they *knew* they didn't have a choice. I didn't give them one.

And they don't deserve it, either, because many of them have forgotten what they did to my family after my father died.

Nikolai Petrov might have committed the biggest betrayal, but the others aren't blameless. They all tried to take a piece of what's mine, coming through side channels because they thought I was too wrapped up in grief to notice.

I suppose, in some way, I have to thank Nikolai for being so bold in his claim. If he weren't, I wouldn't have gained the upper hand I now enjoy. Even though his daughter tests my patience every single day and I have to summon every shred of self-control I have when I'm around her.

She's an expert at getting under my skin. It's a damn shame that a woman that gorgeous, with eyes that look like a sunny day and wild curls that tempt a man, would come with a fierce personality like that.

"Sir," Jakob stops me as I near my office door, "I couldn't stop her. She was going to make a scene, and I know how much you hate that, so I... I let her come through."

My eyebrows furrow. "Who?"

"Miss Bianchi."

Lucia?

Hell.

"I'm sorry." Jakob bows halfway.

I shake my head. "It's fine. I'll take care of her."

My lips are curled with displeasure as I walk into my office to see Lucia seated in my chair, her legs crossed on my desk.

"You seem to have forgotten your place, Lucia," I say through gritted teeth.

She shoots me a coy look, slowly removing her legs and taking her sweet time standing up. She's wearing a coat, but I can tell she has very little on underneath.

"I heard you got married," she says, stopping a few inches away. "Why didn't you send me an invitation? Aren't we friends?"

"We're not friends, and you should leave."

Lucia brings her finger to her mouth, slipping it past her lips. I roll my eyes at her failed attempt at seduction.

"Oh? We aren't? Well," she shrugs, "technically, you're right. Because friends don't screw each other every day, taste each other's bodies, lick the sweat off—"

"What do you want?" I cut in, walking past her and heading to my chair.

Lucia and I have a past. We met at a function that her father, a man involved with the Bratva, hosted. She was flirty, I had been drinking, and she didn't say no when I asked her to come to my hotel with me.

But our wild, tumultuous affair ended when I realized that she'll sleep with anyone as long as they are powerful enough. I didn't judge her for it because we weren't in a relationship, but I wasn't the type to share, either.

"What do you think?" she asks, walking back to my desk and pulling out a chair. She sits down and places one leg on the desk, giving me an unobstructed view into her coat.

Once upon a time, I would've locked my door and bent her over my desk.

"If you're not here for something serious, I suggest you leave, Lucia."

"Is it true that you're working with Nikolai Petrov?"

"Who told you that?" I ask, vaguely remembering that I had the same conversation with someone else recently. Was it Alexey?

She shrugs, smacking her lips. "I didn't hear it from just one person. I was at a party yesterday, and your marriage to Anastasia Petrov was all anyone could talk about. You've succeeded in garnering fear, respect, and envy, Dmitri." Lucia smiles. "But I know what Nikolai did to your father. I know what the others tried to do. I thought you'd be interested in knowing that they think you two are allies."

Annoyance and irritation rush through me, but I keep my cool. Even if what she's saying is the truth, I know she's trying to get a rise out of me.

"You shouldn't be a tattletale, Lucia. Your father wouldn't like that."

Lucia stands up from her seat and comes to perch at the edge of my desk. I let her run her fingers over my arm, knowing that the quicker I attend to her whims, the faster I'll get rid of her. Unless my patience wears off first.

"You know, it's working in your favor, being a son-in-law of Petrov's. The only problem is," her finger curls around my tie, and she tugs at it, "he's not exactly paying for his crime. In fact, he's starting to gain more attention. He's now related to the Orlovs, after all. One of the biggest, or," Lucia's nails brush across the stubble on my chin, "should I say, *the* biggest empire in our little world."

Bullshit. I grit my teeth. If I'm the reason Nikolai Petrov is gaining more popularity, then I'd rather burn him and everything he has to the ground.

When Lucia's thumb brushes my lips, I smack her hand away and glare at her.

"Don't you dare. The only reason I'm still entertaining you is because you're not enough of a nuisance to warrant extra measures. I could easily tell your father that you've been going around frolicking with his enemies."

She gasps. "You wouldn't."

A corner of my mouth curls into a mean smirk. "You want to try me?"

With a huff, Lucia gets off my desk. She stands with her hands on her hips, pouting.

"You're no fun. I used to like you because you were less talk and more action, but you've lost your spark. Is it because of your wife? Is she not pleasing you enough? You know—"

I shake my head when she opens her coat completely, stepping forward and leaving it on the floor. There's nothing on her body but lingerie and a garter. "If you wanted to get married that bad, you could've asked me.

I'm not a fan of commitment, but I would've done it for you."

I scoff. The sight of her body no longer turns me on. That's how easy it is to turn off my emotions, even the strong ones like lust and anger—with anyone at all. The only person I'm having a problem with is Ana.

No matter how much I try, the thought and sight of her evokes a reaction.

Like last night.

When she told me that she wasn't going to be like everyone else, that I'd better give my ego a reality check, or she was going to do it for me. *What the—*

"You could've done things the usual way, you know." Lucia runs her hand over her chest and cups her breasts. "My father has enough influence to buy you connections overseas. Not just here. Now everyone thinks you've forgiven the man who betrayed you. Who didn't even wait until your father's body was in the grave to steal from you. Undermining your ability to lead, to step into your father's shoes."

"Get. Out." My words are deathly cold, and my throat is choked with emotions too hard to swallow. My eyes sink into hers with a fury that has her staggering back out of fear.

Because she knows what I'm capable of.

"You were a pest seconds ago," I say harshly. "But now, the sight of you disgusts me. Leave."

When Lucia doesn't move as quickly as I want her to, I call Jakob.

He walks into the office as she's picking up her coat, and Lucia's face turns red when she sees him. It's a message—*you're worth nothing to me, so if you're going to be on display, you might as well show everyone.*

"See her out."

"I hate you," she whimpers, hastily buttoning her coat and grabbing her bag as she storms out of my office, her heels clicking on the floor.

I immediately raise my fist as the door closes, and it takes every last shred of my will to keep from breaking it on the hard, almost impenetrable wood.

"Fuck." I run my fingers through my hair. "Fuck!"

This is Nikolai's fault.

No. I shake my head. It's mine. I'm the one who chose to take his daughter and nothing more. I should send a message that makes it clear I have no dealings with him.

Nothing at all.

Jakob returns to my office when I call him.

"I want you to round up five men. Take them to any establishment belonging to Nikolai Petrov and give them instructions to cause enough ruckus to send a clear message that we aren't cordial. Got it?"

He nods firmly. "Yes, boss."

"Go."

And if that doesn't work, I'll have to step in personally. For everyone's sake, I hope it doesn't come down to that.

JANET OPENS the door for me, slightly bowing in greeting.

"Good evening, Janet."

She collects my bag and jacket, heading to my room to drop them off. I called beforehand to inform her that I wouldn't be eating dinner again. I didn't tell her it was because I was in a foul mood, which I still am.

I head for the stairs and then decide to go to my study to attend to an email I received on my way home. A meeting with Lucia's father—who must've gotten a call from his whiny, entitled daughter.

In a way, I admire her relentlessness, and I intend to use the meeting to my advantage, but it's pesky and bothersome that she doesn't know when she's not wanted.

At least when it comes to me.

As I walk down the hallway that leads to my study, I hear footsteps coming from behind. Since I sent Janet to my room, I am curious about who's in this part of the house. I turn and take a few steps forward, coming face-to-face with Ana.

She has on a faded blue top and shorts that stop at the hem of the shirt, leaving her legs bare.

Her legs draw me in, asking to be wrapped around something. And I can imagine a couple of places where I'd like them to be. While I do things to other parts of her body, to see just how unruly and untamed she can be. And those lips—

How am I just noticing that she has a pale pink upper lip while the bottom one darkens a little around its curves?

"Can I help you?" Her curt tone pulls me out of my short reverie.

I shake my head, noticing that she's glaring at me.

"No," I respond.

Why was I ogling her?

She's Anastasia Petrov, for goodness sakes. My last name is just an attaché that means nothing but formality. If she were handed a gun and asked to shoot me, she wouldn't hesitate.

"Okay." She shrugs and turns away.

I turn too, but my phone beeps, and I take it out of my pocket.

"I just saw Nikolai Petrov with Alexey. They're sharing a drink. Looks like your alliance is falling apart, big boy."

Lucia. If she was trying to rile me up, she succeeded.

I turn on my heels.

"Ana."

She takes two steps forward before stopping. She's not going to give me an audience, I see.

"Your father isn't allowed to step foot in this house, and you're not allowed to see him from now on."

Ana turns slowly, and I see the confusion on her face, in her raised eyebrows and tilted head.

"What do you mean? I'm not *allowed* to see Papa? That wasn't the agreement we had. I've told you several times, Dmitri. Whatever form of control you have over your men, it's not going to work for me," she increases her pitch with the last word. "I'm not your slave or your toy."

Maybe it's because of the text I just received, the conversation I had with Alexey, or the fact that he went behind my back, but something in me snaps.

I march up to her, taking long strides as I keep my eyes fixed on her. We've been playing this game for far longer than I like, and it's time to make her see things the way she should.

My way.

"You will not see your father again," I repeat. "The day you do will be the last time you'll know his whereabouts."

"Are you going to kill him? Is that what you're saying? Then why haven't you done it already? It wouldn't be your first time, would it? Silencing someone who does the same things you do because you have more power," she challenges me.

Don't let her slip under your skin, Dmitri.

"Your father and mine were as close as brothers. He

might not have told you, but my father helped him build what he has now and didn't ask for anything in return. But the second my father died, yours started reaching out to other *pakhans*, allying. He used them to start a fight against me."

I swallow hard before continuing, "He thought I'd be too caught up in grief to strike back. Your father," I jab my finger in the air, "felt that he was entitled to what was mine because he had an agreement with my father. He didn't even attend his funeral. And you judge me for wanting to take revenge?"

The stubborn look on Ana's face drops, and uncertainty flickers across her expression. Her lips part slightly, and her eyebrows furrow as she stares at me.

"You're fortunate," I say. "Even though you don't know it. Other men would do things to you that would make your life in this house a living hell. And I'm not saying I'm better." I shake my head because I consider acts like that barbaric. "I'm just telling you that you might as well start seeing things clearly."

"I-I . . ." she stutters.

I exhale, regretting already that I so clearly threatened her.

"My order stands. Your father isn't to step anywhere near this house, and you're not to see him. Until I change my mind."

With that, I leave her standing there and head to my room. I've had enough for one night. Hell, I already regret ever proposing this marriage agreement. I should've raised hell, crushing and damning all of them.

FIVE
ANA

I hesitate to open my eyes, even though the sunlight has already flooded the room, casting long beams of warmth across my face. I've been lying here, awake, for what feels like hours, but it's probably only been fifteen minutes. Still, I don't want to move. There's no reason to.

In my old life, weekends meant something. I would've called my father, maybe spent the day at his house helping him with the legal tedium of his business. Or I'd have gone grocery shopping and stocked up on things I enjoyed. My weekends had a purpose back then.

But none of that matters here. Not in this empty, echoing house. Not in this cold, new life where the rooms are too big, silent, and suffocating.

I sigh, throwing the covers off and rolling out of bed with the grace of a sloth, letting myself collapse onto the floor with a dull thud. The pain is minimal, just enough to remind me I'm alive. I drag myself upright, rubbing the spot on my arm that hit the ground harder than intended.

"Why did I do this?" I mutter to the empty room, even

though I already know the answer. It wasn't a choice. Not really.

In the bathroom, I brush my teeth like a robot going through the motions, then step into the shower. The water is too hot, scalding my skin, but I stay under it until I feel like I might start peeling away. I guess I'm hoping to scrub off the sense of regret that clings to me like a second skin. But it doesn't work. It never does.

Afterward, I throw on soft cotton shorts and an oversized plaid shirt. Comfortable. Easy. And utterly devoid of any significance. I sit on the edge of my bed, running my fingers through my hair, staring at nothing.

I could go to the office. At least that would give me something to do. But my bosses have been insufferable ever since I got married. They're convinced I should be using my time for some kind of romantic honeymoon bliss.

"Why don't you go home? Enjoy this period while it lasts. Marriage becomes a chore after the first year—though I'm sure yours will be different."

My boss said that to me just last night, not bothering to hide his confusion at why I was still in the office at nine p.m.

If only he knew.

My stomach growls, interrupting my thoughts. Great. Another reminder that I've been living on scraps for weeks.

Dragging my feet, I head downstairs, gripping the railing as if the steps might give out beneath me. The house is eerily quiet. Dmitri has been AWOL for almost three weeks now, and while I should probably be worried—or at least curious—I'm not. If anything, his absence is a blessing. The less I see of him, the fewer chances there are for my blood pressure to spike dangerously.

In the kitchen, I open the pantry and pull out a loaf of

bread and some eggs. I make myself toast and an omelet. I eat in silence at the kitchen island, and then clean up after myself. The monotony is numbing.

And then it hits me. *What now?*

I can't just go back upstairs and stare at the ceiling. I need something to occupy my time, to fill the hollow hours that stretch endlessly ahead of me.

Shopping.

The idea pops into my head out of nowhere. I've never been one for retail therapy, but it'll kill a few hours. I change into a summer dress, throw on a knitted sweater, slip into some flats, and grab my bag. Before I leave, I scribble a note for Janet, letting her know where I'm headed. Not that it matters. Not that anyone cares.

BLOOMINGDALE'S. The one place that has everything I could possibly need, though I hardly *need* anything. Clothes, shoes, cosmetics—they're all distractions, but at least they're distractions that don't talk back or expect anything from me.

I wander aimlessly through the aisles, stopping at the cosmetics section. Perfumes. I need something that will soothe my mind, something to help me forget that I share a house with a man who makes my skin crawl.

As I browse, one of the sales associates recognizes me and approaches with a smile. "Good morning, ma'am. Welcome back. Looking for something specific today?"

I tap my chin, pretending to consider. "I need something that puts me in a Zen mood. You know, the kind of Zen where no one, not even the most insufferable person in your life, can bother you."

The woman's smile falters slightly, her confusion evident. I quickly realize I've said too much.

"I'm joking," I add with a forced laugh. "Just something new and fun will do."

She nods, pointing out a few options—Spring, Agua, Chanel. I end up choosing Sol de Brazil and place it in my cart, eager to move on from the awkward exchange.

As I turn, I catch a glimpse of a man standing a few feet away, watching me. He's dressed in a full suit, which seems wildly out of place on a Saturday. Our eyes meet, and he quickly looks away.

What the hell?

I frown, glancing around. What's a guy like him doing here? It doesn't make sense.

But then again, none of this makes sense. My life hasn't made sense in weeks.

I shake my head, trying to brush it off. "None of my business," I mumble to myself as I turn around, continuing down the aisle.

But something about the man lingers in my mind. Maybe it's the way he looked at me—like he knew something I didn't, like there was some invisible string tethering him to me. Or maybe I'm just paranoid, which wouldn't be surprising given the circumstances. After all, I'm living in a nightmare I didn't choose.

I try to shake it off, losing myself in the racks of clothes. Ten minutes go by as I sift through Alice and Olivia pieces, trying to decide whether buying something new is even worth it. A dress catches my eye, and I'm almost certain it will fit, so I decide to grab it. I'll need black heels to go with it, something simple.

But as I round the corner, there he is again. Same man, same uneasy feeling, but this time, he's not alone. Another guy stands next to him, trying way too hard to look interested in the new Theory collection.

An alarm bell starts ringing in my head. It's subtle, but years of watching my father's associates—and the people who've shadowed him—have taught me how to spot an oddity. And these two? They stick out like sore thumbs.

I leave the dress on the counter and march straight toward them.

"What is it?" I demand, not bothering with pleasantries.

The first man blinks, feigning ignorance. "What?"

"You've been following me," I say, my voice firm. "The security cameras will prove it. So, you can tell me what you want from me, or I can call the cops. Your choice."

The second man clears his throat, dropping the pretense. His dress shirt is too crisp, too pressed for someone casually browsing a women's section. His posture screams alertness. I was right. They're not here to shop.

The first man straightens his tie, a telltale sign of someone trying to regain control. "Ma'am, Mr. Orlov sent us to keep you safe."

I blink, caught off guard.

Dmitri sent them?

"He sent you two," I say, gesturing at them, "to *keep me safe*? Bodyguards?"

They nod, serious as ever.

"Yes, ma'am."

I shake my head, refusing to believe it. But they're standing here, in front of me, and I can't deny the physical evidence. "Why?"

The word slips out, but I already know the answer. Of course. This has to do with that conversation Dmitri and I had about my work habits. Clearly, he listened and sent these guys—who couldn't be more conspicuous if they tried

—to follow me around like I'm some kind of helpless damsel in distress.

"Since when?" I ask, irritation seeping into my tone.

"Two days ago," the first man responds.

Two days? Two whole freaking days, and I didn't notice?

My hands clench into fists as I try not to let my temper flare. How the hell did I not see them?

"You've been following me to work?" I ask.

They nod.

"And I didn't spot you?"

They shake their heads.

Suit Man speaks again, calm and measured. "We decided it was best not to draw attention. Staying too close would've alerted the security team in your building."

I run a hand through my hair, feeling a mixture of frustration and embarrassment. I should've seen them. I should've *known*. But the real kicker? Dmitri—who hasn't even bothered to show his face in three weeks—didn't tell me.

I square my shoulders. "I'm Anastasia Petrov. My father is Nikolai Petrov, which means I'm more than capable of looking after myself. I don't need you two."

Suit Man shakes his head, unfazed. "I'm sorry, ma'am, but we're under strict orders from Mr. Orlov to watch you at all times. We've determined that this location is vulnerable to potential threats."

"Threats?" I hiss, furiously. "This is *Bloomingdale's*! Who's going to harm me here?"

I see them exchange glances, clearly not swayed by my anger. They're immovable, just like Dmitri.

"Stay away from me," I snap, but even as I turn and walk away, I know they won't listen. They cling to my shadow like I'm a target under siege.

The frustration builds inside me, bubbling until I can't enjoy the shopping trip anymore. After a while, I decide to cut my excursion short, heading for the exit with an irritated sigh. Glancing over my shoulder, I see them still trailing me, always keeping their distance but never far enough to disappear. I turn back to the two men, who stand stoic and unmoving.

"Can you give me some space?" I hiss through clenched teeth. "You're not helping."

They don't listen, of course. They're just like their boss —impervious to reason, stubborn as hell. I toss my shopping bags to one of them, not in the mood to carry them myself. If they're going to shadow me, they might as well make themselves useful.

"I'm done here," I say. "Where are you parked?"

One of them opens the car door for me as if I'm some kind of royalty. I roll my eyes and slide into the backseat, settling in with a sigh.

As we pull away from Bloomingdale's, a thought strikes me. "You know what?" I say, leaning forward. "I think I'd like lunch. There's a place I know, it's about twenty minutes from here."

I rattle off an address, leaning back and closing my eyes. I don't actually want to go there, but if they're going to ruin my day, I might as well take them along for the ride.

AFTER A FULL DAY of dragging these bodyguards around with me, enduring stares from every corner, I finally decide it's time to head home. I slide into the car, exhausted, and scroll mindlessly through my phone, trying to speed up the journey back.

That's when I remember my father.

I haven't heard from him since the day after the wedding. I've been so caught up in surviving this mess of a life that I didn't even realize how long it's been. He hasn't called either, but that's not unusual for him. Which is why I spent most weekends at home, making up for it.

Sighing, I dial his number, thinking of the last time we spoke—his voice thick with emotion, something I'd rarely heard from him. The phone rings once, and then nothing. Not unusual. He probably left it somewhere. I wait a few minutes before trying again. No answer.

Five minutes go by. Then ten. Fifteen. An hour passes. Still nothing.

In all the years I've lived away from him, this has never happened. He doesn't always answer on the first try, but by the third or fourth ring, he picks up. Always.

Something isn't right.

I try again, heart pounding. My calls continue going to voicemail, and my mind starts racing. What could've happened? What's different now? The uneasy feeling in my chest intensifies, and then a chilling thought creeps into my head—Dmitri.

I remember what he said three weeks ago, how my father was banned from coming to the house, how I wasn't allowed to see him anymore.

He wouldn't. He couldn't.

I shake my head, chuckling bitterly. Dmitri didn't make my father ignore my calls. Nikolai Petrov, despite all the twisted circumstances that landed me in this mess, would never let anyone—*not even Dmitri*—cut him off from his daughter.

But that thought lingers, gnawing at me. What if he did?

"No," I mutter aloud, trying to convince myself. "Something else must've happened."

I scroll through my contacts, finding Daria's number—my father's secretary. It's the weekend, but I know she'll help. She's always been loyal, and if anyone can reach him, it's her.

The moment she picks up, I don't waste any time. "Daria, I'm sorry for calling you like this, but could you try reaching my father? I've been calling him, and I'm getting worried."

She pauses. "Is everything okay?"

"I don't know," I admit, my voice tight. "He wasn't answering, and now I can't even dial his number. Could you call him? Don't tell him I asked you to."

"Of course. I'll do it right now."

I hang up, and the wait feels like an eternity. Seconds turn into minutes, and I catch myself biting my cuticles—an old habit I'd kicked, which seems to resurface whenever Dmitri's involved.

My phone rings. The moment I hear it, I snatch it up, pressing it to my ear. "Yes?"

"You were right, his phone's still off," Daria says, her voice careful. "But I called his second line, and he picked up. He told me to tell you he's fine."

I freeze, processing her words. His *second line*? I didn't even know he had another phone.

"Did he say anything else?" I ask, the knot in my stomach tightening.

"No, Ana. Just that he's fine."

My forehead wrinkles in confusion, and anger begins to simmer under my skin. "He didn't say he'd call me back?"

She hesitates. "No."

I'm about to say something, but I stop myself. I'm frustrated, but it's not her fault. "Thank you, Daria," I say softly. "I appreciate your help."

"You're welcome. And Ana, congratulations on your wedding. I couldn't attend, but I heard all about it."

A bitter laugh bubbles up in my throat. Who did she hear it from? The same father who's refusing to speak to me?

I can feel the truth sinking in—Dmitri must have forced him into this. He must've done something, exerted some kind of pressure to make my father cut me off. It's the only explanation. And the more I think about it, the angrier I get.

Dmitri acted on his threats. He actually did it. My fingers curl into tight fists, my nails digging into my palms. I can't let this go. I can't just sit back and take it. Dmitri needs to understand that I won't be bullied, not by him or anyone else.

By the time the car pulls up to the house, I'm seething. I storm out, slamming the door behind me, and march up the steps, ready for a confrontation. The door opens just as I reach for the handle, and I nearly collide with Dmitri.

Perfect.

"Oh no, you don't," I say, stepping in front of him, blocking his path. He's dressed like he's about to leave, but there's no way I'm letting him walk out now.

He frowns, his brow furrowing. "What are you doing?"

"What did *you* do?" I hiss, my voice low but filled with anger. "You threatened my father, didn't you? You told him to stay away from me, to cut me off. And you have your minions following me around!"

Dmitri smooths his tie, seemingly unfazed. "We'll talk about this when I return."

I spread my arms, standing firm. "When you return? So you can disappear for another three weeks? No, Dmitri.

You're going to call off your henchmen, and you're going to stop messing with my family. You already have me," I add bitterly. "What more do you want?"

He glances past me at the guards standing outside, including the two who've been tailing me all day. "We'll talk about this inside. I have ten minutes."

I glare at him, unwilling to budge. "I'm going to say what I need to say no matter how long it takes, and then you can go off to whatever hole you've been hiding in."

I storm into the house, not even waiting for him, but I don't go further than the foyer. I stand my ground, arms crossed, glaring at him as he stops in the hallway.

"Call off your men," I demand. "Now."

He turns, his expression unreadable. "I won't. They're there to protect you. I told you before, there are people who might harm you to get to me."

I scoff, not buying his excuse for a second. "Call them off, or I'll leave and never come back."

His eyes narrow, something cold flashing across his face. "I won't let you."

A humorless laugh escapes me. He still thinks I'll obey him. He thinks his threats will keep me in line.

Not a chance.

I take a step forward. "Try me. You've already done more than enough. It's time you realized I'm not someone to be toyed with."

His eyes darken as he stares me down, but I don't flinch.

"If you do manage to leave without my guards stopping you, your father will pay the price," he says quietly, his voice dripping with cold arrogance.

The words hit me like a punch to the gut, but they don't scare me. They don't break me. My father's already been lost to me since the day I walked down the aisle. If Dmitri wants to chip away at whatever's left of me, he'll have to try harder.

"I hate you," I whisper, my voice steady, devoid of emotion. "I regret the day I married you."

Before he can respond, I turn on my heel and walk out of the house. I don't know where I'm going, but anywhere is better than here.

Anywhere is better than Dmitri Orlov.

SIX
DMITRI

"Dmitri Orlov," Igor announces as he strides into my office, grinning like the fool he is.

I know exactly why he's smiling. He's just secured a deal using *my* name, thinking I wouldn't catch on. But I did. Of course, I did. I let him believe he's clever, though—it's far more entertaining to watch him dig his own grave.

For now, I play along. I turn off my laptop and close the file on my desk before rising to meet him. "Let's go to the conference room. The others are waiting."

Igor's grin falters just slightly. "You don't look like a happy man, Dmitri. Trouble at home?"

I shoot him a sidelong glance, my voice cold. "Would you like trouble in *your* home, Igor?"

He chuckles nervously, his bravado faltering. "I didn't mean to pry. Just concerned."

"You don't need to be concerned. You're here for business, nothing else." My tone leaves no room for argument. "Alexey and Bianchi are already seated, and your business is... lesser, compared to theirs. Let's not waste more time. Time is money, Igor."

"Lesser business?" He laughs, but it's the laugh of a man who thinks he holds a trump card. He doesn't. "I just secured a deal with—" He catches himself, barely, his mouth twitching. "Someone who's promised to finance the opening of my casinos in Vegas."

I let the bait dangle for a moment, pretending indifference. Casinos? Interesting, but not enough to engage just yet. If I stay quiet, his need for validation will have him spilling more.

"You know I never cared for gambling," he continues, babbling on. "But the money in it? Hard to ignore. I'll be opening six casinos in high-end areas. We'll move products through them, of course, but the real profits are in the chips. Big money."

I've heard enough. Igor doesn't realize that I already know about his little deal. He doesn't know that the previous owners of those casinos are brokering something far more lucrative—something I'll be taking from under his nose before he even gets a whiff of it.

This is why he'll never be more than a pawn. He's loose-lipped, careless. He's already part of the group that tried to steal from me, and no matter how long it takes, I'll make every single one of them pay.

We enter the conference room. I survey the faces seated around the table—Igor, Alexey, Bianchi, Romanov, Peterson. Five men, each one carefully slotted into my plans for revenge. They don't know it yet, but their time is coming.

"Thank you all for taking the time," I say smoothly, taking my seat. "I know you have busy schedules."

Alexey interrupts, always the disrespectful one. "We sure do. Couldn't we have done this somewhere else? We don't always need to come to your office. You could make the effort for a change."

Under the table, my hand clenches into a fist, but I don't let it show. Alexey has always been a thorn in my side, but his time will come. For now, I respond with a calm, almost mocking smile. "This is our third meeting, Alexey. If you didn't want to be here, you could have declined. But I'm sure you'd prefer we convene at your place next time, right? What with your current... *situation* with the Italian Mafia?"

Alexey's face blanches, and the room goes silent.

"That's right," I continue, savoring the moment. "Word is, they've been pushing your men back, and now you're scrambling to hold onto your territory. So, I understand if you'd want us at your place—it might make you look stronger, no?"

Everyone's eyes shift to Alexey, watching as his face turns red with barely contained anger. "That's not it," he snaps, his voice rising. "I never asked for you to come to my territory. I just don't see why we always meet here. You act like you're better than us."

Because I am better than you. You tried to steal from me, and you failed miserably.

I chuckle softly, shaking my head.

Bianchi, ever the slippery one, laughs heartily, though I can see the calculation in his eyes. "We're all equals here, gentlemen. Although, I did hear that my daughter once had her sights set on you, Dmitri. Too bad Anastasia Petrov snatched you up. Tell me, does your wife know how lucky she is?"

His words are a veiled jab, one meant to test me, but I give nothing away. "We value loyalty over familial ties," I reply smoothly. "That's why I chose Anastasia. Not for any gain from her father, but for the respect it brings."

And because marrying her gave me leverage.

Leverage I'll use when I decide to take everything Nikolai Petrov has left.

But I sense the suspicion rising around the table, so I pivot, changing the subject before they start probing too deeply.

"Now," I say, my voice sharp, cutting through the tension. "Let's get to the matter at hand."

The room quiets instantly, and I see the fear in their eyes. They don't trust me. They *shouldn't* trust me. Each of them has wronged me in some way, and each of them will pay.

But not today.

Today, they still think they're in control.

And that's just how I want it.

HOURS LATER, I slide into the backseat of my car and tell the driver to take me home.

Home.

The word feels foreign. It's been four weeks since I last slept in that house. Four weeks spent avoiding it, avoiding *her*. Except for that brief visit to grab an important document when I ran into Ana, spitting fire, throwing her words at me like they could hurt.

They didn't.

At least, that's what I've been telling myself.

I've been staying in my penthouse in the city, keeping my distance to avoid getting tangled up in emotions I never intended to feel. Since the wedding, things have changed. I find myself thinking about her at random moments. The defiance in her eyes when she tells me I have no right to control her life. The stubborn set of her chin when she demands I fight my own battles, leaving her out of it.

I shouldn't be thinking about her, but I do. Too often.

The worst part? I wasn't even angry when she called me a hypocrite for doing exactly what her father did, only with more power. I should've been, but all I could think about was how she masked her fear and stood toe to toe with me, unflinching. No one's ever done that before. Not even Alexey, who came crawling with an apology after today's meeting to avoid the inevitable consequences.

But Ana got under my skin. She told me she *hates* me. Those three words echoed in my mind all night, twisting and turning until I couldn't sleep. Why the hell do I care? I'm not in the business of making people like me. I don't need approval. I need power. Control.

I close my eyes, leaning back against the leather seat as the car speeds through the city.

It doesn't matter. She's Nikolai Petrov's daughter, after all. A pawn in a bigger game. I'm not interested in her opinion of me.

The car stops in front of the house, and I open my eyes. With a sigh, I step out and head to the front door.

"Welcome, sir," Janet greets me as she opens the door.

I hand her my bag and jacket. "I don't need anything tonight," I say, waving off her offer for food. "It's late."

She nods and disappears as I make my way through the foyer, fatigue settling in after the long day. When I reach the living room, I see someone curled up on the couch—a small figure, tucked into a fetal position, buried in the cushions.

Ana.

I take a step closer, curiosity pulling me in before I can stop myself. She's sleeping, her face half-buried in the armrest, legs folded under her body like she's trying to protect herself from something. The room is warm enough, so why does she look so small, so cold?

I click my tongue softly, considering waking her up. Janet could do it. I could leave her here and forget this ever happened. But I hesitate.

Her hair is spilled in wild curls across the cushion, her long lashes casting shadows on her cheeks. She sighs softly, lips slightly parted as she breathes. Something stirs inside me—something I don't want to acknowledge—as I take in the peaceful vulnerability on her face. There's a strange beauty to her in this moment, something I hadn't noticed before.

I reach out, my hand moving of its own accord, and then stop, yanking it back like I've been burned.

What the hell am I doing?

This is the woman who despises me, the woman I should be indifferent toward. So why do I suddenly feel this pull toward her, this strange sense of... *something*?

I shake my head, disturbed by the foreign thoughts creeping into my mind.

"Sir," Janet's voice cuts through the silence, startling me.

"I'm going to bed," I say quickly, stepping away from Ana as if I've been caught doing something wrong. "Wake Mrs. Orlov."

"Of course, sir."

Without another word, I make my way up the stairs, gripping the banister tighter than necessary, my mind replaying the moment over and over. What's wrong with me? There's no reason I should be thinking about her this way.

Frustration bubbles up inside me. I head to the shower,

turning the water hotter than usual, hoping it'll burn away the thoughts swirling in my head. I scrub my hair, my body, anything to feel clean again—anything to erase the image of Ana's sleeping face from my mind.

But the more I try to wash it away, the more it lingers, like a stain I can't remove.

And that irritates me more than anything else.

SEVEN
ANA

"Mr. Benjamin," I say, rising from my desk as the door opens. He walks in, all smiles and swagger. I know who he is immediately—one of those state-level politicians who once ran for governor and lost spectacularly. His opponent was just more conniving, more willing to play dirty.

"Mrs. Orlov," he greets me, extending his hand with that politician's grin. It's wide, practiced. His shake is too firm, borderline painful. I pull away quickly and rub my hand against my skirt, sitting back down and reminding myself this is just another client.

"I've read through your case, Mr. Benjamin," I start, trying to keep it professional. "I want to assure you that I'll do everything in my power to—"

"You're married to Dmitri Orlov, aren't you?" he interrupts, leaning in with that same grin.

I nod, my stomach tightening. I hate when people bring up my marriage, especially in the office. It's like they don't see me anymore—just his name, attached to mine.

"Nice," he says, still smiling, like he's just uncovered

some hidden gem. He reaches out again, taking my hand, and I resist the urge to pull back. "I know your father. Nikolai Petrov—nice man. But it's your husband I've been trying to meet. Dmitri Orlov. I need his help with something."

His grip tightens on my hand, and I pull it back sharply this time, my irritation barely contained. What does this have to do with his case?

"He's a busy man," Benjamin continues, lowering his voice like he's sharing a secret. "But I'm running for governor again, and I know he has influence. Could you set up a meeting? Tell him about me?"

And there it is. I should've known.

I take a deep breath, trying to keep my voice even. "What does this have to do with your case, Mr. Benjamin?"

His grin widens, the kind of grin that tells me he thinks he's being clever. "Oh, nothing, really. I just needed to see you. Figured you could help me with your husband." He shrugs like it's no big deal, like he didn't just waste my time. "I didn't mean to lie to your boss, but I wasn't sure you'd see me otherwise."

The nerve.

I clench my jaw, but keep my tone polite—too polite, considering how I feel. "If you don't have business here, Mr. Benjamin, I suggest you leave. I have other clients to attend to."

He leans in again, that same stupid smile on his face, as if he hasn't understood a single word. "So, will you tell your husband? I'm free tomorrow, and the—"

"No," I snap, cutting him off. I've had enough. "I won't be acting as a middleman between you and anyone, Mr. Benjamin. If you want to see Dmitri, go to his office, not mine."

He frowns, finally moving out of my personal space, clearly not understanding why I'm angry. Of course, he doesn't. Men like him never do.

"All you have to do is mention my name," he says, as if I didn't hear him the first time. "I can't exactly make an appointment like everyone else, given my position."

I rub my forehead, exasperated. I'd love nothing more than to wave a magic wand and banish him to some remote corner of the world.

"This is all the time I have for you, Mr. Benjamin," I say, standing up. "If there's anything else, my superiors will be more than capable of handling it."

He finally gets the hint, standing slowly, as if I've somehow offended him. "I see. Have a nice day."

"You too," I mutter through gritted teeth, following him to the door and closing it firmly behind him.

I run my fingers through my hair, frustrated beyond belief. My office was supposed to be my safe space from all things Dmitri, but now even that's tainted.

Dmitri Orlov is taking over my life, I think bitterly. And the worst part is, Benjamin probably won't be the last person to come to me expecting access to Dmitri. He's just the first one bold enough to ask directly.

I groan, scrubbing my face with my hands. Should I change my last name back to Petrov? At least that would make it clear I'm not some extension of Dmitri. But then again, wouldn't that raise questions? Cause more drama?

"Who am I kidding?" I mumble, sinking back into my chair. "Changing my name now would just bring more attention." And the last thing I need is more people poking around in my life.

I sigh heavily, deciding to focus on work. That's all I can do, really. Maybe this whole thing with Benjamin was just an unfortunate incident. It's regrettable, sure, but it won't happen again.

At least, I hope it won't.

HOURS LATER, with the sun long set and exhaustion creeping into my bones, I pull into the driveway, immediately noticing the unusual number of cars parked outside. A strange sight, and one that sets off alarm bells in my head.

What the hell is going on?

Men in suits are standing around, and they're not the usual guards. They're on high alert, like something is about to go down. It reminds me of when my father would heighten security around the house when he expected trouble.

Dmitri wouldn't be meeting Bratva associates here, would he?

I park the car with a growing sense of unease. Surely, he wouldn't be that stupid. It's not just *his* house anymore.

As I step out of the car, the front door opens, and a couple walks out hand in hand, dressed like they're heading to a cocktail party. My frown deepens.

A Bratva meeting normally doesn't involve sequins and black tie.

Another woman follows them, her long black gown shimmering in the faint light. She spots me and makes a beeline in my direction, a bright smile plastered on her face.

"Mrs. Orlov," she greets me like we're old friends, taking my hand before I can even react. "We were starting to think you wouldn't show! Your husband told us how hard you work."

Her grip is light, but her words make me want to pull my hand back and punch something. I stare at her, confused and increasingly irritated.

"But you don't *have* to work," she adds with a patronizing tone. "That's why we marry these men—they have their guns, and we have their money."

I blink, confused.

What in the world is this woman talking about?

"Sorry, I don't know you," I say, forcing a smile despite the bile rising in my throat.

"Oh, silly me!" She laughs breezily, completely unfazed. "I'm Freya. Igor's wife."

The name means nothing to me, but I smile anyway. "Nice to meet you," I manage to say. "Is there a party going on?"

"Of course!" She beams. "It's your wedding party, silly. Since we all couldn't attend the wedding, your husband decided to celebrate with his friends here. He sent out the invitations last week."

That bastard.

A kettle whistle of rage goes off in my head. How dare he throw a party in my name without telling me? Typical Dmitri. He's a man who believes everyone should bend to his will, but he's mistaken if he thinks I'm going to be his good little puppet.

"You should go change," Freya says, completely oblivious to my seething anger. "Everyone's waiting for you."

Oh, they're going to get something alright. But it's not going to be what they expect.

Still in my office clothes, tired and annoyed, I storm through the front entrance. If Dmitri wants to make me play hostess, he's about to regret that decision. I'll show these guests exactly who I am—no fancy dress, no smiles, no playing the obedient wife.

But instead of finding a crowd in the living room, I run straight into *my husband.*

"What's going on?" I snap, barely keeping my voice level. "Why did you invite people without telling me? I come home to strangers ogling me like I'm some prized possession."

His expression is infuriatingly calm. "Does it matter?" he says, shrugging. "All you need to do is go upstairs, put on one of your pretty dresses, and play hostess."

"Hostess? What am I, your trophy wife?"

His face hardens, and his next words cut deep. "Why do you think I married you? You're here to make me look better, Anastasia Orlov. You'll play your part, or we'll have a problem."

I snicker, unable to believe his audacity. "You're unbelievable."

"Janet took one of your dresses so we could give your measurements to a personal shopper. There are a few choices in your bedroom. You'll find something appropriate."

"I'm not going to wear a stupid gown," I hiss, the anger rising in my chest.

He simply shrugs again, already walking away. "We'll see about that."

I stand there, mouth agape, watching him disappear further into the house. His arrogance is so overwhelming that, for a moment, I'm stunned into silence. But then, a dangerous idea starts to form. If he wants me to play the part, I'll play it.

But I'll play *my* way.

In my room, I find the gowns laid out on the bed, each

one more beautiful than the last. One dress, in particular, catches my eye—a deep emerald green with a beaded bodice and a silken skirt that falls like liquid around the waist. It's exquisite, and I can't help but imagine the scene I'll create in it.

I slip it on, and it fits like a glove, molding to my every curve. As much as I hate to admit it, the dress is perfect. I could almost feel like royalty if I didn't loathe the man who arranged this whole charade.

But why play modest? Dmitri didn't specify what kind of hostess he wanted, so I'll be the kind he never saw coming.

With matching heels and a string of pearls, I make my way downstairs. As I approach the garden where the party is in full swing, I hear the hum of voices, laughter, and clinking glasses. The whole setup is extravagant—Dmitri spared no expense.

"Mrs. Orlov," a man greets me as I step into the crowd. "You look stunning this evening."

I smile sweetly, letting the compliment wash over me. "Thank you."

Another man steps closer, his gaze immediately dropping to the neckline of my dress. "I didn't think Dmitri could do any better than marrying Nikolai Petrov's daughter. I was right."

I chuckle, covering my mouth just enough to let him think I'm modest. "Oh, you're exaggerating. It's just the dress."

His eyes linger a little too long on my cleavage, exactly as I expected. The dress emphasizes my curves just enough to leave little to the imagination. I may not seek attention, but tonight, I'm going to make sure I get plenty of it.

There are more people here than I imagined, some of

them familiar faces from my father's world, others complete strangers. And yet, they're all here, smiling, mingling. I wonder how many of them are here because of me. Because I'm *his wife*, the shiny new accessory.

If they came for a show, I think darkly, *then I'll give them one.*

Lifting my chin, I stride through the crowd, eyes following me, some with open admiration, others with envy. A man in a blue suit approaches, his importance evident in the way he carries himself.

"Mrs. Orlov," he says, taking my hand and pressing his lips to it. "I'm Igor Pavlov. A close friend of Dmitri's."

Freya's husband, I recall, remembering her earlier introduction. He oozes fake charm, just like the others.

"Nice to meet you, Mr. Pavlov. Are you enjoying your evening?"

"Igor," he corrects, his eyes straying to my cleavage, lingering too long. "Please, call me Igor."

I give him a coy smile, letting his gaze roam where it pleases. "Of course, Igor."

Out of the corner of my eye, I spot Dmitri. He's standing with a woman who's talking animatedly, but his eyes are trained on me—and on Igor. The way his jaw tightens, the way his eyes narrow... It's not just annoyance.

It's jealousy.

I stifle a laugh, letting the thrill of it wash over me. Dmitri Orlov is jealous, and it's delicious.

"Well, Igor," I say, batting my lashes. "I'm not very familiar with these people. Could you introduce me to everyone?"

Igor beams, eager to please. "Of course! I know everyone here. Let me show you around."

As I take his arm, I glance back at Dmitri, meeting his furious gaze head on. If looks could kill, I'd be dead on the spot. But instead, I smile at him—a slow, Cheshire Cat smile.

I win.

EIGHT
DMITRI

Even though it's been a week, I can't shake the image of Igor holding Ana's hand. It's etched into my mind, like a splinter I can't dig out. Every detail from that night keeps replaying in my head—her in that emerald dress, her body practically sculpted by the fabric, the way the neckline teased just enough to drive me mad.

I remember how I first saw her that night, walking into the garden like she owned the place. The dress clung to her curves, her cleavage perfectly framed, leaving me hard as a rock just from looking at her. The way she carried herself was infuriatingly captivating, each step drawing every eye in the room, mine included.

I told myself it was nothing. That I didn't care. After all, I'd thrown that damn party to show her exactly what she was—a trophy. Nothing more. But when I caught one of the men staring at her too long, a possessive anger surged inside me.

Why the hell would I be jealous?

I don't even like her.

Or so I keep telling myself.

It doesn't matter, I thought then. *She's just another pawn in a bigger game.*

"Sir," Janet's voice cuts through my thoughts, pulling me back to the present. "Mrs. Orlov asked for another thirty minutes. She needs time to change."

Of course she does. I smirk to myself. Ana is likely stalling, dreading going to the event we've been invited to. I anticipated this, so I told her we needed to leave an hour earlier than necessary. Even if she drags her feet, we'll still be on time.

My phone buzzes, and I pull it out, seeing a message from Lucia.

Will you bring your wife? You know you don't have to, right?

I roll my eyes and toss the phone to the far end of the couch, just as I hear the unmistakable click of heels on the hardwood floor.

I turn around, and every thought in my mind evaporates.

Ana stands there, just a few feet away, dressed in a deep red gown that hugs her body in all the right places. The satin fabric shimmers in the light, draping her figure like it was made just for her. Around her neck, a simple diamond necklace glimmers against her skin, but it's her lips—painted a bold, sultry crimson—that draw my gaze. They look utterly, undeniably kissable.

My breath hitches. *Fuck.* All the blood in my body seems to rush south as I stare at her, and for the first time, I can't deny it. I'm attracted to Anastasia Orlov. She's like a fire, thawing out the ice I've kept around my heart for far too long.

She clears her throat, her curt tone snapping me out of my daze. "Are you ready?"

I blink, struggling to pull myself together. "You took your sweet time," I say, though my voice lacks its usual edge. Her beauty has dulled my sharpness, and that realization grates at me.

I'm in trouble.

She doesn't bother to respond, just walks past me toward the exit. I can't help but watch her, the gown flowing with every step, accentuating the curve of her hips. Her ass sways with a rhythm that makes my mouth dry.

I'm starving. *For her.*

THE CAR STOPS in front of the event, and I step out first, walking over to open Ana's door. She takes my hand, sliding one leg out just enough to reveal a glimpse of her calf through the slit of the dress. My jaw tightens.

The instant she steps out, all eyes are on her. The red carpet flashes with camera lights, and every lens is fixed on my wife.

My wife.

The thought crashes through me like a wave. She's here to show the world who I am—what I can control, what I own. Nikolai Petrov's daughter, draped in the finest gown money can buy. A woman most men can only dream about, standing next to me.

I offer her my arm, faking a smile for the cameras. It's all part of the performance, after all. But inside, there's something else—a possessive need to keep her close, to remind the world that she's mine.

Inside the hall, Ana lets go of my arm as soon as the doors close behind us. The mask drops, and I know what's coming.

"Did I put on a good enough show for you?" she hisses, her voice laced with venom.

I turn to her, frowning. "What?"

She rolls her eyes, frustration oozing from her every pore. "You said it yourself. I'm your trophy wife, right? Isn't that why you had your designer bring over a gown like this? It must've cost a fortune. I hope it was worth it for the impression I made."

Her biting tone makes my blood boil, but I manage to keep my expression neutral. "It was. You did well."

Ana scoffs, the sound filled with derision. "I see. Well, I'm going to get drunk now, so if I have to play the part of the good little wife again, I won't feel like throwing up while praising you."

She starts to walk away, but I grab her wrist without thinking. She turns, eyes blazing with fury, and for a moment, we're locked in a silent battle.

"You don't want to do this here," I warn quietly, my voice low and dangerous. "It's your reputation that will suffer, not mine."

I release her wrist, the unplanned action already irritating me. I didn't mean to grab her. But the thought of her getting drunk, of another man leering at her the way they did at the garden party... It twists something inside me I can't control.

"Don't drink too much," I add, covering my mistake. "I won't have you embarrassing yourself—and the last shred of pride I left your father."

Her chin lifts defiantly, her gaze never wavering. Then she storms off, making a beeline for the nearest waitperson. She grabs two glasses of champagne, downing both in quick succession.

Weirdly enough, I'm impressed.

But also, furious.

The rest of the night, I can't stop watching her. I can't stop thinking about how her presence in that dress, with that fire in her eyes, sends my mind into chaos. She isn't just a pawn, not anymore. She's something else, something I refuse to admit.

Something I want.

I can't stand here, watching her, not when I have more pressing matters to attend to. But it's not easy tearing my eyes away from Ana, laughing with those men like she has no care in the world, like she's not my wife.

I force myself to move, to shake off the tension gripping me like a vice. There's business that needs handling, and I'm not the kind of man who lets emotions stand in the way.

But no matter where I go in this room, no matter who I speak to, the image of her keeps creeping back into my mind. That fucking dress. The way she looked at those men, as if they mattered more than the man she married.

Me.

An hour later, I've had enough. I cut off the conversation mid-sentence with the person I was meeting and make my way through the crowd, out into the cool night air, needing a moment to clear my head. I barely make it five steps when a hand grabs my arm.

Lucia.

"What are you doing?" I growl, shaking her off.

She smiles, stepping closer. "Keeping you company, Dmitri. Like old times."

I give her a warning look, but she presses on, her fingers trailing up my arm.

Annoying as hell.

"I know you don't want a scene," she purrs. "I'd hate to cause one."

"You're walking a fine line, Lucia," I warn, my patience wearing thin. "This isn't the time or the place for your games."

She taps her chin thoughtfully, her eyes gleaming with mischief. "What if I told you that your wife seems already... occupied?"

That catches my attention. I scan the room, trying to find Ana, but she's nowhere in sight. Lucia, ever the snake, points toward the far end of the room, where a large potted fern obscures part of the seating area.

"Over there," she says, a satisfied smirk tugging at her lips. "Looks like she's enjoying herself."

I follow her gaze and spot Ana, lounging on a plush couch, surrounded by three men. One leans in, whispering something in her ear that makes her toss her head back and laugh, carefree and radiant. Her hair has come loose, spilling over her shoulders, and for a moment, I'm frozen, watching her like a predator stalking his prey.

My fists clench at my sides, a cold rage building inside me.

How dare they?

Lucia leans in again, her voice dripping with venom. "Seems like she's getting all the attention tonight. Maybe you should take a lesson from her—learn to unwind a little."

Her touch crawls up my arm again, and I brush it off with more force this time, my eyes never leaving Ana.

"They're vultures," I mutter, the words coming out like a growl. "Circling what's mine."

Lucia gasps dramatically, as if she's discovered something groundbreaking. "You're jealous!"

I glare at her, but it only makes her grin wider.

"I didn't think you were the jealous type, Dmitri," she teases. "Are you sure you're not in love with her?"

Love?

The idea is laughable, but something dark and twisted uncoils inside me at the thought. Love has no place in my world, yet the idea of someone else laying a hand on Ana sends me into a cold fury I can barely contain.

Lucia steps in front of me, forcing me to tear my gaze away from Ana. "This isn't like you," she presses. "When we were together, you didn't care. You cut me off like I never meant anything. But it's different with her."

I hate that she's right. I hate that I care.

I shove past her, walking briskly toward the exit, needing to put some distance between myself and the party, between myself and Ana. My mind is swirling with conflicting emotions—rage, jealousy, desire—and I need a moment to clear my head.

As I step out onto the balcony, the cold night air hits me, and I take a deep breath, trying to steady myself. But before I can find any peace, I hear voices.

"—she's fine as hell," one man says, his tone lecherous. "Dmitri's a lucky bastard."

The other man chuckles. "Yeah, but you know it's not a marriage of love. She's probably dying to get away from him."

"I wouldn't mind stealing her away for a night or two," the first one says, his voice thick with lust. "She looks like the kind of woman who'd be a hell of a time in bed."

"And those lips," the second one adds, snickering. "Imagine having them—"

I step out of the shadows, my voice colder than the night air. "Imagine having them where?"

Both men freeze, their eyes wide with terror as they realize who stands before them.

"Dmitri," one stammers, his face draining of color. "We didn't mean—"

"You didn't mean what?" I step closer, towering over them. "Didn't mean to talk about my wife like a couple of fucking degenerates?"

The second man, the one with the loose mouth, tries to backtrack. "We were just talking. It wasn't serious."

"Not serious?" I repeat, my voice dripping with menace. "It sounded pretty fucking serious to me."

The first man shakes his head, his hands trembling. "We didn't mean any disrespect, Dmitri. Really. It was . . . It was just a joke."

"A joke," I say, my tone low and dangerous. "Here's a joke for you: I break every bone in your body and leave you in a ditch. How's that sound?"

They both pale, stammering apologies, but I'm not listening. My hand itches to grab one of them by the throat, to make an example out of them.

"I'll give you a word of advice," I say, stepping back slightly, just enough to let them breathe. "Keep your filthy thoughts to yourselves. If I ever hear you talking about Ana like that again, I won't just break you. I'll erase you."

They nod furiously, practically shaking with fear.

Satisfied, I turn on my heel and head back inside, my fists still clenched at my sides. The rage hasn't subsided. If anything, it's grown. I've never felt this level of anger over a woman before, never cared enough to let something like this affect me.

But Ana's different.

And that terrifies me.

NINE
ANA

I stride across the lobby, eyes locked on the elevator, ignoring the buzz of my phone reminding me about an upcoming meeting. Not now. Nikolai Petrov is going to see his daughter today, whether he likes it or not.

If he won't come to me, I'll find my way to him. Simple as that.

"Miss Petrov!" I hear my name being called from behind, and I come to a sharp stop, sighing as I turn around. It's Ivan, my father's aide—a man with a huge family. I watch impatiently as he hurries toward me, taking his time while the elevator doors open and close like a ticking clock.

"Ivan," I say, forcing a smile. "It's been a while."

He nods, but then his face flickers with realization. "I'm sorry," he stumbles. "It's Mrs. Orlov now, isn't it?"

Oh, right.

I barely noticed. Being Mrs. Orlov doesn't sit quite right, and honestly, I'm still more Nikolai's daughter than Dmitri's wife. Always will be.

"It's fine. Is my father in his office?"

Ivan scratches at his beard, thinking. "I'm not sure. I

haven't seen him today, but that's because I haven't been upstairs. He's usually at his desk unless something urgent has come up."

"Thanks, Ivan." I take the opportunity to slip into the elevator before another interruption can slow me down.

The ride to the top floor is quick, and soon I'm stepping out onto the plush carpet that leads to my father's office. His door is at the end of the hall, but I've got to pass through Daria's space to get there.

When Daria sees me, she stands up quickly, clearly surprised. "Ana! What brings you here?"

"I'm here to see Papa," I say, glancing toward his door. "Is he in?"

She hesitates, and that's my first red flag. "I'm sorry, Ana, but he's not in his office right now. You could leave a message, and I'll make sure it reaches him."

This feels weird. If he wasn't around, Daria wouldn't have hesitated. She's hiding something, and I'm not about to let it slide.

I move closer, resting my hands on her desk, looking her straight in the eye. "Daria, did Papa tell you why I married Dmitri?"

She sighs, eyes darting to the door before she looks back at me. "No, but I figured it wasn't exactly a love match."

"Exactly." I nod. "And he wasn't thrilled about it, as you can imagine. But now he's avoiding me, and I can't figure out why. If he's in there, I need to see him. It's important."

Daria shakes her head, her expression soft with sympathy. "I swear, Ana, he's not here. I wouldn't keep you from seeing him if he was."

I fold my arms, skeptical. "Then why did you hesitate?"

She sighs again, rubbing her temples. "It's just... he came in this morning looking stormy. I asked him what was wrong, but he wouldn't tell me. Just mumbled something about 'handling things,' and then left quickly."

My brow furrows. "Handling things? Have you ever seen him act like that before?"

She shakes her head. "No, that's why it stood out. Your father's always so composed, even when things get heated. But this morning he wasn't himself."

This doesn't sound like my father at all. He's a calculated man, always in control. Something is definitely off, and it's starting to make me nervous. Did Dmitri do something? God, I hope not.

"Thanks, Daria," I say, but my mind is already racing through a dozen worst-case scenarios.

She nods, and I force a smile before turning to leave. My phone starts buzzing again—Steve, of course—but I ignore him. I'll have to deal with work later. Right now, I need to get to my father's house.

If he's not at the office, there's only a few other places he might go. I'm going to find him. Before something bad happens.

BY THE TIME I'm packing up my things at the end of the day, it's already fifteen minutes past six. I toss my paperwork into my bag when Steve, who has decided my office is a nice place to loiter, looks up.

"You're leaving already?" he asks, almost incredulous. "Since when do you leave before dark?"

"Yup," I mutter, not bothering to explain as I shove the last of my things into my bag. "Which means you should probably pack up too because I'm locking the door."

"Huh," he says, like he's got something more to add but is biting his tongue. Fine with me.

"You were never in a hurry to leave early before," he presses. "Things getting better at home?"

I pause, brow furrowing. "What are you talking about?"

Steve shrugs, piling his papers into a neat stack. "Well, it's not really my place, but . . . I just noticed you've been working late a lot recently. I figured something was up."

I give him a sharp look, crossing my arms. "And?"

He holds up his hands, quick to retreat. "Hey, I didn't mean anything by it! Just making an observation."

I shake my head, exhaling in exasperation. "Well, you're right—it's not your place. Now, if you don't mind, I've got somewhere to be."

Steve stutters a quick apology before scurrying out of my office like a scolded puppy. Shaking my head, I grab my bag and lock up behind me. There's only one reason I'd leave this office before sunset, and it's definitely not to have dinner with Dmitri.

I'm going to see my father.

The drive to Papa's place takes longer than usual—typical New York traffic—but eventually, I pull into the driveway of his Long Island home. Familiar faces greet me as I step out of the car, but no one mentions Dmitri. They know better.

The house hasn't changed since the last time I was here, and nostalgia hits me as I walk through the hallway. It's quiet—too quiet.

Oh well, I sigh to myself. *Sacrifices, right? You gotta make them when there's no one else to carry the burden.*

I walk into the living room and spot Maxim immediately. His face lights up, arms open wide in that fatherly way of his—one of the few people left who hasn't put distance between us.

"Anastasia. It's been a while."

There it is—*Anastasia*. Maxim's the only one who still calls me by my full name and hearing it from him is like a warm hug I've been needing. I hadn't realized how much I missed it until now, how much I've missed *home* in all the ways that matter.

"Maxim," I say, managing a small smile. "I came to see Papa. Is he around?"

At my words, his expression changes, his warm demeanor faltering. He shifts on his feet, looking uncomfortable. Something's up, and I'm already tired of the secrets.

"Ah, Anastasia," he says, his voice softer. "Your father is unavailable right now. Perhaps it's best to come back another time."

I narrow my eyes, already suspicious. "Maxim, what's going on? Out with it. What are you hiding?"

Maxim glances around, his gaze flickering nervously. Without another word, he gently takes my elbow and leads me into a quieter corner of the room, out of earshot from anyone else.

My heart starts racing. Did something happen to my father? Is he sick? Worse?

Once we're alone, Maxim lets go of my arm, and I turn to face him, squaring my shoulders. "What happened?" My voice is sharper than I intended, but I can't help it. I need answers.

He sighs heavily, running a hand through his thinning gray hair. "Your father doesn't want to see you. Not yet, at least."

My stomach drops, the floor seemingly disappearing

beneath me. "What?" The word comes out harsher than I mean. "Is this Dmitri's doing? Because if he—"

Maxim shakes his head quickly. "No, no. It's not Dmitri. Your father doesn't want to see you because he can't bear to face you after what happened."

I stare at him, the confusion twisting into frustration. "What do you mean 'after what happened'? What did he do?"

Maxim looks at me with a deep sadness, like he's been carrying this weight for too long. "Ever since your marriage to Orlov, your father's been beside himself. He blames himself, Anastasia. For letting you carry his burden, for putting you in a position where you had no choice but to marry him. He's been trying to find a way to make things right, but... he can't face you until he feels like he's done that."

I can't believe what I'm hearing. My father—*my Papa*—has been avoiding me, not because of Dmitri, but because of his guilt?

"He thinks I'm angry with him," I mutter, the realization hitting me like a punch to the gut. "But I married Dmitri because it was the only option. We both knew what had to be done."

And now, after everything, he's just going to disappear and leave me to deal with the consequences alone?

"I thought we were past all that," I say, my voice rising, heat building in my chest. "I agreed to marry Dmitri so Papa wouldn't have to pay the price for his mistakes. Now he's going to push me away? Abandon me? After everything?"

My emotions are spiraling now, years of pent-up frustration crashing against the surface. I tried not to feel this way —I really did—but now it feels like I'm drowning. I was forced into this life, into this marriage, and now my father is too ashamed to face me?

"After everything I've sacrificed for him, the least he could do is *stand by me*!" I snap at Maxim, the words spilling out before I can stop them. "He's the one who left me to deal with the fallout of all this. And now I'm supposed to just accept that he's refusing to see me?"

Maxim sighs heavily, his hand resting on my shoulder again. "Anastasia, I understand how you feel. But give him time. Your father is a proud man. He can't face you until he feels he's made things right."

I laugh bitterly, shaking his hand off. "Time? I've already given him *time*. I've done everything I can to protect him, to save him from this mess. But if he can't face me now, after all of this, then maybe I'm better off without him."

I take a step back, anger and sadness swirling together in my chest, the weight of everything pressing down on me. Tears prick at the corners of my eyes, but I blink them away quickly.

"I won't reach out again," I say firmly, my voice cold. "If he wants to talk to me, he knows where to find me. But I won't be waiting."

Before Maxim can say anything else, I turn and walk away, my footsteps echoing through the quiet house. Each step feels heavier than the last, but I refuse to stop. I refuse to let the tears fall.

I've never felt this alone before. But I'm strong, stronger than this fucked up situation.

I am still Anastasia Petrov. No matter what, I refuse to lose myself.

And they'll see that. One way or another.

TEN
DMITRI

I scowl at my door, the sound of a knock grating against my already fraying patience. My focus on the work at hand fades the moment my stepsister, Yelena, breezes in like a gust of uninvited chaos.

"Brother!" she sings, dropping her leather luggage with a thud. In seconds, she's latched onto me, squeezing me tight with her arms, as if she's trying to suffocate me with affection.

"You look good!" she chirps, clearly ignoring the fact that I can barely breathe.

"And I'm going to be blue and cold if you don't let up, Yelena," I rasp, tapping her arm to signal my surrender.

"Oh!" She releases me, stepping back with a sheepish grin. "Sorry. I just missed you. Wanted to soak in all the *you* I could."

I stretch my arm out, keeping a safe distance between us. "You can soak in the 'me' with your words, not your death grip," I say, cutting her off before she decides to smother me again.

She pouts, dramatically releasing me. "Right. I forget

how much you hate physical contact. Always the brooding type. You and your thoughts, all alone in your little castle of seriousness."

Typical Yelena. Always poking, always pushing. I don't rise to it. "What brings you back?" I ask, cutting straight to the point.

She shrugs, tossing her hair back like the world revolves around her whims. "What do you think?"

I tilt my head, feigning curiosity. "You got bored traveling the world? Fell in love with some poor fool and realized it wasn't love after all, so you did what you always do—ran?"

She clicks her tongue at me. "You make it sound like I have no depth, Dmitri. I came back because I missed you. You may not think about me, but I think about you all the time. Miss our time together, even when you're scowling at me."

My hand runs across my mouth, suppressing the grin that threatens to appear. "I'm not scowling."

"Sure," she says, waving her hand dismissively. "But, brother, I've got one question. Is your wife anything like you?"

The question takes me off guard, but I recover quickly. *Like me?* Ana is the furthest thing from me. If I'm winter, she's summer. She burns where I freeze. She commands attention where I make people retreat. The thought of her, of her fire, brings an uncomfortable tightness to my chest.

"She's nothing like me," I say, my tone flat.

Yelena raises a brow, intrigued. "Good for you. But why did she marry you, then?"

I don't answer right away. Yelena doesn't know the real story. She doesn't know this marriage wasn't born out of anything real. No love, no affection, just strategy. I had kept her away from the wedding, away from the truth, and she didn't push.

"It doesn't matter," I redirect, unwilling to open that door. "Why are you back?"

She sighs, a weariness settling in her eyes. "Needed a break. Traveling nonstop wears you down eventually. And yes, maybe my heart wavered for a bit. But I remembered what happened two years ago and thought it was time for a reality check." She spreads her arms wide like she's presenting herself to me. "So, here I am."

I nod, accepting her vague explanation. "How's your mother?"

Yelena pinches the bridge of her nose, her face a mixture of frustration and fondness. "Getting married again. Fourth husband this time. You know how it is." She rolls her eyes. "Every time she calls, she somehow manages to bring you up."

The corner of my lips twitch into the barest hint of a smile. Her mother always had a strange attachment to me, despite never really being present in my life. She wasn't the motherly type, but there was something there—a soft spot, maybe.

"I wonder if she wishes you were her biological child instead of me," Yelena muses, her voice distant for a moment before she snaps out of it and flashes her usual grin. "But now that I'm back, we get to make up for lost time. I'd like to stay with you. You think your wife will mind?"

"It's my house," I say reflexively, though the words taste hollow as soon as they leave my mouth.

"But she's your wife," Yelena counters, eyes glinting with amusement. "Don't tell me you invite people over without consulting her. That's just rude, Dmitri."

Ana said something similar at that damn party. *Is it rude?* Why should I need Ana's permission? It's not as though we're living like a married couple. We don't share meals, barely even cross paths unless forced to. We're more like strangers sharing a space, bound by a name and nothing more.

"If she has a problem with it, you can stay at a hotel," I mutter, not wanting to think too hard about why Yelena's question is bothering me more than it should.

Yelena shrugs, unfazed. She moves to her bag, unzipping it and pulling out a bottle of wine, holding it up with a grin. "Care to join me?"

I shake my head, disapproving. "It's not even noon."

She shrugs again. "It's five o'clock somewhere. Come on, live a little. The world's not going to collapse because you take a break, Dmitri."

It might, though. I let my guard down once, and Nikolai Petrov nearly took everything from me. If I let it down again, who knows what kind of chaos could unfold?

It's just wine, Dmitri. Relax.

The voice in my head sounds suspiciously like Yelena, her words always managing to crawl under my skin. She's right, though. It's just a glass. And I haven't seen her in over a year. What's the harm?

"I'll tell Jakob to bring the glasses."

She pumps her fist in the air like a child. "Party time!"

I SEE Ana's car parked just outside the house as I pull up—a sign that she's home. My brows scrunch together as I turn off my car's engine.

It's weird for her to be back at this time of the day. Typically, she comes back from work long after the sun has set.

Yelena is already racing through the door before I manage to intervene, passing Janet in the doorway. The only thing I can do is stare at the scene, wondering what'll happen when the two finally meet and I'm not the one making an introduction.

But I'm met with a surprise. My stepsister has her arms around Ana, who looks polished and pulled together in her work clothes.

But that's not all.

Ana, who's never once shown any expression other than anger or displeasure toward me, has the biggest smile on her face as she's hugging Yelena back.

"Oh, it's so good to meet you finally," I hear Yelena say as she pulls away and cups Ana's cheek. "I knew the pictures I saw didn't do you justice."

"Mr. Orlov," Janet is the first person to notice my presence, and three pairs of eyes turn to me where I stand. "Welcome home."

Yelena rushes over to me, dragging Ana along. "How did you get this sweet, beautiful woman to marry you?" Her tone sounds more like an interrogation than a question, and she stares at me like she's waiting for a confession.

I glance at Ana.

Should I tell her about your father?"

"I'm not always sweet." She laughs, picking up on my hint.

"Nonsense," Yelena disagrees. "You've the cutest look on your face, and you let me hug you before I even introduced myself. You're a gem. My brother, on the other hand," she says, giving me a side glance, "is allergic to people."

"Janet," I divert my attention to the housekeeper, handing her my coat and bag, before Yelena goes on to embarrass me further, "here."

"Yelena, Janet will show you to your room. If," I glance at Ana for a second, "it's alright with you that she stays with us for a while."

Ana smiles, and I freeze momentarily, taken aback by the change in her facial expression. I know she's smiling because I mentioned Yelena's name, but the fact that it's aimed at me stirs up something in my heart.

No.

Nope. We're done with the feelings.

It ended after the party, where I almost assaulted two men because they were talking shit about her.

"I'll turn in for the night," I announce. "See you in the morning."

"Oh no, you won't." Yelena quickly blocks my path, shaking her head. "You just came home from work, and your wife arrived mere minutes before you. Aren't we having dinner?"

Dinner?

The same look of surprise that's on my face is mirrored on Ana's. Yelena doesn't seem to notice the reactions, though, because she turns to Janet.

"Is there anything to eat?"

Even the housekeeper, who's never served husband and wife dinner since we got married, is flustered. She scratches her head.

"Ah, no, ma'am. They don't . . . I mean dinner isn't—"

I clear my throat loudly. "It's been a long day, Yelena, and I'm sure you're jet-lagged. We'll have breakfast together tomorrow."

But she doesn't give up. Grabbing Ana's arm again, Yelena asks, "You're hungry, aren't you?"

Ana nods and side-eyes me. "Y—yeah?"

"Good!" Yelena says loudly. "And I'm hungry too. It's two to one, Dmitri." She lifts two fingers. "You're eating with us whether you want to or not."

Forty minutes later, Ana, Yelena, and I sit around the dining table eating baked chicken Parmesan that Janet quickly assembled.

Ana is sitting beside me, and I'm all too aware of her presence. I can smell her perfume as it wafts through the air, settling around me like a warm caress.

"So," she rubs her palms, "tell me, Anastasia. Wait, should I call you that?"

My wife laughs—a soft sound that carries a hidden lilt.

"Yes, that's fine. Although there's only one other person that calls me by my full name."

"My brother?"

She shakes her head. "No. Just someone I used to see as a father figure."

Yelena nods. "Well, I like your name a lot. As I was saying, how does it feel to live under the same roof as my brother? I've had years to get used to him, but it's like living with a ghost—a man without feelings. Sometimes you just want to shake him until the screws that keep his emotions under lock come undone."

Ana's gaze cuts to me, and her raised eyebrows, with the slight tilt of her head, convey her astonishment.

I press my lips together, my gaze penetrating hers. "You know why I'm like this."

She arches one brow. "I see."

"Am I interrupting something?" Yelena's voice has us both turning to her at the same time.

Ana shakes her head. "Nope. Nothing. It's like you said," she smiles, pulling her hair to the side, "he barely shows any emotion. But then again," she cuts me with a glance, "it's not like he owes me anything. I'm fine being the only funny one."

Yelena throws her head back and laughs.

"I knew there was a reason why I liked you! You have the sense of humor that my dear brother is sorely lacking."

Ana delivers a reply that's meant for me. "We can't all be detached tyrants. Some of us need to have upbeat personalities."

I don't have to be told to my face to know who I am in this scenario.

"I'm curious about you, though," she changes the subject while I stab my chicken. "Where have you been?"

While my sister entertains Ana with her travels, I stare at my plate, trying to burn holes into it. I nibble my Caesar salad while I try not to listen to their conversation. My attempts have me staring at random places in the dining room until my eyes softly land on Ana.

Her hand reaches up to the back of her neck, fingers lightly grazing the delicate skin. The simple gesture pulls my gaze in, fixating on the graceful curve. When she drops her hand back down, I catch a glimpse of the thin necklace resting against her throat, the tiny pendant drawing my eyes to the pale column of her neck.

The smooth skin begs to be touched.

I can't help my thoughts as they imagine tracing the line of her throat with my fingertips, feeling the subtle pulse beneath the surface.

As she tilts her head slightly, I'm entranced by the elegant slope, wishing I could press my lips against that vulnerable spot just below her jaw. I'm reminded of the night I saw her sleeping on the couch, when I was drawn to her for the first time since we got married.

Then, the party.

The dress she wore, the way it hugged her curves, transformed her into a sensuous, almost irresistible creature. It seems the night she fell asleep on the couch unlocked a part of me that can no longer see Anastasia Petrov as a means to an end.

Every time my gaze falls on her, I'm reminded that she's a beautiful woman with words that can cut through stone. She's gorgeous, smart, spirited, more than I bargained for.

"Dmitri?"

I hear Yelena call my name, and I blink rapidly, pushing away my thoughts to focus on the present.

"Yes?"

She rolls her eyes and sighs dramatically. "You were thinking about work, weren't you?"

No.

"Yeah. Anything you need?"

Yelena clicks her tongue. "Nope. Nothing. I just wanted to see where your mind was at. Ana and I were having a wonderful conversation."

Ana turns to me just then, and her tongue darts out to lick the salad dressing from the corner of her lips. The simple gesture sends a jolt of desire down my throat, and it makes its way quickly to my chest.

Her lips look so soft. I wonder what it would feel like to kiss them.

Just once.

No. No. No.

I push my chair back, standing up. "Since you two are having fun in each other's company, I'll go up and get the sleep I need."

"You should loosen up and have fun, brother! Life's not going to go kaput if you do!"

No, it's not. But it will force me to spend more time with Ana, and my resolve, which is slowly chipping away, will end up breaking down completely.

The emotions I feel make me weak. And I promised myself, years ago, after my father died, that I would not let myself be used or tricked by anyone.

Anastasia is still Nikolai Petrov's daughter. I can't forget that.

Ever.

ELEVEN
ANA

"I hope you don't mind me stopping by. I was in the neighborhood and thought I'd pop in to see my favorite sister-in-law."

I look up from my desk, and my face instantly brightens at the sound of Yelena's voice. She's like a breath of fresh air, completely opposite to her stone-cold brother, Dmitri.

My husband.

"No, no," I wave her in, shaking my head. "You're always welcome. What brings you to the city?"

Yelena strolls in, dropping onto the chair opposite me with a dramatic sigh, a bag clutched in her hand. I can see the neck of a bottle peeking out, and judging by the size of the bag, there's more than just champagne in there. This is Yelena, after all.

It's been a week since she moved in with us, and the house has never been livelier. Every time she goes out, she returns with some kind of gift. Dresses, shoes, even random trinkets she thought I'd like. It's sweet, in a way. A little overwhelming, sure, but sweet.

She flashes a mischievous grin. "Okay, so I lied about

being in the neighborhood. I was bored at home. Didn't feel like shopping, didn't want to deal with my friends. So, I figured, why not hang out with you?"

"Oh." I nod, smiling. "That's fine. I'm working on a closing statement—it'll take me a couple of hours. But if you want to stick around, I'd love the company."

She pulls out the champagne bottle and two glasses from her bag like it's the most normal thing in the world. "Say no more."

I laugh, shaking my head. "As much as I'd love to join you, I can't. Work rules."

Yelena waves her hand dismissively. "Oh, don't worry. One glass is for me, and the other is for me after I finish the first one."

Her grin is infectious, and despite myself, I chuckle. She's a force of nature, but one I can handle. I mean, give me Yelena over her brother any day. At least she doesn't make me want to tear my hair out every time she walks into the room.

"You don't have to entertain me," Yelena says, settling in comfortably. "I'm just here to keep you company. I'll quietly send you good vibes."

Nodding, I turn back to my screen, trying to focus on the case in front of me. The closing statement I'm drafting should be airtight, but I can't shake the feeling that the plaintiff's attorney might have a trick up her sleeve. I just need to go over it one more time to be sure.

But then, Yelena's face pops up in my peripheral vision. "I still don't know why you married my grumpy brother."

I freeze for a second, my hands pausing over the keyboard. Here it comes.

"You're fun, smart, beautiful," she continues, leaning in like we're sharing a secret. "No offense, but I always thought if Dmitri was going to get married, it would be to someone . . . well, like him."

I rest my chin on my hand, smiling faintly. The truth teases the edge of my tongue, but I hold it back. As much as I like Yelena, as much as we've bonded, she's still Dmitri's sister. There's a line I can't cross. And anyway, it's not my story to tell. Not fully.

Still, a part of me wonders how she'd react if I told her that her dear brother forced me into this marriage. That I'm paying the price for a crime my father supposedly committed.

Yelena's voice softens. "Or . . . is it true?"

I tilt my head slightly, studying her. "True?"

Her eyes dart around nervously, and for the first time since I've known her, she seems unsure of herself. She bites her lower lip, hesitating.

"I heard something through the grapevine. But it's not my place to ask." She scratches at her chin, clearly uncomfortable.

I keep my face neutral, but my mind is racing. Does she know? How much does she know? I don't want to confirm or deny anything by accident, so I tread carefully.

"What is it?" I ask, keeping my tone light.

She shifts in her seat, her discomfort obvious now. "It's probably nothing. You know how rumors can be. I must've had too much to drink one night and started believing the nonsense people talk about."

I nod slowly, giving her a way out. "Right."

Yelena waves her hand like she's brushing off her own words. "Forget I said anything! Honestly, it's just silly talk. You get back to work, and I'll just sit here and enjoy my champagne."

She picks up her glass, but the way her eyes avoid mine

tells me she's holding something back. There's more she wants to say, but for now, she's keeping quiet.

I glance at her as I try to refocus on the statement. There's something about her expression that sticks with me—like she knows more than she's letting on but doesn't want to admit it. Maybe she's heard whispers about my arrangement with Dmitri. Maybe she's putting the pieces together.

She knows. Or at least, she suspects.

But she's not ready to say it. And honestly, I'm not sure how I feel about that.

Grateful? Apprehensive?

I sigh softly, telling myself I'll figure it out in time. For now, Yelena's the closest thing to a friend I have in this house. I'm not going to risk that over a conversation neither of us is ready to have.

"LET'S GO FOR A DRINK." Yelena grabs my hand as we head out of the office.

"Are you sure you can have more?" I ask, giving her a sideways glance.

She nods enthusiastically. "Yup. I only had three glasses, and that was hours ago. You know," she leans her head against my shoulder, her voice dropping, "when you go through something that messes with your head just enough, you build up a tolerance pretty quickly."

Her tone takes on a strange wistfulness that makes me pause. I turn my head slightly to study her expression, but her gaze is far off, fixed on some distant point. There's sadness in her eyes that I hadn't noticed before, a heaviness she hides well under her usual brightness.

. . .

WE STEP into the elevator in silence, and Yelena lets go of my hand, wrapping her arms around herself as if to ward off the weight of whatever thoughts are pulling her down. I'm no expert in reading people's emotions, but even I can see that something's bothering her—something she's not ready to share.

"So, what do you say?" she asks, her voice picking up that false cheerfulness again. "Shall we get a nice drink and some food? You know, in case Dmitri's written us off for the evening."

I chuckle, taking her up on the offer. "I'm sure if he could avoid eating with us for the rest of his life, he'd be thrilled."

Yelena giggles. "I know, right? But," she lowers her voice dramatically, "it's all a facade."

"A facade?" I raise an eyebrow.

She leans in closer, her voice conspiratorial. "Between you and me, Dmitri likes to act all tough, but deep down? He's a cinnamon roll."

I nearly snort in disbelief. Dmitri, a cinnamon roll? The man who threatened my father, who forced me into this sham of a marriage? Yeah, right. That's as likely as pigs flying.

"Are you sure about that?" I reply, trying to keep the skepticism from my voice.

Yelena grins, unfazed. "Oh, I know it's hard to believe. But I've seen it. Under the right circumstances, with the right people, that gruff exterior melts away. Although," she pauses for effect, "I might be the only one who's ever seen it."

I raise an eyebrow but say nothing. I don't doubt that Yelena, with her infectious energy and warmth, brings out a side of Dmitri that no one else could. But me? I've only ever gotten the coldest, most brutal version of him.

"You don't believe me, do you?" Yelena nudges me as we step out of the elevator.

"I don't know," I admit as we walk toward the parking lot. "From what I've seen, it's hard to imagine."

She slips into the passenger seat of my car. "Well, you'll just have to take my word for it. Dmitri grew up without knowing what it felt like to be loved. All he understands is duty," she says with a note of affection in her voice. "He was trained by his father to forge connections and to trust no one."

I nod, letting her words sink in. Even if I want to sympathize with Dmitri's tough childhood, it doesn't erase the fact that he's been nothing but a bully since the moment we met.

TWO HOURS LATER, I'm practically dragging Yelena out of the car, her arm slung over my shoulder as she sways unsteadily.

"There we go," I mutter, using my body to keep her upright. She's had way too many drinks, but something about the sadness that hung over her all night made me let her. If she needed to drown whatever was haunting her, who was I to stop her?

Janet opens the door after the second knock, her eyes widening briefly when she sees the state Yelena's in. She quickly steps in to help me, guiding us both inside. As we make it to the living room, Dmitri rounds the corner, his sharp eyes locking onto us.

His gaze flicks from Yelena to me, then back to her, his expression unreadable but tense.

"I'll take Miss Romanov to her room," Janet says quietly, clearly sensing the shift in the air.

I hand Yelena over to her, rubbing my sore shoulder from supporting her weight. As Janet disappears with Yelena, I feel Dmitri's eyes still on me.

"What happened?" he asks, his tone flat, but there's something probing in it—like an interrogation.

I resist the urge to snap back. "We went for dinner."

His arms fold over his chest. "And she comes back like that?"

I shrug, trying to keep my tone neutral. "You saw her. If you want to know why, you can ask her in the morning."

His gaze narrows, lingering on me in silence. I can feel the weight of it, the judgment, the questions he isn't asking but wants to.

"I had a long day," I add, taking a few steps past him. "Goodnight."

But Dmitri isn't done. "Did you drink?"

I stop, glancing back over my shoulder. "Yes. Why?"

He sighs, and for a second, it sounds like he's disappointed. "You should've called a cab instead of driving."

I turn to face him fully, trying not to roll my eyes. His words sound almost caring, but I know better. It's not concern—it's control. Dmitri doesn't care if I'm safe; he cares about keeping everything and everyone in line.

"I had one drink," I snap, keeping my voice steady.

His eyes bore into mine, searching for the truth. We stand there for a long moment, locked in a silent battle of wills. Finally, he breaks eye contact, running a hand through his hair.

"Thank you for bringing Yelena home safely," he says, his voice softer than I'd thought possible.

And then he walks away, leaving me standing there, thrown off by the sudden shift in his tone.

Thank you? Since when does Dmitri thank me for anything?

I watch him retreat, still processing the exchange. Yelena's words from earlier drift back into my mind.

All he understands is duty.

Could she be right? Is there a side of Dmitri I haven't seen yet?

I rub my chin as I make my way upstairs. Maybe there's more to him than the ruthless exterior he shows the world. But how deep would I have to dig to find it? And more importantly, do I even want to?

TWELVE
DMITRI

I'm halfway down the stairs when I hear footsteps behind me. My instinct sharpens, and for a moment, I slow, thinking it's Ana. The thought makes my mind wander, unbidden, back to last night.

Thank you for bringing Yelena home safely.

The words still echo in my head. They weren't what I intended to say. Hell, they felt wrong even as I said them. But there was something in Ana's expression, that defiant tilt of her chin, like she was waiting for me to tear into her, waiting for the usual criticism. And in that split second, I saw it—how I was missing the bigger picture. She brought Yelena home in one piece. Yelena, who doesn't stop until she's blind drunk, was safe because of Ana.

I don't know how the thanks slipped out of my mouth, but they did. And somehow, it felt okay. Almost natural. The look of shock on her face was unexpected, but the real surprise was how light I felt afterward, like I'd broken some unspoken rule between us by not turning it into an argument.

Lately, everything with Ana feels new. Too new. It's unsettling.

I'm drawn to her, more than I'd like to admit. The way she carries herself, her beauty—hell, even the stupid necklace that rests on her collarbone makes me envious. I want her. And I hate that I do. This wasn't supposed to happen. I married her for revenge. And yet, the desire is there. Growing.

I need to get a grip.

"Don't tell me you're leaving without breakfast?" Yelena's voice jolts me from my thoughts.

I glance over my shoulder at her standing at the top of the stairs, looking far too chipper for someone who drank enough to drown a sailor last night.

"How's your head?" I ask, already knowing the answer.

"Never been better." She grins. "I took the liberty of making you and Ana breakfast. Mostly for her, since she saved my life last night, but I made extra for you."

"I don't have time," I say, my fingers itching toward my buzzing phone. "I've got a meeting."

She blocks my path, spreading her arms wide, her smile too innocent to be genuine. "You're the boss, Dmitri. You can take ten minutes to eat breakfast with your wife."

I sigh. "Dinner. We'll do dinner."

Her smile vanishes, replaced with a disappointed frown. "Studies show that couples who eat together grow closer over time. It reduces divorce rates and—"

"Divorce?" I raise a brow, cutting her off. "Since when did you become a marriage counselor?"

Yelena tuts. "Since I've had to force you to sit in the same room as Ana. It's like you're allergic to her. You're sending the message that you can't stand to spend time with your own wife. Do you even care about her, Dmitri?"

I stiffen at the question. "I never said I didn't."

"You don't have to say it. Your actions are doing all the talking," she shoots back. "Ana's warm, kind, and loving. If I were you, I'd be doing everything in my power to keep her by my side instead of pretending I don't need anyone."

Warm. Kind. Loving.

The words twist in my gut. I've seen her interact with others—she's all of those things to them. But not to me. To me, Ana is a storm, fierce and unyielding. Still, Yelena's right about one thing—I've never given her the chance to be anything else with me.

Maybe I pushed her away the moment we married. I left her outside the church that day, told her Janet would show her to her room, and disappeared into my own world. I made sure she knew there would be no affection between us. She is Nikolai Petrov's daughter, and that was all I needed to know.

Would things have been different if I hadn't built that wall so high?

Yelena breaks into my thoughts again, her voice softer this time. "Don't worry. Ana and I can eat without you. You're practically invisible anyway."

Something about her words digs at me. Invisible? Is that really how I've been?

Before I can stop myself, I say, "I'll eat. I haven't had bacon and eggs in a while."

Yelena's face lights up, and I silently curse myself for giving in. But maybe breakfast won't kill me.

We walk into the kitchen, and there's Ana, already seated at the table, her eyes flickering up when she hears us. She looks as surprised as I feel.

I catch her gaze for a brief moment, and something stirs inside me—something I don't want to acknowledge. I take a seat across from her, the tension between us almost tangible, and Yelena slides two plates of food in front of us with a grin, oblivious to the charged atmosphere.

"See? This isn't hard," she chirps, settling into her own seat with satisfaction.

Ana doesn't say anything. Neither do I.

We eat in silence, the clink of silverware the only sound in the room. And yet, despite the quiet, my mind keeps drifting to her, watching the way her lips move as she takes a bite, the way her fingers brush against the edge of her plate.

This wasn't supposed to happen.

I wasn't supposed to want her. But I do. And it's a problem I can't afford to have.

Because no matter how much I might be drawn to Ana, she's still Nikolai Petrov's daughter. And I can never forget that.

YELENA'S SHOES click on the hardwood floor as she strides into my office. I follow her, and the second I sit down at my desk, dropping my bag carelessly onto the table, she's already spinning around like she owns the place.

"You didn't have to come with me, you know," I mutter, leaning back in my chair, eyeing her with mild irritation.

She ignores the tone, planting both hands on my desk with a mischievous grin. "Yeah, but if I'm going to learn how things work, I need to stick with you for a while, right?"

I arch a brow. "And what exactly do you think learning 'how things work' entails?"

Yelena plops down in the chair opposite me, her fingers tapping rhythmically on the polished mahogany. "I've decided I want to settle down. For good this time. Get a job, make some money—work for you."

I shake my head before she even finishes her sentence. "You're not working for me, Yelena. What I do isn't safe. You went to business school; you can find a job anywhere else that doesn't come with the possibility of a bullet to the head."

Her stubbornness kicks in, and she meets my gaze without flinching. "I don't want to work anywhere else, Dmitri. I know this isn't a family business, but we've been apart for too long. I've been running from things that won't go away until I face them."

I stare at her, sighing internally as I set my hands on the desk. "If you want to keep living with Ana and me, fine. As long as she agrees. But this," I gesture to the office, to the world we both know I live in, "isn't the life for you. I take risks every day. I always have to watch my back. I don't want that for you."

Yelena places her hand over mine, squeezing it in that affectionate way she's always had.

"You know," she begins, her voice softer, "after I first found out we didn't share the same mother, I always wondered why you were so nice to me. I'm not your real sister."

"You are my real sister," I snap, cutting through her words.

She rolls her eyes, brushing it off. "You know what I mean. You're the only one who ever cared about me. My mother was always chasing her next boyfriend, and your father was more interested in this life."

She's not wrong. But caring about her didn't come naturally. When my mother died and my father brought Yelena and her mother into our home, it took me a while to feel any sort of attachment. She was just a kid, barely one year old. But over time, it felt like a duty—protecting her, watching out for her. My father made sure I knew the weight of my responsibilities, and looking after her became one of them.

"I know you're more worried than ever because of what happened two years ago," she continues, her voice barely a whisper now. "But I'm fine, Dmitri. I've been going to therapy, working through it. It took time, but I'm getting over him."

I search her eyes, looking for cracks in her armor. Yelena has always been able to hide behind that smile, lighting up the room with her laughter while keeping her pain buried. But I know better.

"Are you sure?" I ask, my voice uncharacteristically gentle. I'm not used to this—showing concern. But I can't help it with her. I remember the wreck she was a year ago, pretending everything was fine when it clearly wasn't.

Her lip quivers slightly, but she keeps it together. "I fell in love with a man who used me. In every way possible. It takes time to heal from that, especially when I almost married him. But I'm okay now. I promise."

I nod slowly, though doubt lingers in the back of my mind. If I don't believe her, it means I don't trust she's healing. And what kind of brother would that make me?

"Alright," I concede, watching her eyes light up in victory. "But I'm not letting you near the dangerous stuff. You'll handle the accounting, maybe review some of the business ideas I've been working on. That's it."

Her grin is instantaneous. "That's more than enough! When do I start?"

I glance at the clock. "I have a meeting in fifteen minutes. How about right now?"

"Works for me," she chirps, then pauses. "There's just one more thing, Dmitri."

I raise a brow, pausing as I reach for a document. Her tone shifts, and for the first time since she entered my office, there's seriousness in her eyes.

"Just because our parents didn't understand love doesn't mean it doesn't exist. It might not start out that way, but sometimes, love hides in the places we least expect."

She smiles, but her words hang in the air, heavy and pointed.

My thoughts immediately turn to Ana—whether I like it or not. Yelena's earlier comments from this morning replay in my head, a mental loop I can't shake off.

Is there something more beneath all the tension? All the fights?

I sigh inwardly, irritated by the questions bubbling up that I'd rather ignore. I'm not the type to believe in happiness or love, especially not for someone like me.

But still...

Is it possible? Could there be pockets of happiness, even for me?

The thought lingers, uncomfortably lodged in my mind as I try to push it aside.

Focus on the work. Always focus on the work.

THIRTEEN
ANA

I drag myself out of the car, my feet heavy as lead as I make my way to the graveyard behind the gated fence. Every step feels like I'm wading through thick mud, weighed down by the endless tears I've cried and the hollow ache in my chest. I don't even know how I made it here, but somehow, I keep moving.

I push open the gate with trembling fingers and let my legs carry me to the headstone. The graveyard is quiet, almost untouched, the few bodies buried here belonging to people connected to my family. It's a private place, away from the world.

It's where my father buried my mother. Every year since I was two, he brought me here to visit her.

"*Mamochka*." I fall to my knees, letting my body crumble in front of her grave. The tears spill freely now, rolling down my cheeks as my shaking hands brush the dirt off the headstone.

Maria Petrov. Mother and Wife. Gone, but never forgotten.

I trace the letters with my fingertips, as if touching her name might somehow bring her closer to me.

"Mom." My voice cracks, choking on the lump of sorrow lodged in my throat. "I wish you were here. I don't know what I'm doing anymore. Papa won't see me. He's avoiding me because of what he made me do—because of this marriage to Dmitri Orlov."

The sobs rack my body again, my chest heaving as I struggle to catch my breath.

"I'm alone, *Mamochka*. Completely alone, and I don't know what to do. If you were here, maybe everything would be different. Maybe I wouldn't feel so . . . trapped."

I press my forehead against the cold marble of her grave, feeling the icy stone against my burning skin. "It's not fair," I cry, my voice barely above a whisper. "I never asked for this. I never wanted this life. But I'm stuck in it. I'm a prisoner, and no one cares."

The sobs tear through me, leaving me shaking as I curl up against the gravestone, wishing more than anything that my mother could reach through the earth and hold me, comfort me the way only a mother could.

"I miss you so much, Mom," I whisper into the silence, my voice dissolving into raw, broken weeping. "Please . . . if you can hear me, send me something. A sign. Anything. I just need you."

But the air remains still, the weight of my grief too much to bear.

BY THE TIME I get back home, it feels like I've been hollowed out. The grief still clings to me like a second skin, making every movement feel like I'm dragging an anchor behind me. I barely make it through the door before Yelena's voice reaches me.

"Anastasia?" Her tone shifts from light to concerned as soon as she catches sight of me. She rushes over, her face full of worry. "What happened? Are you okay? What's going on?"

I try to speak, but my throat is too tight, my emotions too raw. My legs buckle beneath me, the strength drained from my body.

"Yelena . . ." I choke on her name, tears blurring my vision again.

Before I collapse completely, she's there, holding me tight, her arms wrapping around me like a lifeline.

"It's okay," she soothes, guiding me to the couch. "You don't have to say anything yet. Just sit down and breathe."

I can barely catch my breath, but Yelena's voice is calm and steady, just what I need right now.

"In and out," she whispers. "Just breathe. You're safe here."

I follow her instructions, taking shaky breaths until the weight on my chest lifts just enough to let me speak. When the worst of it passes, I tell her everything—the memories of my mom, the annual visits to her grave, how my father has refused to see me, and how it feels like I've been abandoned by the one person who should always support me.

"He wasn't there today," I say, my voice breaking. "He's never missed any of her death anniversaries. I don't know what to do anymore, Yelena. It's like I'm drowning, and there's no one to pull me out."

Yelena shakes her head, squeezing my hand. "You're not alone. You've got me, okay? I might've just gotten here, but I'm not going anywhere. I'm pretty good at offering shoulders to cry on." She offers a small smile. "I even give out discounts for extended use."

I let out a weak laugh, the sound more of a broken sob.

"Oh yeah? And what's your rate?"

She grins, her eyes lighting up with warmth. "One hug per day should cover it."

I reach out, pulling her into a hug. "You're a much better deal than anything else I've got going."

We sit in silence for a while, Yelena's presence a balm for the raw ache in my chest. When I finally pull away, I head to my room to take a nap, hoping that sleep will numb the pain for a little while. But as soon as I sit down, alone again, the grief rushes back. My hands shake as I run them through my hair, the weight of everything pressing down on me all over again.

I step into the bathroom, needing something—anything—to wash away the feeling. The hot water from the shower beats against my skin, but it doesn't do enough to drown out the sadness that clings to me.

Wrapping a towel around myself, I step out of the bathroom—and freeze.

Dmitri is standing by the door, his eyes widening the second he sees me.

For a moment, neither of us moves. The air between us crackles with tension, and I realize with horror that I'm standing here, wet, in nothing but a towel.

"What are you doing here?" I snap, my voice sharper than I intended.

He rubs the bridge of his nose, sighing deeply. "Yelena told me you weren't feeling well. I came to check on you."

"I'm fine," I bite out, crossing my arms over my chest, trying to cover the vulnerability I feel.

He takes a step forward, his expression softening in a way I've never seen before. "I know about your mother's death anniversary."

I shrug, turning away from him. "So? That doesn't have

anything to do with you."

But Dmitri doesn't move. "I'm not here to offer empty sympathy, Ana. I just—"

"Just what?" I spin around, tears spilling down my cheeks. "Just want to ease your guilt? I don't need it. I don't need *you*."

"Ana—" he starts, his voice low, but I cut him off.

"Please, Dmitri," I whisper, my voice breaking. "Not today. I can't deal with this. Not now."

He stands there for a moment, watching me as I turn my back on him, retreating to my closet to find something to wear. But then, I feel his presence behind me, and before I can say anything, his arms wrap around me, pulling me into his chest.

"I'm sorry," he murmurs into my hair. "I'm so sorry."

My first instinct is to push him away, but I don't. The warmth of his arms, the steady rise and fall of his chest, it all feels too much like the comfort I've been craving.

He turns me to face him, and I sob against his chest, my body shaking as he holds me tighter, refusing to let go.

"Take it out on me," he says softly. "Hit me. Scream at me. But don't keep it in, Ana. You'll only hurt yourself more."

I finally try to push him away, but my strength is gone. All I can do is cling to him, the man I've spent months resenting, as the sobs rack my body.

"That's it," he whispers, his voice gentle. "Breathe. Just breathe."

For the first time in a long while, I feel like maybe, just maybe, I'm not as alone as I thought. When I calm down somewhat, I open my eyes, realizing that my fingers are digging into his arms. I loosen the grip, and the red marks I left behind make me gasp.

"Oh gosh," I mutter incoherently.

Dmitri smiles. It's the first time he's ever smiled at me that way. Warmth touches every inch of his face, making his eyes look brighter and bluer, his cheekbones softer.

Unable to stop myself, I reach up and touch his lips with my thumb.

His smile drops, and I snatch my hand away as though burned.

"I'm sorry. I'm so sorry."

"For what?"

"Uh, I just—" I hesitate. "I haven't seen you smile at me since we got married. I mean, there was the one time when Yelena was there, but it was because of her..."

I don't finish, and silence follows.

We stare at each other, and it feels like an eternity. Something shifts between us, the air now charged with an undercurrent I can't define but feel all the way down to my bones.

What's going on?

I open my mouth to ask what's changed, what this charged energy means, but the words die on my lips.

"I'm going to kiss you now."

Dmitri surprises me by speaking first, his voice low.

My heart stutters in my chest. I don't know what's brought about the sudden change in the way he sees me and treats me, but I'm not about to question it.

One large hand comes up to cradle my cheek as his head dips low.

Then his lips are on mine, soft yet decisive. I gasp quietly at the unfamiliar yet overwhelming sensation. This is no peck or cursory kiss—it feels like an earthquake, shaking me to my core.

One kiss turns to two, three, forgetting to count as I lose

myself. All the months of hostility between us seem to melt away as I circle my arms around his neck.

His thumb strokes my cheek as our lips move together, and I realize with startling clarity that I *like* this. More than I thought I ever would.

Reluctantly, Dmitri ends the kiss but stays close, our foreheads touching as we both catch our breath.

I keep my eyes closed, afraid of what I might see in his when I open them. I don't want this moment to end.

"Anastasia," he whispers my full name. "I want more. If you want me to stop, you need to say it."

This is uncharted territory.

I should take a step back and evaluate.

"Don't stop." My lips move, birthing the words.

He nods and leans in again, kissing me deeper this time. There's no question of patience or subtlety. We both know this is more than a kiss—we know where it will end. I let my towel fall when his hand touches the part where I tucked it in, and he ends the kiss to stare at me, sucking in a deep breath.

I feel exposed under his stare, but he looks at me like I'm something unbelievable. It erases my vulnerability. His gaze is pure adoration, and his hands, when they cup my breasts, do so gently.

"Dmitri," I murmur his name, leaning in as his fingers tease my nipples to hardened peaks, awash with need and desire.

Dmitri claims my lips again as his muscular arms encircle my body, closing the space between us. He nudges my legs apart, stepping in with a muscled thigh.

I pant as his tongue slides into my mouth, and his hand cups my ass, kneading hard. Every part of me screams his name, wanting to be touched and set aflame by his hands.

"Bed," he whispers, lifting me off my feet.

I throw my arms around him with a breezy laugh, which dies when he lays me down, and I notice his gaze. Dark and intense, Dmitri's eyes send a shot of pleasure through me, while a steady pulse kicks between my legs.

He braces his weight on his arms as he hovers above me and one hand caresses my cheek.

"You're beautiful," Dmitri utters as his thumb strokes the spot behind my ear. "So beautiful."

My cheeks turn rosy, and the flush spreads across my face. I've been complimented a lot before I met Dmitri, but I've never been with someone who called me *beautiful* while looking at me like he wanted to devour me.

With a promise that I'll enjoy every moment of it.

His lips touch my forehead. "Gorgeous. When I saw you walk into the garden that night, I couldn't keep my eyes off you."

Does he mean it? I wonder, searching for the truth in his eyes.

My thoughts melt away when his lips touch my chin—kisses peppered down my neck and my collarbone. His hands run over my arms, my stomach, and between my legs.

I gasp when his thumb brushes over my clit, tilting my pelvis and riding his hand. His finger slips inside me, and he touches my g-spot, rubbing against it until I'm panting loudly, sinking my fingers into his hair.

My walls clench around his finger, greedy for more and craving release. Dmitri pushes me until I'm close—moaning and panting and begging him with heavy sighs, then removes his finger.

I open my mouth to protest, and he swallows my words with another kiss. My impatient hands reach for his shirt, getting it off quickly while the sound of his zipper echoes in the background.

Then he stops abruptly, and I open my eyes to see him staring down at me with an unreadable expression on his face.

"What?" My voice comes out squeaky. I clear my throat and try again. "What's wrong?"

He sighs and rubs his forehead. "I don't have a condom."

"Just be careful."

He nods, smirking. "Where were we?"

I'm once again swept away by his kisses, and I suck in a deep breath when he pushes into me inch by inch until my body stretches to accommodate him.

"Are you okay?" he asks.

I can't trust myself to speak, so I nod, wrapping my arms around his neck as his thrusts increase—harder, faster, filling every inch of me. My hips rock to match his tempo, and I lose myself in the waves that pull me under repeatedly, taking over my mind, body, and everything else.

He hikes my legs around his waist, and I lock them tight.

"*Kotyonok,*" Dmitri whispers in my ear. "You feel so wet. So fucking wet and tight."

My entire body trembles when he changes position, pushing my legs close to my chest.

"*Yes. Yes.*" My hands fall on the bed, and I cling to the sheets, fisting them tight.

My climax hits me without warning and I go taut for a second before I explode, falling apart with shudders. He doesn't stop, though, and a tightness rolls through me as I come again.

I hear Dmitri's low groan, and I feel him pull out as I close my eyes, basking in the euphoria of release.

Minutes later, after returning from the bathroom and climbing back into bed, I lay next to him with my limbs feeling like limp noodles.

He pulls me to him, but neither of us utters a word.

Where do we go from here?

It's obvious that this is a one-time thing. We don't even like each other. It's easy for only sexual chemistry to exist between two people when they can go their separate ways after. But what happens when they're married?

FOURTEEN
DMITRI

I wake slowly, blinking against the sunlight spilling through the window. I can feel warmth on my face, the rare sensation of peace wrapped around me. That's unusual, considering I barely sleep more than five hours on a good night. The weight of endless responsibilities usually keeps me half-awake, always vigilant. But this morning feels different.

Something shifts in the bed beside me.

I turn my head, and there she is. Ana.

I freeze.

What is she doing here?

And then it hits me—*last night*. The memories come flooding back as I glance around the room, seeing the telltale signs. The way we tangled together, the heat between us as she clung to me, the feel of her skin under my hands. We fucked, and I let myself fall asleep with her in my arms.

I shouldn't have.

I should've walked away, should've left the room before things got messy. But instead, I stayed, and now I'm lying here like a damn fool, watching her sleep.

I try to reason with myself, to dismiss the strange pull in my chest. *Who am I kidding?*

My eyes linger on her face, the peaceful rise and fall of her chest as she breathes, her eyelashes fluttering softly against her cheeks. Anastasia Orlov, *my wife*, lying next to me like she belongs there.

My hand moves almost on instinct, fingers itching to touch her, to trace the curve of her cheek. But I stop myself just inches away. If I touch her, if I give in to that urge, it'll break the spell. And I know as well as anyone that the moment the spell breaks, we go back to what we were—strangers under the same roof, a marriage built on business interest and revenge.

This thing between us won't last. It *can't* last.

I swallow hard, trying to bury the gnawing feeling inside me, but it's there, persistent and irritating.

Her eyelids flutter open, and I can see the confusion in her gaze as it lands on me. She gasps and rolls off the bed, hitting the floor with a loud *thud*.

"Ouch!" she yelps, cradling her knee.

Without thinking, I'm off the bed in a second, crouching down beside her. "What the hell was that?" I laugh, even as something tugs at me.

She lets out a girlish giggle but quickly catches herself, waving it off with a flick of her hand as a frown erases the glimmer of playfulness. "Forget it. I'm fine."

I stand. I start to reach out to help her up, but she holds out a hand, stopping me. "Can you give me some space, please?"

There it is. The pushback.

I feel the cold wash of rejection settle over me, and I know it's coming. She's pulling away already, setting the boundary between us. But still, I perch on the edge of the bed, watching her, waiting for her to say what I know is coming.

It would be smarter to walk out, save myself from hearing it. I know exactly what she's going to say. And yet, a part of me—some weak, foolish part—waits.

Ana sighs, closing her eyes as if steeling herself. "Thank you for being there for me. But what happened," she hesitates, "it was a mistake. We both know that. It would be silly to think otherwise. Right?"

"Right," I say, my voice flat, the word leaving a bitter taste in my mouth.

I shouldn't feel this way. My chest shouldn't ache like this.

I stand abruptly, the weight of her words settling over me like a cold, heavy blanket. "I should go. I'll see you later."

As I make my way toward the door, her voice stops me in my tracks.

"Dmitri?" she calls my name softly, and something in me stirs, like a flicker of warmth in the icy distance. I turn my head slightly, just enough to hear her. "Thank you," she says quietly.

A spark.

But it fades just as quickly as it came, snuffed out by the sound of her footsteps retreating toward the bathroom. I stand there for a moment, feeling the emptiness return, then head back to my room.

I scrub my face with my hands, the cold water doing nothing to wash away the lingering frustration. I shouldn't be thinking about her like this. *It was a mistake*; she's made that clear. I need to let it go, move on.

But the truth is, I can't stop thinking about last night.

About how her body fit against mine, the way she whispered my name, the way she let me in.

I step into the shower, the scalding water cascading over me, but the heat doesn't stop my mind from wandering back to her. It's stupid, but I can't shake it. She's gotten under my skin in a way I wasn't prepared for, and it's messing with me.

There's no going back to the way things were between us. No matter how much we both pretend it was an accident, we've crossed a line.

So where do we go from here?

I don't know, but one thing is clear: she's not leaving my mind anytime soon.

"IGOR," I say, the second I see him hovering by the elevator as I step out.

Typical. He's been circling like a vulture for days. "What brings you to my office?"

"I was hoping I could have a word with you," he says, trying to match my strides as I make my way down the hallway.

I know what this is about before he even opens his mouth. Igor's been sweating the Las Vegas deal for weeks now, unable to close it. I knew he would come to me sooner or later. I let him twist in the wind and watched him scramble. He's desperate now, and desperate men are easy to control.

We reach my office door, and he halts, shifty-eyed, fidgeting like a kid about to confess.

Here we go.

"Okay?" I ask, pausing to let him gather whatever courage he has left.

He avoids my gaze, staring at the floor, the walls—anywhere but at me.

Pathetic.

I already know what he wants, but I let him grovel. It's more fun.

"You remember when I told you about that good deal in Vegas?" His voice is laced with anxiety. "A billionaire investor interested in my casinos?"

I arch a brow, barely able to conceal my disdain. "*Your* casinos? Did you actually buy them?"

He scratches the back of his head, avoiding the question entirely. "Well, no. Not yet. But I met with the owners. They're willing to move forward, it's just . . . there's a time factor."

I stare at him, pretending ignorance. "And what's stopping you? You've got your investor, right? You've got the parties lined up. All you need to do is close the deal, buy them out. Profit rolls in."

Igor shifts nervously, and I can practically see the beads of sweat forming on his forehead.

Just say it. Admit your failure.

"Well," he falters, looking like he'd rather be anywhere else. "The thing is, the investor wasn't going to give me the money outright. He wanted shares. And then, after some time, I'd pay him back half."

I nod slowly, enjoying the way he squirms. "So, you're telling me you just realized you were about to get played? That the investor was ready to screw you over?"

Igor's eyes widen with panic. "Yes. Yes, exactly! I should've listened to you. You warned me about outsiders. I thought I could handle it, but—"

I raise a hand to stop his rambling.

Pitiful. I can almost feel sorry for him.

Almost.

"Let me guess," I say, the edge in my voice unmistakable. "You're here to ask me to fix this for you."

He flinches at the bluntness of it, but nods. "Yes, Dmitri. I need your help."

I let the silence stretch, drumming my fingers against my thigh as he stares at me like a drowning man reaching for a lifeline.

He's mine now.

"Okay, Igor," I finally say, placing a hand on his shoulder like a father about to offer sage advice. "You made a mistake. A terrible one. But it's not the end of the world." My voice lowers, calm and calculated. "I'll help you. But there's a catch."

His eyes light up with desperate hope. "What do I need to do?"

"Leave it all to me," I say simply. "I'll handle the investment, the handover, everything. Your name will be on the papers, but I'll be running the show. Agreed?"

Igor hesitates, his brows knitting together as he tries to process the offer. His eyes dart to mine, searching for the catch, but there's no hidden motive. It's all right there, laid out plainly for him.

I control everything.

"You have concerns about my methods?" I challenge, turning slightly as if ready to leave.

"No, no," he blurts out quickly. "I'll do it. I'll do whatever you think is best."

I suppress a smile, turning back to him with a slight nod.

That's more like it.

"Good. Send whatever documents you have to my secretary. I'll go over them and let you know the next steps."

Igor breathes out in relief, like a man who just got pulled from the jaws of death. "Thank you, Dmitri. Thank you."

I dismiss his gratitude with a wave, already bored of the conversation. "Don't mention it. Just remember—your loyalty is the only thing I expect in return."

He nods fervently, his grin returning. "Of course. That's why you're Dmitri Orlov. Your father was the same."

My jaw tightens, the mention of my father stirring something dark and bitter inside me.

No, he wasn't.

My father wasn't ruthless enough. He trusted the wrong people, let himself be deceived, manipulated. That's not a mistake I plan to repeat.

"I have a meeting," I say, my voice colder now. "I'll see you later."

I turn sharply, striding down the hall as my fingernails dig into my palm.

Your father was the same.

No. My father was weak in ways I'll never allow myself to be. I won't let sentiment or misplaced trust cloud my judgment. This empire will be stronger, more unshakable than his ever was. And people like Igor Pavlov? They'll be the ones who fall in line—or fall entirely.

As I reach the elevator, my thoughts flicker back to Ana.

No.

I can't afford to think about her now. Feelings make you weak, and weakness gets you killed. I tighten my grip on the situation with Igor, reminding myself of what I do best. Control. Power. Ruthlessness.

That's what keeps me at the top.

FIFTEEN
ANA

"Do you know what time it is?" Yelena's voice pops into my office like a bright, yellow ray of sunshine.

I glance up from my paperwork to see her head peeking around the door, a grin already plastered on my face. "What time is it?"

The door swings open wider, and there she is, in all her mini-skirt glory, her arms thrown wide like she's about to announce a surprise party. "Shopping time!" she declares, as if it's a national holiday.

I laugh, shaking my head and pointing at the mountain of paperwork threatening to swallow my desk. "I'd love to, but I've got work, Yelena. Crime doesn't take a day off."

She plops down into the chair opposite me, dramatically sighing like I've just told her there's no wi-fi. "These papers will still be here tomorrow, but the perfect handbag? The statement shoes? They'll be gone. Come on, let's take the afternoon off."

I pull my hand away from her outstretched one with a regretful smile. "As tempting as that sounds, I can't. I think my bosses might frown on me neglecting my legal duties for retail therapy."

Yelena's eyes twinkle mischievously, and I narrow mine. I know that look.

"What did you do?" I ask, already dreading the answer.

She leans back in the chair, twirling a strand of her hair like a schoolgirl caught red-handed. "Oh, nothing much. Just told your bosses you were working on a super important case for my brother and me. Might have mentioned unless you could meet with us all the way in Long Island today, the Orlov family would have to take their legal business elsewhere."

I groan, burying my face in my hands.

Of course, she did.

"Yelena!" I drag out her name but can't help my curiosity. "What happens when they ask me about this 'case'?"

She waves a dismissive hand. "Easy. I'll get Dmitri to send one of his guys to you. They're always in some kind of trouble."

Oh, God, no. The last thing I need is Dmitri's involvement. I can practically hear him now, lecturing me on the dangers of working too late and refusing to quit my job. He'd probably toss in something about how it's bad for my health and terrible for his image.

"Bad idea," I say firmly, shaking my head. "It's not good to mix business with . . . whatever it is that my life has become."

She sighs dramatically, leaning back in her chair. "Fine. But after work, you're coming with me. Dmitri won't let me do anything fun at his office, and I'm dying of boredom over there."

I chuckle despite myself. "Alright, after work. But what are you going to do until then?"

She stretches like a cat, her smile full of carefree mischief. "Oh, I don't know. Find some trouble to get into. Have a little fun."

I can't help but feel a small pang of jealousy as I watch her glide out of my office, her carefree attitude so effortless. Yelena seems to breeze through life, and while I know there's more to her than meets the eye, I sometimes wish I could borrow that lightness of being.

But my life is complicated. My work, my marriage to Dmitri, my estranged father—it all weighs heavily.

I rub my temples, feeling a headache coming on. "Screw it," I mutter, standing up and grabbing my bag. I might not be as free as Yelena, but I can take one afternoon off. "Work can wait."

"WHAT DO you think of this one?" Yelena holds up a brown Hermes bag for inspection, her eyes gleaming.

I tilt my head, trying to appreciate it. "It's nice, but not really me."

She huffs, taking it back. "Yeah, I figured. Too drab for you. If I'm going to spend that much, it better scream when I walk into a room."

I laugh. "Agreed."

Yelena's energy is infectious, and I find myself enjoying the time away from work, letting her drag me from store to store.

She waves her hand toward a display of shoes. "Pick something you like, it's on me. After this, we'll grab coffee, and then I'm getting you flowers."

"Flowers?" I raise an eyebrow. "Why flowers?"

She shrugs, grinning. "Why not? Everyone deserves flowers."

A soft smile tugs at my lips. When was the last time anyone gave me flowers?

A few minutes later, Yelena's voice pulls me from my thoughts. "I've been meaning to ask—do you have any siblings? I don't think I've seen anyone come by the house."

I nod, running my fingers over the buttery leather of a black Prada bag that catches my eye. "I have a half-brother. Viktor."

Her eyes widen. "You do? Why haven't I met him?"

"He doesn't live in the country," I say, pausing to admire the bag's craftsmanship. "We don't have the same mom. My father had... well, I guess you'd call it a 'past life' with Viktor's mother. She never wanted anything to do with the Bratva, refused to raise her son anywhere near it. So she stayed in Europe, kept Viktor with her in London, away from all this."

Yelena strokes her chin thoughtfully. "And your father let her? That doesn't seem... typical."

I let out a soft laugh, glancing at her. "No, it's definitely not. But he let them go when he met my mother. He was so wrapped up in her, he didn't fight it. He just... left them both alone."

"Wow. That's..." She trails off, clearly trying to process it.

"We talk regularly," I add, offering a small smile. "But Viktor's world is different from mine. He's always been the one who got away, the one who wasn't marked by all this. Sometimes I think he got lucky."

She gives me a curious look, as if trying to see beneath the layers I don't often show. "Do you ever wish you had that option?"

I shrug, glancing away as we start toward the shoe section. Her question hangs in the air between us, making me wonder about her own family. Dmitri doesn't talk much about their shared history, and it leaves a lot of blanks.

"What about you?" I ask, turning the focus back on her. "Does Dmitri talk to your mom?"

She snorts, holding up a pair of kitten heels. "My mom? She wishes. She's obsessed with the idea that Dmitri is somehow her son by default, just because she had an affair with his father."

She rolls her eyes, but there's something underneath the nonchalance—something heavier.

Before I can dig deeper, a voice interrupts us.

"Hi."

Yelena and I turn, and my gaze lands on a blonde woman dressed in pink with a sneer that could cut glass. Her hand is on her hip, and she's staring right at me.

"Hi," I say slowly, unsure of what this is about. "Can I help you?"

The woman smirks, her tone dripping with condescension. "Oh, darling. I doubt you could help me with anything. I just thought it was time we met."

What the hell?

"Um, okay? I don't know who you are, so—"

"I'm Lucia," she says, her voice sickly sweet. "Lucia Bianchi. Dmitri's lover." She rolls her eyes as if the title bores her. "Well, ex-lover. That's the downside of falling for a man who'd rather stay in a loveless marriage than enjoy life."

My stomach tightens. *Lover?* I've never heard of this woman, but the jealousy that stirs in me is undeniable.

Yelena steps forward, her tone ice cold. "Get lost."

Lucia smirks, unbothered. "Oh, Yelena. Still bitter

about the man who used you? How's your broken heart? And your body?"

I see Yelena's fists clench, and I step in, gently pushing her aside.

No one talks to Yelena like that.

Not while I'm around.

Lucia wants to play games? Fine. Let's see how she handles it when I'm standing toe to toe with her.

"Look," I say, my voice low, steady, a tone I reserve for moments when I refuse to be rattled. "I don't care about your past or present relationship with Dmitri. That's between you and him. I don't see you as competition, and frankly, you're not even worth my time."

Lucia's sneer deepens, her chest puffing out as she tilts her head back like she's about to deliver a crushing blow. "Oh really? You think I don't know the reason why he married you? Your father—" she scoffs "—a pathetic man, lost his daughter in a game of chess. My father and Dmitri are business partners, and there's more respect between them than Dmitri will ever have for your family."

Her words hit hard, right in the chest, like someone took a swing and found my weakest spot.

Papa. A reminder of the weight I've been carrying, the guilt, the constant uncertainty about whether Dmitri sees me as more than just a pawn in some elaborate game. But I refuse to let her see how deeply she's cut. I lock my jaw, steady my breathing, and force my expression into something cold and distant. She won't see how much it stings.

I let out a breath, slowly, purposefully, before meeting her gaze again. "What exactly do you think this little performance is going to achieve?" I ask, raising an eyebrow. "You think you're going to intimidate me? I'm the one with his last name," I continue, my confidence creeping back with each word. "You claim to know why he married me," I pause, letting my words linger in the air before the punchline hits, "but why didn't he choose you? If he wanted you so badly, I think we both know he'd have found a way."

I see the shift in her, the crumbling of that arrogant front. Her arms, once cockily crossed, slowly drop to her sides as the reality of my words sinks in.

She's scrambling.

I step in closer, my voice soft but sharp. "Spare me the theatrics, Lucia. I'm very secure in my position as Dmitri's wife. If you want to be his mistress," I shrug casually, "go ahead."

Lucia's face contorts with fury as she spits out her parting shot, "You'll regret your words when I'm moving into your house and sleeping in his room, right under your nose."

With that, she turns on her heel and storms off, her heels clicking sharply against the floor, the sound ringing in the aftermath of her departure.

Yelena steps forward, eyes wide, mouth agape. "You—you're a beast!"

I manage a smile, but my hands, still trembling from the exchange, are hidden behind my back. My heart is pounding so loudly in my chest I can barely hear anything else. A beast? No. I don't feel like one. I feel vulnerable.

"You're the best sister-in-law ever," Yelena gushes, throwing her arms around me in a tight hug. I return the embrace, but I can't shake the unease settling in my stomach.

I said what I had to say to Lucia, but her words are still echoing in my mind. What if there's something I don't know? What if, despite everything, she is right about

Dmitri? If she's had him once, what's stopping him from going back to her?

We might share a home—we might have fucked once—but there's no real commitment between us. Nothing binding him to me except a last name and a contract. If he decides to see other women, I won't be able to stop him.

The real question, the one that gnaws at the edges of my confidence, is what I'll do if I find out I'm not the only one sharing his bed.

SIXTEEN
DMITRI

I slide the file across the desk, watching as Igor Pavlov scrambles to open it like it holds the secret to saving his skin. It does—just not in the way he thinks. He flips through the pages hurriedly, glancing up at me with those darting, nervous eyes. Desperate men never read the fine print. That's why I like doing business with them.

"As I promised," I say, tapping the folder with my finger, "the paperwork for the casino project. All you need to do is sign."

I push the pen toward him, watching him swallow hard. The clock's ticking, and I know he's feeling the heat. He needs this deal to go through. The former owners gave him a deadline, and he's on the edge of losing everything.

He won't bother reading the part where I take full control after a year. Not until it's too late.

Igor hesitates when he gets to the signature page, looking up at me with a pathetic attempt at confidence. "How're we working out the investment? What's the interest? How long do I have to pay you back?"

I drum my fingers on the desk, letting the tension build

before I respond. "I'll take ten percent of your annual profits for ten years. No payback necessary."

His eyes widen like I've just handed him the winning lottery ticket. "That's . . . generous. Too generous."

I lean back in my chair, keeping my expression calm. "Is it? With the plan I've got, those casinos will bring in more than double the purchase cost in the first year alone. You'll be swimming in money."

His tongue flicks out nervously to wet his lips. He doesn't realize he's about to sign away his empire.

"I see. Okay," he mutters, his voice shaky, but he picks up the pen anyway. I don't take my eyes off him as he scribbles his name on the dotted line. The ink dries, and with it, his fate.

"Thank you," I say smoothly, pulling the file back toward me, tucking it away. "I'll be in touch."

Igor leans forward, his desperation showing again. "Don't you need me for something? I mean, I get to have a say in the renovation, right? I've got ideas I thought about implementing."

I stifle the urge to laugh. His ideas? Not happening. I give him a quick shake of my head. "Don't worry. I'll consider your suggestions. But for now, let me handle things. I didn't leave you hanging, did I? You should trust me by now."

He chuckles nervously, trying to keep up appearances. "I trust you, Dmitri. Hell, I was one of the few people who supported you when the alliance was first proposed, remember?"

Oh, I remember. I also remember how he tried to stab me in the back when I was grieving my father. But I don't show that. Not yet.

"Why don't we celebrate?" Igor's trying to lighten the

mood, offering an olive branch he doesn't realize I'll break over his head later. "I know the perfect place. Hell, I'm thinking of buying the bar next. Elite clients, beautiful women—"

I cut him off, my voice cold. "What about Freya?"

Igor sputters, caught off guard. "W-we could just drink. Hang out, nothing more."

I stare at him, unblinking. It's fascinating how quickly they forget what matters. Igor, Alexey, and the rest—they're older, used to thinking their years somehow give them an edge. But in this world, age doesn't mean anything. Power does. Control does. Rank and loyalty are the currency here, and they're sorely lacking.

"I'll be there," I say, deciding to play along for now. "Might come a little late. Things to attend to."

He stands, adjusting his jacket, looking relieved like he's just escaped a firing squad. He reaches for the file, but I'm faster.

"Why don't I hold onto this?" I suggest, my tone sharp. "For safekeeping. You know as well as I do there's no replacing that document if something happens to it."

He pulls his hand back slowly, nodding. "Right. But you'll keep me updated, yeah?"

I flash him a smile, the kind that makes men like him uneasy. "Of course."

As he turns to leave, he throws me a grin, thinking he's still in the game. "You're the man, Dmitri. I'll save you a seat and a bottle."

I watch him go, the file safe in my hands. He has no idea that he's already lost. By the time he realizes it, I'll have what I need, and he'll have nothing.

This is how it's always been. Control. Power. They never see it coming until it's too late.

I ARRIVE at the Gentleman's Club, already regretting my decision. The hostess leads me to the VIP room where Igor and Bianchi are deep in conversation, along with some guy I barely know. Alexey's absence is obvious, but no surprise. He's always been more selective about these gatherings.

Igor, already drunk, attempts to stand when he sees me. "My good man!" he slurs, wobbling as he clutches a bottle in one hand and a glass in the other.

"You're going to break someone's head," Bianchi says, laughing as he takes the bottle from Igor, his gaze shifting to me. "Dmitri, I didn't think you were the type to drink at night. Formal parties, sure, but this? It's a surprise."

I sit down, already regretting my presence. I don't do things like this unless I have a reason, and tonight's no different. Igor's drunk, the man next to him is distracted with a blonde, and soon enough, I'll have Bianchi to myself. He's next on my list.

I raise my glass toward Bianchi. "Pour me a glass."

He looks me in the eye, filling my glass. "Something's going on with you."

I don't bother denying it. Bianchi's not stupid and playing coy won't get me anywhere. "Yeah, there is. But I can handle it. I hear there's trouble on your end. Need help? I could step in. You'll owe me, but who doesn't?"

Bianchi shakes his head, laughing as he takes a sip from his drink. "You know, Lucia's not backing down."

"Backing down from what?" I ask though I already know.

"She wants you, Dmitri. For all of Lucia's games, she's never been with a married man. But now? She's dead set on you. I've tried to stop her, but if you know my daughter—and I think you do—you know better. She's not giving up."

The man sounds stressed, and I don't blame him. He's never been able to control Lucia. He just enables her, covering her mistakes when things go sideways.

I place my glass on the table and face him squarely. "She's going to have to learn, Bianchi. I'm married. I'm committed to my wife. I'm not bringing anyone else into our relationship."

Bianchi shrugs, a tired acceptance in his expression. "I understand."

We sit in silence for a moment, the tension palpable. Then, as expected, he leans back, folding his arms. "Can I ask you something? You like her? Your wife, I mean. Because, let's be honest, most Bratva heads don't stay faithful. Hell, Pavlov over there," he nods toward a passed-out Igor, "doesn't even pretend. Loyalty to the men is one thing. But marriage? That's different."

Do I *like* Anastasia? "Like" doesn't even begin to describe it.

Every time I look at her, something shifts inside me. There's a pull, a need that I've never felt with anyone else. When I kiss her, it's like a surge of adrenaline, something deeper than just desire. It confuses me, this feeling. I didn't expect it, didn't want it. I married her for reasons that had nothing to do with affection. Yet, here I am.

"I'm a faithful man, Bianchi," I say, not fully answering his question. "I protect what's mine. That includes my marriage."

He raises an eyebrow, clearly not expecting that. "Then I'd better warn Lucia about the heartbreak to come. She told me she met your wife while shopping, said Anastasia was cold and rude. Though, I'm guessing Lucia wasn't exactly friendly herself."

My mind spins at his words. Ana met Lucia? Why didn't she tell me? Did Lucia mention that we'd been together before? What does Ana think of me now? Does she think I'm a man who sleeps with every woman that crosses his path?

I run my fingers through my hair, tension building in my chest. I need to talk to Ana before this blows up in my face.

Standing abruptly, I grab my jacket. "I've got to head home. Tell Igor I had a good time."

Bianchi gives me a nod. "I'll make sure he gets home safe. Have a good night, Dmitri."

I leave the club, ignoring the women who call out to me, their hands grazing my shoulders as I walk past. They mean nothing. My mind is elsewhere, back at home, with Anastasia.

The drive is a blur. All I can think about is what Lucia might have said to Ana. The sex we had might have been a mistake, but Ana deserves to hear the truth from me. I have to tell her that Lucia and I have been over for a long time, and there's no place for her in my life now.

When I step into the house, it's Yelena I find in the living room, casually eating bread with jam while watching TV. She turns to me with a teasing grin.

"About time you came home. I was starting to think you had another family."

"Why are you still here?" I quip back. "You didn't come home last night. Thought you'd moved out."

She stands, popping the rest of the bread into her mouth. "I wanted to give you and Ana some space. I mean, you're my brother and Ana's becoming my best friend. Didn't want to be the third wheel."

I stay quiet, but she scurries over, rubbing her shoulder against mine with a mischievous smile. "Did something happen last night? Anything... interesting?"

I brush her off with a hand. "You're nosy for someone who doesn't want to be a third wheel. Where's Ana?"

"Asleep."

"Asleep?" I frown, glancing at the clock. "It's only ten. She doesn't sleep this early."

Yelena steps in front of me, her face serious now. "How would you know that, huh? Something going on between you two?"

I ignore her, heading for the stairs, but she stops me, her tone shifting to something more somber.

"I know why you married her. I know it wasn't for love."

Her words freeze me in place.

"But Ana's incredible," Yelena continues. "She's sweet, smart, and tough. She'd do anything for the people she cares about. Like when she stood up for me against Lucia. When I froze, Ana stepped in. Protected me."

I grip Yelena's shoulders, my mind racing. "What else did Lucia say?"

She hesitates, clicking her tongue before answering. "Lucia implied you chose Ana for business, but she's the one who has your heart. She made it clear she thinks she will have you again."

My jaw clenches. Lucia's playing a dangerous game, and if she thinks I'll let her meddle in my life, she's gravely mistaken.

Ana doesn't deserve this. And Lucia? She's about to find out what happens when you push Dmitri Orlov too far. "Never," I say strongly, shaking my head. "Lucia and I are a thing of the far past. I ended things way before Ana and I got married. I'd never betray Ana like that."

Yelena's words hit me harder than I expected. They linger in my head like an accusation I can't shake off. She's right—Ana's been carrying the weight of her father's guilt, my resentment, and the mess of a life she didn't choose. I let my anger toward Nikolai Petrov blind me to the fact that his daughter wasn't the one who betrayed me. Yet, I've punished her all the same.

"I need to check on Ana," I say quietly, the weight of guilt tightening in my chest.

Yelena steps aside, offering a small nod. "Do what you need to do. I'm going to bed."

As I make my way to Ana's room, each step feels heavier, like I'm walking toward something I can't undo. I push the door open carefully, not wanting to disturb her. The dim light from her bedside lamp casts a soft glow on her face, and for a moment, I just stand there, staring.

She's breathtaking in her sleep. So peaceful, so vulnerable. The opposite of what I've always made her feel. She deserves more—more than I've given her, more than this cold, transactional life we've fallen into.

"*Kotyonok*," I whisper, my fingers tracing the air just above her skin, close enough to feel her warmth but not touching her. "I'm sorry. I didn't mean to put you in this situation. I was angry—angry at your father, at the world, but I shouldn't have let that fall on you. None of this is your fault."

I lean down, my lips brushing the air near her cheek. "I should've been kinder," I breathe, hoping somehow the words will reach her, even in her sleep. "I'll deal with Lucia. I'll fix this. I promise."

I stay there for a while, watching her. It's strange how

the simple rise and fall of her chest can bring me a sense of calm I haven't felt in years. She reaches out in her sleep, her hand brushing against mine, and my heart stumbles in my chest.

"Dmitri," she whispers my name, her eyelids fluttering briefly as if she's caught between the dream world and reality.

A rush of emotions surges through me—things I can't explain, things I don't *want* to explain. I gently pull my hand away from her grip, retreating like the coward I've become when it comes to her. Standing by the door, I look back at her one last time. She's already settled back into peaceful sleep, unaware of the storm inside me.

It's a shame, really—a damn shame—that I'll never be able to say these things to her when she's awake. Because men like me don't get to have peace. We make promises in the dark, and they disappear with the daylight.

SEVENTEEN
ANA

"Flowers for you," Steve announces as he strides into my office, holding a massive bouquet of white and red roses like it's the most normal thing in the world for me to receive. "Met the delivery guy on my way in. Figured I'd do him a solid and bring them up."

I stare at the bouquet suspiciously. "What about my signature?" I ask, wondering who would send me something like this. The only person who might send me roses is Yelena, and she's more of a chocolates and cocktails kind of girl.

Steve shrugs. "I signed for you."

Of course, he did. Because that's totally normal. I should probably ask how, since delivery guys don't just hand things over without verification, but I can already imagine him pulling some fast-talking nonsense. Not worth the effort.

I get up and take the roses from him, their scent hitting me as I inhale deeply. It's nice—unexpected, but nice. A small smile creeps onto my face, though I can't shake the curiosity gnawing at me. Who's responsible for this?

"This came with it," Steve says, holding up a pink envelope between two fingers like it's a classified document.

I roll my eyes and snatch it out of his hand. "First, you shouldn't sign for things addressed to me. Second, my personal life is none of your business. And third," I gesture at the mountain of paperwork on my desk, "I've got a lot to do, so if you don't mind..."

He clicks his tongue, then heads for the door, lingering for a beat, hoping I'll crack and read the letter in front of him. When I don't, he finally leaves.

As soon as the door clicks shut, I rip open the envelope, curiosity winning over. Inside is a folded note and when I see who it is from, my stomach drops. *No way.*

The note is short and to the point:

Anastasia,

I'd like us to have dinner. I'll send my stylist to set you up with a dress. Or several.

—Dmitri

I read it again, just to make sure I'm not hallucinating. Dinner? Shopping? *What?*

I hold the letter up, staring at it like it might suddenly change into something that makes more sense. *Dmitri* sending flowers and asking me to dinner? Is this his version of an apology? Or worse . . . guilt over what happened between us?

It's been days since we slept together, and while I've been trying to compartmentalize it—as in, shove it into a drawer and never look at it again—this is not how I expected him to follow up. I thought maybe we'd just avoid each other until the awkwardness faded into a distant, foggy memory.

But dinner? A stylist? The whole thing feels so transactional. Of course, that's exactly how Dmitri operates. I've been invited to a business meeting with a wardrobe requirement.

"What is this? A summons?" I mutter to myself, shaking my head.

The thought crosses my mind that he might be feeling guilty. But no, Dmitri doesn't do guilt. Or if he does, it's buried under layers of icy detachment. Besides, he hasn't exactly made an effort to see me since we slept together.

I glance at the flowers again, my heart speeding up despite my better judgment. It's the first time he's ever given me a gift. Probably sent by his secretary, but still. It's the thought that—nope, I'm not doing this. I can't afford to get my hopes up.

"Dmitri wouldn't know how to be thoughtful if it slapped him in the face," I mutter, trying to tamp down any stupid expectations.

But damn it if he doesn't know how to make a woman feel like a goddess in bed.

I give myself a mental shake. Focus, Ana. Flowers don't mean feelings, and dinner doesn't mean, well, anything, really. It's probably a power move, and I'm not about to fall for it.

Just as I'm setting the note aside, there's a knock at the door.

"Come in," I say, half expecting Steve to barge back in with another nosy comment.

Instead, a smartly dressed woman with a perfectly cut bob and designer sunglasses strides in. She's wearing a tailored blazer paired with a boho-chic skirt—an outfit that would look ridiculous on me but somehow works for her.

She smiles and extends a hand. "Hi, I'm Andrea. Mr. Orlov sent me. You're Mrs. Anastasia Orlov, right?"

I blink, connecting the dots. *The stylist.* Of course. "Uh, yeah. That's me."

"Great," she says, all business. "It's past noon, so I was thinking now's the perfect time to go shopping."

Shopping. Right. For dinner.

"I've got a lot of work to do," I say, motioning to my desk full of paperwork. "Maybe in a couple of hours?"

Andrea shakes her head with the air of someone who's had this conversation too many times. "I understand, but we're not shopping for just any dinner. Mr. Orlov is taking you to a six-star establishment. You don't just throw on any old dress for something like that. I have the expertise, but we need *time.*"

Six-star? Is that even a thing? Isn't five stars the top? I'm clearly out of my league here, and Andrea knows it.

"I might get fired if I leave now," I mumble, glancing at the pile of work on my desk. But honestly? Why am I even fighting this?

She waves her hand like my job is a minor inconvenience. "Mr. Orlov has already taken care of that. You're free to leave when you want."

I blink at her. Of course he did. Why would my actual job matter when he's decided I need a makeover?

"And people will talk," I add, grasping at straws. "If I keep leaving early, they'll say I'm slacking off."

Andrea leans in, dead serious. "Are you?"

"No."

"Then why should you care?"

Unfortunately, she has a point.

INSTEAD OF GOING for a classic red dress, Andrea insisted on sage green, a color I'd never have thought of but now realize was an inspired choice. The dress is understated but elegant, hugging my body like a glove with a fitted satin bodice that flares from the knee down. It's almost off-shoulder, exposing just enough skin to feel both sophisticated and daring. The silver jewelry—a simple necklace and delicate half-drop earrings—completes the look without competing for attention. My hair is styled in an artfully messy updo, something I'd never manage on my own, and I have to admit, I look nice. Maybe even more than nice.

"You're beautiful, Mrs. Orlov," Andrea had said as the car pulled up to take me to the dinner. "Beauty like yours turns heads."

I laughed it off, trying to dismiss the compliment. I don't usually think of myself as the kind of woman who turns heads, more like someone who blends into the background unless I'm actively trying not to.

But as I step into the restaurant's grand entrance, I'm reminded that this is no ordinary dinner. The place is stunning, with soaring ceilings, soft lighting, and live music drifting through the air. Everything about it screams opulence, like I've walked straight into a 1920s movie set. A smartly dressed host greets me with a polished smile.

"I'm meeting Mr. Orlov," I say, trying to sound like I belong here, even though I'm not quite sure I do.

"Of course, right this way," he replies, leading me deeper into the elegant space. Every detail—from the gleaming chandeliers to the rich tapestries—makes me feel like I've been transported to another world. A world where sage green gowns are appropriate, and Dmitri Orlov is waiting for me.

When I spot him, my breath catches. He's standing by

the table, impossibly handsome in a dark tailored suit. His hair is slicked back, and there's something about the way he's looking at me, dark and intense, like he's seeing right through me.

He stands as I approach, extending his hand with a small smile. "Mrs. Orlov."

"Mr. Orlov," I respond, taking his hand. Though my heart's racing, I feel more like a teenager at her first prom than a grown woman. I'm trying to play it cool, but I hear myself blurting, "I wouldn't have missed this for the end of the world." Great, now I sound overenthusiastic.

Dmitri just nods, his expression unreadable as always. He pulls out my chair with a quiet efficiency that feels more business than personal. "Please sit. I assume you're hungry."

I nod, sitting down and placing my bag on my lap, trying not to fidget. I'm hyper-aware of how fancy this place is, how out of my element I feel, and how Dmitri is both so close and so distant at the same time. The silence stretches on until my curiosity gets the better of me.

"I mean, I appreciate this. The flowers were nice. But . . . why?" I ask, unable to help myself.

He shrugs, his answer as cool as ever. "You're my wife. No other reason."

"Huh." I try not to let the disappointment show, but I feel it settling in my chest. His answer is so mechanical, like he's ticking off a box. I study his face, trying to read him, but it's impossible. The Dmitri I know is all walls and armor, and tonight, even though we're not fighting, I still can't tell what he's thinking.

And before I can stop myself, I blurt out the question that's been nagging at me. "Is it the sex? Are you trying to apologize for that night? Because if so, you don't have to. It was mutual, and this," I gesture to the table, the whole evening, "really isn't necessary."

For a split second, I think I see a flicker of amusement on his face, but it's gone just as quickly. He leans back slightly, his lips curling into a small smile. "I'm not doing this because of what happened that night, Ana. You're my wife. It's expected that I treat you right, regardless of our... situationship."

Situationship. Right. I'd almost forgotten that's all this is—a weird situation. Not a real marriage, not a real relationship. Just a deal.

I sigh softly, letting the disappointment creep in again. "I see."

Dmitri tilts his head slightly, watching me, and I wonder if he can sense the shift in my mood. "What's wrong?" he asks.

"Nothing," I lie, forcing a smile. "Everything's fine."

He hands me the menu. "What would you like to eat?"

I glance at it, the words blurring together as I try to focus. I don't really care about the food, but I pick something anyway. "Roasted beet salad to start. Lamb chops for the main."

He nods approvingly. "Good choice. I'll let the sommelier pair the wine."

We fall into silence again, the weight of unsaid things pressing down on me. I try to act like I'm fine, but it's hard when I can't shake the feeling that this dinner is just another one of Dmitri's moves. A way to control the narrative, to keep up appearances. I glance at him from beneath my lashes, wondering what's really going on in his head.

How can someone be so attentive in one moment and so distant in the next?

"Excuse me, I need to use the ladies' room," I say, standing up quickly, needing a moment to clear my head.

As I walk away, I feel his eyes on me, that same intense gaze that always makes my heart stutter. I don't look back, but I can feel the weight of his stare, like he's trying to figure me out. Like maybe, just maybe, he's as confused by this whole thing as I am.

"Can I help you, miss?" a hostess asks as I stand there, momentarily lost in thought.

I blink, snapping back to reality. "Oh, yes. I'm looking for the restroom."

As I follow her, I can't help but wonder what I'm really looking for, because it's definitely not just the bathroom.

She gives me the directions, and I hurry away, trying to push down the urge to turn around again. Why does everything with Dmitri feel so intense, even when nothing's really happening?

By the time I return, a server is already at the table with our starters and mains, setting down a bottle of wine. I sit back down, nodding at Dmitri, but my mind is a whirlwind of thoughts. We eat mostly in silence, and I poke at my salad, completely distracted by all the questions bubbling inside me.

What happens now? Where do we go from here?

I stare so hard at my plate, I feel like I could burn a hole through it with my eyes. I try to focus on the meal, but my thoughts are louder than the clinking of silverware.

How long does he plan to keep up this charade? Was tonight just another check on his list of duties?

"THAT WAS A LOVELY DINNER," I say as we step into the house, both of us lingering at the foot of the stairs. The food was, admittedly, incredible. The company . . . not so much.

Dmitri nods, his expression unreadable as usual. "Yes, it was. Thank you for joining me."

Thank you for joining me? The words feel so formal, so cold. I offer him a small smile, even though I feel like screaming. "Of course."

An awkward silence falls between us, and we just stand there, staring at each other. My heart's beating a little faster now because, even though this evening has been emotionally confusing, there's a pull I can't deny. His eyes drift to my lips, lingering there in a way that sends a ripple of warmth through me.

Maybe he's going to kiss me. Maybe he's waiting for the right moment.

I stand there, frozen, waiting for him to make the first move. But the seconds stretch out, and nothing happens. It's like we're in some kind of silent standoff, neither of us willing to take the plunge.

Come on, Dmitri. Do something. Anything.

He doesn't.

I take a step back, feeling the disappointment sink into my chest. "Uh, I should go to bed," I mumble awkwardly. "I'll see you tomorrow."

For a second, it looks like he is about to ask me to stay, like maybe this could still turn into more. But he just nods, his face as unreadable as ever. "Alright. Have a good night."

As I turn to head up the stairs, I'm hyper-aware of his presence behind me. Every step feels heavier, like I'm dragging my feet through quicksand. I could turn around, ask him to kiss me, or just do it myself. But I don't. I keep walking, feeling this huge weight of regret building inside me.

At the door to my room, I hesitate for a second, my hand on the handle. It would be so easy to go back down and bridge this maddening gap between us. But I push the door open and step inside, closing it softly behind me.

And just like that, the moment is gone. The night feels long and endless, and I have a sinking feeling that sleep won't come easy.

I should've said something. But instead, I'm left with this hollow feeling in my chest and the thought that tomorrow, everything will go back to normal. Whatever normal even is with us.

I lean against the door, sighing. Yeah, it's going to be a long night.

EIGHTEEN
DMITRI

"Have I ever told you that I like this new you?" Yelena's voice drips with amusement as she lounges on the sofa in the corner of my office. Her legs are crossed, a playful pout on her lips. "Everyone says it's impossible to change a man set in his ways, but Ana's a magician."

I stare at the bouquet sitting on my desk, my eyes narrowing. "How?"

Yelena uncrosses her legs, strolling over to my desk with her usual air of confidence. She pulls out the chair across from me and sits down, her gaze fixed on the flowers. "Did you pick these out yourself?" she asks, her tone teasing.

"I didn't," I reply bluntly. "I had Jakob take care of it."

Her eyes flicker with amusement, and I can sense she's about to crack a joke. I scowl, my patience already running thin. "What's your point, Yelena?"

She gives me a shrug, but there's a glint of mischief in her expression that makes my jaw tighten. Finally, she relents with a smirk. "It's nothing, really. Just... I've never seen you buy flowers for anyone. Not even me." She lifts the bouquet slightly. "And you got her red and white carnations."

I frown, not seeing the point. "And?"

Yelena raises an eyebrow. "You do know red carnations symbolize deep love and admiration, right?"

My lips part in surprise. "Deep love?" I scoff, more irritated than amused by her little revelation. "I didn't choose them. You're the one who insisted I send her flowers in the first place. What are you trying to get at?"

She bursts into laughter, doubling over at the look on my face. My temper flares, the sharp edge of annoyance cutting through me.

"There's nothing funny about this," I snap.

"I'm not laughing at you," she gasps, still struggling to contain her giggles. "It's just . . . the irony. You, stone-cold Dmitri Orlov, sending flowers that scream *love* to your wife. It's poetic."

I glare at her, but the image of Ana from last night creeps into my mind uninvited. The way she looked at me, her eyes soft, like she was waiting for me to make a move. A move I didn't—couldn't—make.

"Should I have done something?" The question slips out before I can stop it.

Yelena perks up. "What was that?"

I shake my head, dismissing the thought. "Nothing," I mutter, annoyed with myself for even thinking it.

The truth is, Ana lingers in my mind far more than I'm willing to admit. There's something about her, pulling at me in ways I don't want to acknowledge. But acting on those feelings would only lead to my downfall.

"Yelena?" I turn to her, my voice clipped.

"Yup?"

"Get rid of these," I say, nodding to the flowers. "Get some roses. They're more common."

Yelena clicks her tongue, exasperated. "So, you've changed your mind?"

"It wasn't my idea in the first place," I respond flatly.

She stands, picking up the bouquet with a dramatic sigh. "I'll give these to Ana and tell her they're from me. Don't worry, brother, I won't let you send the wrong message."

"Good." The word comes out more curt than I intended, but her comment leaves a sour taste in my mouth. There's a part of me that hates the idea of passing off the gesture as someone else's. But I bury that feeling down deep. Feelings are a weakness, and I've had enough of those for one lifetime.

Minutes after Yelena leaves, Alexey, Igor, Bianchi, and the rest of the men filter into the conference room. The usual suspects. I take my seat, the weight of my role settling back onto my shoulders as the door closes behind us.

"I saw your sister as she was leaving," Bianchi says, a grin tugging at his lips. "She's all grown up now. Last time I saw her, she was still wearing braces. Is there a man in her life?"

"If you've got designs on Yelena, you'd be smart to drop them," I reply coldly. "For your own good."

Bianchi chuckles, but there's an edge to it. "You're saying she's not available?"

"I'm saying she'd make you regret it. And it wouldn't be personal," I add, letting my gaze sweep the room. "But you'd regret it all the same."

Yelena didn't crawl out of an abusive relationship just to be tied down to another man. She's stronger than that, and anyone stupid enough to try will find themselves on the wrong side of her wrath.

Bianchi leans back, shaking his head. "Dmitri isn't like the rest of us. We buy our wives whatever they want, and while they're busy unwrapping presents, we find ourselves mistresses. But we pretend they don't know about it. Like you, Pavlov," he says, nodding toward Igor. "Freya already knows about your new girl."

Igor's jaw drops, caught off guard. Idiot. He's so careless, it's almost embarrassing.

"What makes you different, Dmitri?" Alexey chimes in, his voice sly, his beady eyes watching me too closely. "You didn't marry Anastasia because you love her. We all know the real reason. So, what is it? Is she that good in the sack?"

Something in me snaps. Before he can finish the sentence, I'm across the room, my fist clutching the front of his shirt. I shove him back into his chair with a force that sends the air rushing out of his lungs.

My voice is ice. "You will never speak of Ana like that again. Understand me?"

Alexey's face pales as my fingers tighten around his collar. He sputters, struggling to breathe under my grip.

"I will cut out your tongue and make sure you choke on it if you ever disrespect her again," I growl, my tone deadly serious.

I release him, watching as he gasps for air, his hand clutching his throat. The room is dead silent, every eye on me.

I turn, my voice calm once more as I head back to my seat. "Now that we've settled that, let's get on with the meeting."

AT EIGHT O'CLOCK SHARP, I toss my bag into the backseat of the car, the weight of the day pressing against my shoulders. It's a typical New York evening—traffic clogging every inch of the FDR, slowing me down as I navigate through the endless sea of brake lights. I grip the steering wheel harder than usual, my mind circling back to Ana.

I asked Yelena to give her the flowers. Red and white carnations.

Love and admiration.

My chest tightens as I pull into the driveway. I could have chosen roses, something simple, but no—I had to be difficult. I'd chosen carnations, flowers that *meant* something, and I don't even know if Ana is the type to care about that kind of thing.

What's worse, I'd allowed Yelena to lie and say the flowers were from her.

The door swings open, and I step into the quiet foyer, the scent of freshly popped popcorn drifting from the living room. My feet slow as my mind replays last night, the dinner, the tension, and the words I didn't say.

I sent them because you're my wife.

I could've come up with something else, *anything* to break through that wall between us, but that was what came out. Cold. Dismissive. Like everything I've done with her since this sham of a marriage began.

Yelena is sprawled across the couch, engrossed in a wrestling match, popcorn in hand.

"I think I'll move out next week," she says casually, as if we were discussing the weather. She throws another handful of popcorn into her mouth, barely glancing in my direction.

I stop mid-stride and shrug. "Okay."

Yelena's always unpredictable, so I don't question it.

She could be serious, or she could be toying with me—either way, I don't bite.

Before I can head upstairs, she pipes up again. "If you didn't see Anastasia's car, it's because it broke down at work today. She came home pissed off, didn't want to eat, and went to bed early." She lifts the popcorn bowl as if offering me a solution. "I made my special popcorn for her, but she didn't have an appetite."

That catches my attention. I turn to face her fully, brows furrowing.

"And you think I had something to do with that?" I ask, my voice sharper than intended.

Yelena leans back on the couch, looking at me like she's amused by how clueless I am. "I don't know, Dmitri, did you send her a message? Or did you screw it up in some other way I'm not aware of yet?"

"No," I grunt. "I didn't. I told you, I didn't want to mislead her." But now I'm regretting every part of that decision. "You said she was upset. Was it just the car?"

Yelena sighs, waving her hand dismissively. "That's what she called about, but no, I don't think that's why she's mad. She was home by seven, went straight to her room without a word."

Something shifts in my gut, a familiar knot of dread. The last time Ana came home early, she didn't eat dinner either. That was the day Lucia approached her.

I rub my chin, piecing it together. "You don't think—"

Yelena pops another kernel of popcorn in her mouth, watching me like she's waiting for the obvious to sink in. "You did something, Dmitri. You're just too blind to see it."

"What exactly did I do wrong?" I snap, the frustration boiling up. "I didn't even talk to her today."

"Maybe that's the problem," she says simply, standing

up and brushing crumbs off her lap. "You don't talk to her. You think she's going to stick around forever, waiting for you to get your shit together?"

I scowl at her, but her words hit too close to home. I don't like it. Yelena smirks, strolling past me with her bowl. "Don't worry, big brother. You'll figure it out. Eventually."

Left standing there in the quiet hallway, I replay Yelena's parting words over and over, trying to make sense of them.

Why is Ana avoiding me?

It's not like I've given her a reason to stick around. But still...

I head upstairs, the tension building in my chest as I stop in front of Ana's door. There's a faint light peeking from under the door, but the house is quiet. I consider knocking, but something holds me back.

What if she doesn't want to see me? What if I've already done too much damage? My hand hovers over the door for a long moment before I let it fall to my side. Maybe I should have done something last night. Maybe I shouldn't have let her walk away.

I shake my head, jaw clenching.

I'll figure it out.

NINETEEN
ANA

Daria's face says it all as I approach her desk.

Great. Just great.

"Let me guess, he's pulled another disappearing act?" I ask, my heart sinking. I thought giving Papa some space would make him miss me, but apparently his ego's gotten so big it's pushed out any paternal feelings. At this rate, I'll be collecting social security before he decides to grace me with his presence.

Daria shakes her head, oozing sympathy. "Sorry, hon. I wouldn't hold your breath waiting. You know how he gets."

My shoulders slump like they're trying to touch the floor. "Right. Because heaven forbid Nikolai Petrov face his only daughter." A spark of defiance flares up. "Maybe I should just camp out here. He can't ignore me forever, can he?"

I see the pity in Daria's eyes as she offers me a chair. "If you think it'll work. Or I could tell you where he is. If you're feeling brave enough to make a scene—"

"No, no," I cut her off, shaking my head so hard I'm

surprised it doesn't fall off. "Can't embarrass the great Nikolai Petrov. God knows I was raised too well for that." I laugh, but it comes out sounding more like a wounded animal. "If only he'd been a worse father, maybe I'd have the guts to go all paparazzi on him."

Daria's laugh is gentle. "You've always been a good kid, Anastasia. Remember how you used to follow him around, arguing your way into meetings? Such a serious little face, even when you had no clue what was going on."

I collapse into the chair, feeling about as deflated as a week-old balloon. "Yeah, well, he was my hero. I wanted to be just like him." The irony is so thick you could cut it with a knife. "Fat lot of good that did me."

"He knew you had a mind of your own," Daria says softly. "That's why he let you study law. Figured if he couldn't keep you out, at least he could channel it."

A tear sneaks down my cheek, the traitor. I swipe it away, cursing my inability to keep it together. "So why push me away now? Last I checked, I'm still his daughter. Or did I miss the memo where he disowned me?"

"The Bratva and their pride." Daria sighs. "They'd rather eat glass than admit they've screwed up. He used to talk about how badly he wanted you to be proud of him. Now, I think he feels like he's lost that right."

"That's ridiculous! He didn't have a choice." My voice cracks and more tears betray me. Stupid tear ducts. I'm starting to think they're in cahoots with my heart.

The Bratva code. The reason I'm married to a man who makes icebergs look cuddly. All because dear old Papa couldn't keep his hands off what didn't belong to him. And now I'm the sacrificial lamb, given to Dmitri Orlov like some sort of twisted peace offering.

"And the kicker?" I laugh, but it sounds more like a sob.

"I'm actually falling for the guy. Talk about Stockholm syndrome on steroids."

Daria pushes a cup of coffee into my hands. The warmth seeps into my fingers, grounding me. "I'll try talking to him again," she promises. "Maybe he'll listen this time."

"Thanks," I mumble, taking a sip. The coffee burns my tongue, but at least it gives me something else to focus on besides the gaping hole where my heart used to be.

I stand up, my legs feeling about as steady as a newborn giraffe's. "I should go. Thanks for . . . you know. Everything."

Daria grabs my hands, squeezing them tight. The compassion in her eyes nearly undoes me. "You'll get through this, Ana. And if you need someone, I'm always here."

I nod, not trusting myself to speak. If I open my mouth now, I'm liable to start bawling like a baby. With one last watery smile, I turn and flee the office.

As the elevator doors close, I lean against the wall, feeling utterly drained. I can't go back to that mausoleum Dmitri calls a house. Not now. There's only one place left for me, one person who'll listen without judgment.

Too bad she's six feet under.

"ANA."

I pause as I walk into the living room, and Dmitri, who looks like he's been waiting for a while, gets up from the couch.

"Yeah?" I ask, my voice hoarse from crying.

He frowns. "I've been calling you. Where have you been?"

Where have I been? The question sounds so silly in my head, and I scoff. "Why does it matter to you?"

Dmitri walks toward me, but I step back and stretch my hand out, telling him to stay away.

"Don't," I call out when he doesn't listen. "Don't come closer. I can't deal with you tonight."

"Deal with me?" he growls. "It's past midnight. Your phone is off."

Rolling my eyes, I reach into my bag and bring out my phone. Switching it on, I thrust it at him. "It's on. You happy now? I was busy, okay? I'm sure you know what that means, with your fancy *pakhan* title and your stupid connections and your—"

My rant is cut short when Dmitri grabs the phone from my hand and pulls me in. My brows crease when he begins to sniff at me. I struggle to free myself, but he refuses to let go.

"You smell like alcohol," he says, his tone teetering the line between accusatory and concerned.

I say accusatory because I doubt he can summon up concern for me, but the way he looks at me feels weird. Different.

Even with the alcohol flowing through me, I can read between the lines.

"That's weird," I murmur.

His voice is soft when he says, "What is?"

"You," I point with my free hand. "When you asked me out to dinner, I couldn't tell what you were thinking. You had this poker face," I mimic it, and it makes me laugh. "But now your eyebrows and lips are all funny."

When I try to touch his mouth, he lets my hand go and takes a step back, sighing.

"It's unlike you to get drunk."

I shrug. "I went to see my father, then I went to see my mom, and I didn't want to come back here because I hate this place. So, I went to a bar. And I drank." My lips stretch into a lopsided grin. "It was so much fun."

Dmitri runs his fingers through his hair. "How did you get home, then?"

How did I get home?

I scratch my head, trying to remember the details, but all I feel is this warm, fuzzy feeling in my head. Like I'm floating on clouds but not quite.

"Where's your car?" he prompts.

"Ah!" I smack my temple as I remember. "I drove. Slowly," I drag out the last word, "because I didn't want to get into an accident. Yeah. I drove here."

Panic rushes into Dmitri's eyes for a split second, then he races past me. Seconds later, I hear the door open and slam shut.

I pout. *What's his problem?*

He's sure acting strange tonight.

You're my wife. No other reason.

Who says something like that? I scoff as he rushes back into the living room, taking me by surprise when he grabs my shoulders.

"Why did you drive after drinking? You could've gotten yourself into an accident, or worse, killed."

My chin juts out defiantly as I reply, "And why do you care? You'll be free of me if I'm gone, won't you? After all, I'm just your *wife*. Anastasia *Orlov*," I spit out.

Dmitri falters at my words, and his grip on my shoulders loosens. "Where do you get that from? 'I'll be free of you'?"

"Am I making this up?" I ask. "You sent me flowers and sent someone to take me shopping. When I sat down and asked why you did all that, what did you say?"

His Adam's apple bobs.

"What did you say, Dmitri?" I prompt, growing angrier by the minute.

He sighs. "I said that you're my wife."

"No other reason," I spit. "That's what you said. If you did that out of duty, why should you care if I drink and drive?"

A heartbeat of silence passes between us. Then two. Then four. Dmitri doesn't respond. My heart sinks. I don't know what I was expecting. He's the same Orlov I married, after all.

"Ana," he starts, then stops.

"I'm not mad," I respond, as my emotions have faded to disappointment already. "It's just the way it is. I'm tired," I add, pulling away from him. "I'll head to *my* room now."

As I walk past him, his hand holds my wrist. I stop, but I don't turn.

"Ana," he says with a little force, like if he doesn't hold it together, the dam would break. "Look at me."

I turn my head and throw him a glance, unwilling to open my heart again. "They're just words, Dmitri. It's not hard to string a few together to form a better sentence. I'm tired, please let me go."

He doesn't.

Instead, he pulls me into his arms, and I find myself staring at his face mere inches from mine. My breath hitches, and my eyelids flutter.

He leans in and gently brushes his lips against mine.

It's not the kiss that comforted me when I mourned my mother. Or the one we shared when we were naked.

When his mouth claims mine, it's with certainty. His hands cup my face firmly as he angles his head, taking it further and sending a shiver of desire down my spine. My bag falls on the floor as I wrap my arms around his neck, clinging to his firm, muscular frame.

Desire pools in my stomach as his tongue trails down the slope of my neck, his teeth gently scraping against my skin, nipping and soothing with teasing kisses.

His hands run down my body, caressing my arms. A soft gasp slips past my lips when he pulls me snug against his body, my stomach rubbing against his erection. I moan with need when his hands cup my ass, squeezing firmly.

I want him.

This is how Dmitri makes me feel. I go from hating to needing him with my next breath, craving his hands against my skin, my legs wrapped around his body while he fucks me.

"Ana," he drags out my name with a harsh breath.

I throw my head back when he presses his lips to my neck, inhaling audibly. I can feel that he wants me as much as I *need* him.

"I want to be deep inside you, your walls clenching around my dick, begging for release," he murmurs. "Say you want it too."

I whimper as he slides his hand into my pants, his finger gliding over my sex, making me so wet, I ride his hand shamelessly. I don't care that we're in the middle of the living room because all I can think of is him and the primal urge that burns like wildfire.

He slides his finger inside me, and I gasp, but then I'm riding his hand, bucking my hips and clinging to him with my fingers grabbing fistfuls of his shirt.

My orgasm rips through me, making my shoulders shudder and my legs shake. Dmitri captures my lips in a punishing kiss, swallowing my choked cry.

As my body turns limp, he lifts me and carries me to the

couch, guiding my head to his chest. There's nothing but silence between us as I try not to think about what just happened.

I prefer to enjoy this contentment, even if it doesn't last more than tonight.

TWENTY
DMITRI

I guide Ana onto the yacht's deck, my grip firm on her hand. "Watch your step," I warn, my voice low and commanding. I'm not used to being gentle, but with her, I find myself adjusting.

Her midnight blue dress ripples in the breeze, a stark contrast to the white of the yacht. She moves with a grace that reminds me she's no stranger to luxury. Of course, she isn't, she's Nikolai Petrov's daughter.

"I'm not going to fall," she laughs softly. "This isn't my first time on a yacht."

"I know," I respond curtly, reminding myself of who she is, who I am. This isn't a fairytale romance, it's a strategic move. At least, that was the idea.

I survey the deck, noting the scattered carnation petals with satisfaction. Everything is precisely as I ordered. I'm a man who demands perfection, even in this.

"Carnations?" Ana asks, her voice tinged with surprise.

I nod, keeping my face impassive. "Red and white. I assumed you'd had your fill of roses."

A small smile plays on her lips. "You assumed correctly."

Her reaction pleases me more than it should. I push the feeling aside, focusing on the task at hand. "Would you like a tour? Or perhaps some champagne first?"

Ana nods, her eyes bright with curiosity. I feel a pull toward her that I can't explain—and can't afford.

When did she become more than just a pawn in my game?

I think back to last night, to the moment I almost started a war over a mere slight against her. It was irrational, dangerous, everything I've trained myself not to be. And yet, I can't bring myself to regret it.

I'm Dmitri Orlov. I don't fall in love. Love is a weakness, a liability in my world.

But as I look at Ana, standing on my yacht in that dress, I realize I might have miscalculated. And in my line of work, miscalculations can be deadly.

I need to tread carefully. The stakes are higher than ever now, and I can't afford to lose control. Not even for her.

Especially not for her.

Her skin glows under the faint light, and my groin stirs as I picture her lying under me, her luscious hair fanned over my pillow.

We head into the spacious salon with two plush couches and a bar filled with aged and expensive bottles inside well-polished mahogany cases.

I gesture to the smaller couch, and when she sits, I head behind the bar, opening the glass case at the bottom left. I take out a bottle of champagne and two flutes. Setting them down on the counter, I open the bottle and pour some into the glasses.

"Here." I hand her one, my fingertips brushing against

hers and sending a jolt of desire through me. Mesmerized, I watch as she brings it to her mouth, wetting her lower lip with her tongue, her gaze fixed on my mouth. Her lips part slightly, and my cock strains against my pants as she lazily drags her eyes to mine, taking a sip and smiling. I'm so hot for her, I'm about to burst into flames.

Hold your horses, buddy. Take it slow.

"How about a tour?" I ask, breaking the spell.

"Sure," she agrees, placing her glass down and taking my hand. Her palm is small and warm against mine, and I brush her soft skin with my fingers, looking forward to feeling more of her skin pressed against me. My gaze flickers to her as she walks next to me, taking in her facial features, from her curled lashes to the hair cascading down her shoulders and the subtle blush on her lips. They roam downward to her sandals, and I notice the sheer pink pedicure on her toes.

Everything about Anastasia is beautiful. But it always has been. I've just been blind to it before.

We venture downstairs, stopping at the guest suite.

"These," I point to the two doors facing each other, "are for visitors. Though I rarely have any. But they're fully equipped with everything you'd need for an impromptu trip."

Her head bobs slightly. Moving on, we go into the kitchen. "This is barely in use too. Most of the time, I have food delivered instead of having it prepared here. Although, today's going to be different."

"Oh?" She tilts her head.

Her monotonous answers make me want to see her unravel.

Under me.

We didn't resolve the impression she had of me last

night—about my lack of enthusiasm during our dinner together. Tonight, I have every intention of not holding back and showing her the depth of my desire.

"The chef will be here in thirty minutes."

We go back topside, and I point out the helm station and the fly bridge above. After, I lead her to the bow where string lights drape across the railing, winking to life as dusk falls.

Cushioned lounge chairs are strategically arranged to face the direction of the receding sun. "Let's sit down." I gesture toward them.

Her soft smile grows wider, making my heart skip a beat. "Okay."

We settle in side by side and stare out into the horizon. A comfortable silence grows between us, but the thoughts in my mind keep it busy. I remain quiet, though more because I'm waiting for the right time.

It's odd.

In all my life, I've never felt compelled to make things perfect. Trying to fill in my father's shoes, yes, but not when it comes to cultivating relationships with other people.

I turn to Ana, my gaze calculating and intense. The warm light bathes her in a golden glow.

Something has shifted. This woman, meant to be nothing more than a pawn, has wormed her way past my defenses. It's a weakness I can't afford, but one I find increasingly difficult to ignore.

Ana meets my eyes, and I feel the air charge with tension. I've faced down rival mobsters without flinching, but her gaze threatens to unravel me.

I won't allow it.

"There's something you need to know," I state, my voice low and commanding.

She nods, wary but curious. "What is it?"

I close the distance between us with measured steps, a predator stalking its prey. "You've become . . . valuable to me," I rumble, the words foreign on my tongue. "I believe the feeling is mutual."

Her breath catches, and I note the rapid rise and fall of her chest.

Fear? Excitement?

Both work in my favor.

Without warning, I seize her, pulling her against me. She gasps, her nails digging into my chest.

I crush my lips to hers, devouring, possessing. A primal sound tears from my throat as I break away, my control slipping for a dangerous second.

Ana isn't just warmth; she's third-degree burns. Our mouths clash again, a battle for dominance that I have no intention of losing. She yields, opening to me, and I push forward, claiming what's mine.

In this moment, I'm not just taking Ana. I'm conquering my own weakness, turning it into strength. She may have softened my heart, but I'll use that to make myself more formidable than ever.

Dmitri Orlov doesn't fall in love.

He takes what he wants and makes it his own.

I can feel her nails as she grabs my shoulders to steady herself against me. Her body is soft, slipping across the fabric of my clothes as I pull her in.

"There's something about kissing you. I don't know what it is, but I want to keep doing it," I murmur, and I can't tell if she heard me.

I hope that she did; I don't have the presence of mind to repeat it.

Ana reaches for my face, but I intercept her hand, gripping her wrist firmly.

I'll dictate the pace here.

Slowly, deliberately, I lower my mouth to hers, asserting my dominance with a deep, possessive kiss. I capture her lower lip between my teeth, eliciting a soft gasp from her.

She is compliant and silent, and I prefer it that way. Words could shatter this moment, bring reality crashing back in. I won't allow that. Not yet.

Without breaking the kiss, I feel her hand on my elbow, trying to guide me. I resist for a moment, reminding her who's in control. Then, deciding to indulge her, I allow her to place my palm on her breast. Her heart races beneath my touch.

I growl low in my throat, pleased by her submission. My other hand slides to the nape of her neck, fingers tangling in her hair as I deepen the kiss. I explore her mouth thoroughly, claiming every inch as mine.

She may have softened me in some ways, but in this, I remain unyielding. I am Dmitri Orlov, and what I desire, I take. And right now, I desire her completely.

I can feel the weight of her breast against my palm, the soft poke of her nipple showing her arousal.

She's a beautiful woman.

My wife.

I cradle her face in my hands.

"I want more of you. Everything."

Her moan is shy of a gasp, fast and forceful, as she watches me kiss her hand. A kiss for each knuckle, I trail my way up past her wrist, and soon, I'm at her neck, kissing desperately, trying to mark every bit of her with my claim.

I can't explain what happens next; as she stands before me, eyes partly closed in a daze, I'm overcome with the possessiveness of a man married for more romantic reasons. I want her; I want her because she's mine. I want her because I chose her. I want to please her, to keep this expression on her face forever.

She gasps as I pull down the top of her dress. The slip below follows the outer material as I bare her breasts to me.

My mouth is on them before she can ask me what I mean to do. I should show her now isn't the time for words.

My lips wrap around her nipple as I suck and tease, flicking my tongue against the small pebble. I need no other motivation to go on; her hand against my head, pushing me closer to her chest, is all that's required.

She all but hugs me to her as I taste her, pushing her sensitive nub against my teeth as I pull softly.

"D-Dmitri," she stutters, "someone might come—"

"Let them all see," I growl. "They should know that you're mine."

"Dmitri" is all she manages to say as I guide her to the cushioned chair behind her.

She hurriedly places herself down as I pull up the hem of her dress.

"Dmitri, wait,"

"No more waiting," I interrupt. "You're mine."

I place my head between her legs, marking my trail with kisses along her inner thigh. Her skin is soft, stretched elegantly across her toned form. She quivers as I place my mouth on her, and it spurs me onward. I nibble at her flesh, desperate to mark her, to taste her.

As much as I can, as much as she'll allow.

I find my way to her, pulling her underwear to the side as my breath begins to tease her.

My tongue is against her, and the catch in her breath is

met with the first flick against wetness. Her arousal against my tongue pushes me into delirium.

"That's my beautiful fucking wife, taking my tongue so good. Next it will be my cock," I murmur against her pussy, warm and swollen. She whimpers above me as she struggles to push out my name like before.

She's the only thing I can hear as my tongue dances across her labia, splitting her lips as I take in her juices.

"Look at the mess you're making, you dirty girl." I smirk. "Let me hear you scream," I demand, continuing to flick my tongue around her swollen clit.

My arms wrap around her legs, lifting and placing them on my shoulders. I'm strangely aware of the heel of her shoes against my back.

"So, so fucking good," I hear her moan above me. I'd stop and smile if I weren't so desperate for her taste.

My tongue teases her sensitive nub, drawing wet figure eights across her. Teasing and toying as my mouth bumps into her again and again.

Each time pulls the softest gasp from her as she thrusts against me, as if trying to drag more out of me.

"Oh, fuck. Dmitri. Wait. Please."

I pull myself out from under her dress.

"I need to talk to you," she says as she holds my gaze.

I stare momentarily before standing, never breaking eye contact with her.

"Now is not a good time for a talk," I say as I undo my belt buckle. Soon, I'm free of my restraints and stand before her.

"Take what's yours, Ana."

She stares at me, then at my erection before her, trying her best not to swallow.

"You had me before; don't overthink it."

She abandons the attempt to hide it, swallowing before reaching for me, the initial cool touch of her fingertips morphing into a warmer embrace as she wraps her palm against me.

She doesn't waste time, folding her lips greedily around the head of my cock, taking me in as best as she can.

The sounds of her sucking on me fill the air around us.

She's perfect.

She's mine.

I'm overcome with desire as my hand reaches for her, cradling her face and pulling her up.

"I need to be inside of you, right now."

I place her on the cushioned seat as she spreads her legs for me. Her dress is gathered at her waist, and the sight of her dazed eyes as she waits to take me is breathtaking.

"No matter how you may feel, you're the best of women. I'm telling that to you now. You're my wife."

She doesn't answer me, and I know I'll have to explain myself later.

I move against her, resting my head on her shoulder, whispering in her ear as I slide into her.

Her gasp as I slowly push into her is the only sound in my head. Soon, I'm filling her completely, and we stay motionless for a second, panting against each other.

"Oh please, fuck me," she moans.

And that's all I need.

I begin to pull out of her, slowly, inch by inch, leaving her until only the tip remains. Then I push it all back in.

"Oh, fucking hell," she cusses loudly.

"Easy, you'll be fine; just breathe," I guide her, kissing her neck.

I do it again, slowly pulling out of her and filling her up

fast. The sound of our flesh meeting against each other causes me to throb even harder inside her.

"You feel so fucking good," I whisper into her ear as her moans begin to pour out in short bursts.

I pick up my pace, slowly fucking her as I kiss her neck, her hand steadying herself against the seat.

Nothing can prepare me for her hand against my head as she whispers fiercely, "Fuck me hard and fast. Don't let me think of anything else."

I slip out of her, feeling sorely abandoned as I hang in the cool air around us.

I pull her up and turn her back to me, coming up behind her.

Her moans are louder now, and the space blurs around us as I take her from behind. She times her rocking against my thrusts to slam against me as I fuck her.

"You take my cock so well," I say as my hand holds her by her hip, keeping her steady as I continue thrusting.

"You're so deep in me. Filling me up," she gasps. Her legs shaking, she reaches back to take hold of my arm for stability. "Don't stop. Whatever you do, don't stop."

I pull her up and keep thrusting into her, and she leans against me, her mouth open as she moans with each thrust.

"Look at you, so fucking beautiful."

"I'm coming," she moans as she shakes against me.

Before the words fully leave her mouth, I grab her, a deep groan vibrating through my chest as I join her.

Afterward we sink into the nearby seats. I pull Ana into my arms, holding her in a close snuggle and kissing her hair. Only then do I remember we were supposed to have dinner a while ago.

TWENTY-ONE
ANA

I take Dmitri's hand as I climb out of the limo, trying not to faceplant in these ridiculous heels. Nothing says "Bratva wife" like eating pavement at a fancy party, right?

The night air hits me, and I resist the urge to shiver. Next time I'm bringing a jacket. Or better yet, staying home with Netflix and sweatpants.

Dmitri insisted on being "fashionably late," which I'm pretty sure is code for "I wanted to make an entrance." I half expect a spotlight to shine on us as we cross the street.

He offers me his arm like we're in some period drama.

Who is this guy, and what has he done with my usually detached husband?

I take it anyway, because hey, if he's playing nice, I might as well enjoy it while it lasts.

The security outside looks like they eat steroids for breakfast. Their suits are probably bulletproof too, unlike my flimsy dress.

Dmitri doesn't need to show an invite. Of course, he doesn't. He probably owns half the city by now. He gestures for me to enter first, all gentlemanly. I'm half waiting for him to announce, "After you, m'lady."

I can't help but smile as I walk in. This new, attentive Dmitri is nice. Weird, but nice. A week ago, he told me he has feelings for me.

In his own way, of course, but still, I heard him loud and clear.

Part of me wants to believe him, but the other part is waiting for the other shoe to drop. This is Dmitri Orlov we're talking about. The man who basically blackmailed my father into giving me away.

I push those thoughts aside as we enter what looks like Richie Rich's playground. No foyer, just instant opulence. Chandeliers, artwork, people dripping in diamonds. I suddenly feel underdressed in my measly Vera Wang gown.

"Dmitri!" a voice that could shatter glass calls out. A blonde in a dress that probably costs more than my college education is heading our way. Great. With my luck, she's probably one of Dmitri's exes.

To my surprise, Dmitri takes my hand, lacing our fingers together. I glance down, half expecting to see our hands burst into flames from the unexpected contact.

Blondie air-kisses Dmitri, gushing about how she never thought he'd show. Apparently, she's married to an actual Sultan. Because, of course, that's perfectly normal.

"Grace," Dmitri says, "this is my wife, Anastasia Orlov. She's the reason I'm here."

I'm the *what* now? I must have misheard. There's no way Dmitri "Ice King" Orlov just said that.

Grace gives me a once-over that makes me feel like a secondhand car. "Good evening," I manage, plastering on my best "please don't eat me alive" smile.

She tugs on Dmitri's arm, eager to show him off like a

prized poodle. To my utter shock, he doesn't budge. "I need to get my wife a drink," he informs her.

Who is this man, and what has he done with my husband?

As Grace saunters off, I try to reclaim my hand. "You didn't have to use me as an excuse," I mutter.

"You weren't an excuse," he says, leading me to the bar. "I meant it. Now, what would you like?"

I stare at the selection, suddenly forgetting every drink I've ever known. "Uh..."

Dmitri smiles—actually smiles!—and orders something that sounds more like a spell than a drink. As the bartender gets to work, I find myself wondering if I fell and hit my head on the way in. How can this be real?

Only time will tell, I suppose. But for now, I might as well enjoy whatever bizarro world I've stumbled into.

The bartender returns with what looks like liquid sunshine in a fancy glass. The saffron drink arrives in a *chalice*. It's so blinged out, I'm half expecting it to start singing.

"Cheers," Dmitri says, raising his glass. "This night belongs to us."

I clink my glass against his, thinking, "*Yeah, and I belong in Crazy Town.*"

But you know what? I'm starting to dig it.

FAST FORWARD TO who-knows-how-many drinks later, and the world is a lovely, swirly place. We're leaving the party, and I'm grinning like I've won the lottery. Grace is trying to convince Dmitri to stay, probably hoping I'll turn into a pumpkin at midnight.

Sorry, honey, this Cinderella's keeping her prince.

Dmitri helps me into the limo, which suddenly feels like it's made of marshmallows. So comfy.

"How do you feel?" he asks, sounding suspiciously sober.

I give him an OK sign that probably looks more like I'm trying to catch a fly. "Like a champ!" I announce proudly. "How 'bout you, Mr. Orlov?"

He smiles—still weird—and pulls me close. "I'm fine. You can sleep if you want."

"Nope!" I declare, popping the "P" like it's bubble wrap. "I wanna talk. Hey," I poke his lips with my finger, because apparently that's a thing I do now, "why'd you bring me? You coulda gone stag. I wouldn't have minded."

He looks at me all serious-like. "I wanted you by my side. To show you off."

I blink owlishly. "Show me off? Like a trophy?"

He chuckles, guiding my head to his shoulder. "Sleep, *kotyonok*. I'll wake you when we're home."

I try to argue, but then he kisses me, and suddenly, my brain goes all fuzzy and warm. What was I saying? Oh well, doesn't matter. Sleep sounds good.

And just like that, I'm out like a light, dreaming of saffron rivers and Dmitri.

What a night.

TWENTY-TWO
DMITRI

I find Igor Pavlov waiting in my office like an uninvited pest. His attempt at a disarming smile only serves to fuel my irritation. The audacity of this man never ceases to amaze me.

"What are you doing here, Igor?" I ask, my voice a cold blade.

He stammers out some excuse about the casino project. How quaint. I let him squirm for a full minute before acknowledging him, savoring his discomfort like a fine wine.

Igor launches into his concerns about profits and timelines. Little does he know, those casinos were never his to begin with. The fool signed away his empire without even realizing it. It would almost be pitiful if it weren't so satisfying.

"Everything takes time," I say, feeding him just enough truth to keep him complacent. "There were . . . complications with the previous owners."

I watch realization dawns on his face. He truly had no idea what he was getting into. It's almost too easy.

The conversation shifts to the sultan's party. Igor's

curiosity is palpable, tinged with envy. He thinks he's being clever, probing for information, trying to catch me in some sort of betrayal to the Bratva.

"Isn't that what everyone says about us?" I respond smoothly to his jab about thieves. "That we have the Thieves' Code?"

I can see the wheels turning in his head, trying to decide whether I've given him ammunition or not. He's so focused on the small game that he can't see the larger trap.

I redirect, asking him what he'd do if someone tried to steal his father's territory. It's a test, of course. One he fails spectacularly.

"I'd do worse," he boasts, not realizing he's digging his own grave deeper with every word.

When he mentions calling a meeting about the Italian families, I have to stifle a laugh. He thinks he's making moves, playing the game. In reality, he's just a pawn on my chessboard, and I'm about to capture his king.

"Fine," I agree, already planning three steps ahead. "If there's going to be an issue, we should deal with it now."

I can't wait to watch his world crumble around him. After all, in this game, there can only be one winner. And I've never been one for participation trophies.

TWO HOURS of my life wasted on Igor's paranoid ramblings. He claims it's about New York, but I see through his pitiful attempt at misdirection. His problems in New Jersey are of no concern to me, unless they become useful leverage.

"Are you sure you don't need my help with the casino?" he asks, trailing after me like a lost puppy.

"Opening night will be in a month," I reply, my tone flat and final. "Give me till then."

He reaches out, as if to pat my shoulder, but thinks better of it when he sees my expression. Smart move. The last man who touched me without permission lost three fingers.

As Igor slinks away, I shake my head. Pathetic. Jakob approaches, informing me that my sister is waiting in my office.

Now there's a pleasant surprise.

"Brother!" Yelena greets me with her usual exuberance. I allow her embrace, mentally counting the seconds until I can extricate myself.

"You can let go now," I say after a while.

She chatters away, mentioning lunch plans with Ana. My interest piques, though I'm careful not to show it.

"Do you need a ride?" I offer, aiming for casual indifference.

Yelena's eyes widen comically. "Eh? Are you feeling alright, brother?"

I roll my eyes. "Don't be dramatic."

She sees right through me, of course. Always too perceptive for her own good. "I won't assume you wanted to use me as an excuse to see Ana," she teases.

I consider telling her the truth but decide against it. Some vulnerabilities are best kept hidden, even from family. Especially from family.

"Alright," I say, waving her off. "See you when I see you."

As the door closes behind her, I sigh, running a hand through my hair. This softness I'm feeling toward Ana is distracting.

"It's better you didn't, Dmitri," I mutter to myself. "Some might see that as being clingy."

The very word makes me shudder. I am Dmitri Orlov. I don't do clingy. I'm a man who's just discovered he likes his wife, nothing more.

To prove it to myself, I dive back into work. There are empires to topple and rivals to crush. No time for sentiment in this world of ours.

But even as I focus on spreadsheets and strategic maneuvers, a part of my mind lingers on Ana. On her smile, her laugh, the way she looks at me when she thinks I'm not paying attention.

TWENTY-THREE
ANA

Picture this: me, standing in the airport like a human billboard, holding a sign over my head that says "Welcome back, favorite brother!" Because nothing says, "I missed you" more than potential shoulder strain, right?

I spot Viktor emerging from behind what looks like the entire inventory of a luggage store. He sees my sign and starts laughing.

I drop the sign and run toward him, nearly taking out a few innocent bystanders in the process. We collide in a hug that's part bear, part octopus, and all awkward public display of affection.

"Viktor!" I squeak, probably sounding more like an excited chipmunk than a dignified adult. "Welcome back to the land of the free and home of the Bratva!"

He kisses the top of my head, which is sweet but also reminds me that I'll always be the baby sister. "Your face makes it worth returning to this country," he says, ever the charmer.

As we pull apart, he looks me up and down. "You've grown! What are you now, eighteen?"

I roll my eyes so hard, I'm surprised they don't fall out of my head. "Ha ha, very funny. You know, some of us actually age. We can't all be time-traveling vampires like you."

He pinches my cheek like I'm still four. "Aw, where's my little sister?"

"She grew up and got a life," I quip. "Also, therapy. Lots and lots of therapy."

We head to the parking lot, where Viktor predictably calls dibs on driving. I toss him the keys, silently praying he remembers which side of the road we drive on here.

As we merge into traffic, miraculously without incident, Viktor asks about my job. "Still keeping the scum of the earth out of prison?"

I give him a look that could curdle milk. "Hey, someone's got to keep Papa's friends in business, right?"

Two hours later, we're sitting in a West Village restaurant. Viktor's inhaling his sandwich like he's afraid it might run away.

Then he drops the bomb. "So, how's the old man?"

And just like that, my mood plummets faster than my college GPA. "I don't know," I mutter, suddenly finding my napkin fascinating.

Viktor's eyebrows shoot up so fast, I'm worried they might achieve orbit. "You don't know? Is he okay? Is he, you know, still breathing?"

I nod, feeling like I've swallowed a bowling ball. "Oh, he's alive. Probably plotting world domination or perfecting his disappearing act. You know, the usual Papa stuff."

And just like that, our happy reunion takes a nosedive into the soap opera that is my life.

Welcome home, brother. Hope you brought popcorn.

Viktor drops his sandwich like it's suddenly turned into a live grenade. "Okay, spill. What's going on? Is he sick?

Did he finally tick off the wrong person and end up in concrete shoes?"

I bite my lip, wishing I could just disappear into the upholstery. "No, nothing that dramatic. Though at this point, I'd almost prefer it. He's just . . . gone MIA. Radio silence since I got hitched."

Viktor's face scrunches up like he's just tasted something sour. "Wait, what? Is this Orlov's doing? I knew that guy was bad news. I told Father he should've—"

"Whoa, hold your horses there, cowboy," I cut in. "It's not Dmitri. Well, not entirely. I mean, sure, he started it, but since when has anything stopped the great Nikolai Petrov? I've been to his office, his house, I even considered skywriting 'Papa, call me!' But he's refusing to see me. Apparently, he thinks he's failed me so badly that we can never speak again."

Viktor scoffs so hard, I'm worried he might pull something. "That's the dumbest thing I've ever heard. And I've heard some doozies in my line of work."

"Tell me about it," I groan, throwing my hands up. "I've been racking my brain trying to figure it out. Maybe you can talk some sense into him? Because I'm officially out of ideas and patience."

"This is insane," Viktor mutters, shaking his head like a wet dog. "Our father, abandoning his daughter? The man who once threatened to castrate a guy for looking at you funny? Are you absolutely sure Orlov isn't behind this?"

"Trust me, if Dmitri was capable of keeping Nikolai Petrov away, he'd be ruling the world by now. No, this is pure, unadulterated Papa drama."

Viktor reaches for his phone, but I grab his wrist faster than you can say "family dysfunction."

"Don't," I plead. "I've already tried calling him more

times than I can count. If he answers you now, I might actually lose it. Call him later and let's just have a nice meal? Please?"

He sighs, dropping his phone like it's suddenly become radioactive. "Okay, okay. You win. If he doesn't reach out, it's his loss. You're the best thing in this family anyway."

I blink back tears, suddenly feeling like I'm four years old again, looking up to my big brother. "Thanks, Viktor. I needed that."

"Hey, what are emotionally stable siblings for?" He grins, trying to lighten the mood.

I manage a watery smile. "Right. Because we're the poster children for well-adjusted adults."

As we finish our meal, I can't help but think about Papa. There was a time when he was my whole world. Now? Now I'm just hoping he might consider being a footnote in my life story.

Welcome to the Petrov family circus, folks. We put the *fun* in dysfunctional.

I PULL into the garage around eleven p.m., feeling like Cinderella racing against the clock. Viktor declined my offer to stay with us. Apparently, the idea of sleeping under the same roof as Dmitri was too much for his delicate constitution. Can't say I blame him. Living with Dmitri is like rooming with a grizzly bear. A very sexy, occasionally sweet grizzly bear, but still.

I grab my bag and head inside, plastering on a smile that hopefully says, I'm a responsible adult who didn't just spend the evening gossiping and eating junk food.

Lo and behold, there's Dmitri, lounging on the couch

like he's auditioning for a GQ spread. "Good evening, Mrs. Orlov." He smirks. "You're early."

I can practically taste the sarcasm. "What can I say? I live for the thrill of beating curfew. Did you get my message, or should I have sent a carrier pigeon?"

He nods, crossing the room in two strides and pulling me into a hug. It's warm and comforting, and I'm totally not melting into it.

Nope. Not at all.

"Yeah, I got it. Where's your brother staying?"

"Downtown hotel," I reply. "I offered him our guest room, but apparently, the idea of sleeping under the same roof as you was too much for his delicate sensibilities."

Dmitri makes a noncommittal "Mm" sound, but he's staring at my lips like they hold the secrets of the universe. I'm pretty sure I could tell him I've decided to join the circus, and he wouldn't hear a word.

His thumb caresses my cheek, and suddenly, we're in a rom-com. He kisses me like he's a man starved and I'm a five-course meal. When his hand grabs my ass, I can't help but grind against him.

"You missed me," he says, smug as a cat with a canary.

"Yeah, well, don't let it go to your head," I reply. "Though it seems something already has."

He pulls me closer, and I'm suddenly very aware of every inch of him. "Two options," he purrs in my ear. "Dinner then bed, or bed then . . . more bed."

I give him my best sultry look, which probably makes me look like I'm having an allergy attack. "Are you on the menu?"

His smile is pure sin. "Let's find out."

Before I can unleash my wit, I'm suddenly airborne, tossed over his shoulder like a sack of potatoes. He spanks me with every step, and I'm torn between indignation and arousal. By the time we reach the bedroom, I'm a mess of hormones and anticipation.

He drops me on the bed and looms over me. "You're what's on the menu tonight, Mrs. Anastasia Orlov."

I like the sound of that.

TWENTY-FOUR
DMITRI

I sense Viktor Petrov's arrival before Jakob announces him. His presence carries weight, a formidable energy I've rarely encountered. I've been anticipating this meeting, curious to see what kind of man Ana's brother is.

"Let him in," I command, my voice cool and controlled.

Viktor enters, his stride purposeful and confident. He carries himself with the assurance of a man who's seen the world and faced its challenges. I find myself reassessing my initial assumptions. This is no mere boy playing at being a protector.

"You're Dmitri Orlov," he states, his voice firm and unwavering.

I nod, gesturing to a chair. "And you're my wife's brother. Please, sit."

He takes the seat, his posture relaxed yet alert. Our eyes lock, and I'm met with a gaze as steely and determined as my own. Interesting. Most men falter under my scrutiny, but Viktor holds firm.

I break the silence. "I'm certain you didn't come here for a social call. "It's about Ana, yes?"

Viktor nods, his words measured and direct as he expresses his concerns. He speaks of family, loyalty, and protection with a conviction that's almost admirable. I listen, grudgingly impressed by his composure and clarity of thought.

"You care for her deeply," I observe, my tone neutral. "That's commendable. But you should know, Ana is not just a Petrov anymore. She's an Orlov now, my wife."

Viktor's eyes narrow. "And that's supposed to reassure me? Your reputation precedes you, Orlov. I need to know she's safe and happy."

I lean forward, matching his intensity. "Then perhaps you should see for yourself. Ana invited you to stay with us, did she not?"

A flicker of surprise crosses his face, quickly replaced by determination. "Yes, she did. And I think I'll take her up on that offer."

I nod, a small smile playing at my lips. "Good. You're welcome in our home. See how Ana lives now, judge for yourself."

As Viktor leaves, I find myself reassessing the situation. He's not the naive idealist I expected, but a worthy adversary—or potential ally. Either way, his presence adds an intriguing element to the game.

I WATCH Ana greet her brother with unbridled joy, a rare display of emotion in this house. Viktor's presence brings a light to her eyes I've rarely seen. It's intriguing.

"Her half-brother?" Yelena asks, her tone laced with curiosity.

"Yes," I confirm, my eyes never leaving the pair.

Yelena's gaze sharpens. "And you're okay with this?"

I turn to her, my expression carefully neutral. "He's Ana's family. Why wouldn't I be?"

She scoffs, seeing right through me as always. "You're playing host because of Ana, but we both know you're keeping your guard up."

I allow a small smirk. "Nothing escapes you, does it?"

"Not when it comes to you, brother," she says, her eyes twinkling with mischief.

As Ana introduces Viktor to Yelena, I observe their interaction closely. He carries himself with confidence, but there's a wariness in his eyes when they meet mine. Good. He's not a fool.

Yelena, ever the social butterfly, swoops in to introduce herself. I watch with amusement as Viktor falls under her spell, just like countless men before him. This could be entertaining.

When Yelena insists on a family dinner, I see Viktor's resolve crumble. Poor man doesn't stand a chance against her charm.

Later, in my bedroom, Ana asks, "What do you think about Viktor and Yelena? They seemed to like each other. Would that bother you?"

I pull her close, silencing her with a deep kiss. She melts against me, and for a moment, I forget about everything else.

"If my sister is happy, I wouldn't interfere," I murmur against her lips. "But if he hurts her, there will be consequences."

Ana nods, understanding the weight of my words. I'm about to show her just how much I've missed her when my phone rings. Irritation flares, but I know better than to ignore it.

The news from Jakob hits me like a punch to the gut.

Our shipment, our containers—all up in flames. Rage burns through me, hot and deadly.

I turn to Ana, my voice cold and controlled. "I have to go. Don't wait up."

As I stalk out of the room, my mind is already racing with possibilities. Someone has dared to cross me, to challenge my authority. They've made a grave mistake.

Whoever is behind this will learn why I am feared. And they will pay dearly for their transgression. In blood, if necessary.

The game has changed, and I intend to remind everyone why I always come out on top.

TWENTY-FIVE
ANA

I jolt awake, fumbling for my phone like it's a lifeline. No messages from Dmitri.

Fantastic.

"Come on, you brooding idiot," I mutter, scrolling through my empty inbox. "Give a girl a sign of life."

I've spent the night tossing and turning, my mind conjuring up increasingly ridiculous scenarios. Maybe he's joined a secret underground knitting circle. Or he's been abducted by aliens who needed a crash course in scowling techniques.

As I drag myself to the shower, I catch my reflection. I look like I've been hit by the worry truck. "Please don't be out murdering someone," I plead to no one in particular.

Because that's a totally normal concern for a wife to have.

Welcome to the Orlov family, folks!

Downstairs, the house is quieter than a library run by mimes. My phone buzzes—it's Viktor, with a cryptic "gotta run" message.

"What is this, the Great Bratva Disappearing Act?" I grumble, heading out the door.

At work, I'm a bundle of nerves wrapped in a pantsuit. When my office phone rings, I nearly break my neck sprinting to answer it.

"Hello?" I say, breathless.

"Ana." It's Dmitri, sounding like he's been gargling gravel. "Anastasia."

"Oh, thank God," I breathe. "Are you okay? You left in such a hurry last night, I was worried sick!"

"I'm fine," he says, his voice softening. "I'll be at your office in ten minutes."

Before I can process that, he's here, looking like he's been through a sexy war. His shirt's half undone, there's a cut on his cheek, and his eyes are blazing with fury.

"WHAT HAPPENED TO YOU?" I blurt out. "Did you join an underground fight club or something?"

He doesn't crack a smile. "I need to speak with you, Ana."

I lean back, trying to look nonchalant. "Okay, shoot. Wait, don't actually shoot. That was just a figure of speech."

He doesn't smile at my clumsy joke. "My shipment was burned. All of it." His jaw clenches. "I might need you to help me frame someone for murder."

I blink. Once. Twice.

"I'm sorry, I think I just had an aneurysm. Did you say frame someone for murder?"

He nods, deadly serious. "I think I'd prefer you helping me with my affairs if the need arises than you stop working altogether."

"Dmitri, *husband*," I say, my voice rising, "I defend people who fudge their taxes, not . . . not this! I wouldn't even know where to start!"

"You're smart. You'll figure it out," he says, like he's asking me to pick up a carton of milk.

I laugh, a touch hysterically. "Oh sure, let me just Google 'How to Frame Someone for Murder 101.' I'm sure that won't raise any red flags at all!"

Dmitri leans forward, his eyes intense. "Ana, I need you to trust me."

I throw my hands up. "Trust you? I'm all for working, but framing someone for murder? Dmitri, that's not exactly like asking me to pick up the dry cleaning!"

"I know it's a lot," he says, his voice low. " I don't need you to do anything right now. I just want to know you will have my back."

I snort. "Oh, well that makes me feel so much better."

He sighs, running a hand through his hair. "Look, I just need you to agree in principle. Can you do that for me?"

I stare at him, aware of my rapidly crumbling moral compass. "In principle? That's like being a little bit pregnant, Dmitri. It doesn't work that way."

"Ana, please," he says, and there's something in his voice that makes me pause. "I need to know that you're all in."

I close my eyes, feeling a headache coming on. "Fine. In principle, I agree. But I reserve the right to back out if things get too crazy. And believe me, my bar for 'too crazy' is getting lower by the minute."

Dmitri's shoulders relax slightly. "Thank you. I promise, if the time comes, I'll explain everything."

"Yeah, yeah," I mutter. "I just hope I don't end up explaining myself to a jury someday. And if it blows up in our faces, I'm changing my name and moving to Tibet to become a monk."

Dmitri actually cracks a smile at that. "Deal."

As he stands up to leave, I slump in my chair, wondering if it's too late to change careers. Maybe I could be a professional cat herder. It'd probably be less stressful than this.

Just another day in the life of Anastasia Orlov, reluctant Bratva wife.

"Before I go," Dmitri says, suddenly looming over me like a very sexy thundercloud.

I tilt my head back, ready to make some quip about neck strain, when his lips brush against mine. His hand cradles my face, and suddenly, I'm melting faster than ice cream in July.

The kiss is soft but deep, and by the time he pulls away, I'm pretty sure I've forgotten how to breathe. Who needs oxygen when you have Dmitri Orlov?

"Have a good day, Ana," he murmurs, and then he's gone, leaving me feeling like I've just run a marathon while riding a rollercoaster.

I press a hand to my chest, half expecting to find my heart trying to escape. "Down, girl," I mutter to myself. "He's your husband, not a chocolate lava cake."

But that's how it always is with Dmitri. One touch, and I'm a mess of hormones and want, like a teenager with her first crush. Except my crush is a dangerous Bratva boss who just asked me if I'd be willing to frame someone for murder. In principle.

Totally normal, right?

I clear my throat, trying to regain some semblance of professionalism. "Alright then," I announce to my empty office, "back to work. Time to see which scoundrel I get to save from going to the guillotine."

I turn back to my computer, wondering when my life turn into a soap opera crossed with a crime thriller. And more importantly, why am I kind of enjoying it?

TWENTY-SIX
DMITRI

I stop in front of a florist shop, parking my car and staring at the flower arrangements sitting prettily in the window. "She finds roses ordinary," I say to Yelena on the phone. "I'll get carnations."

She laughs. "Are you sure she likes them, or is it because you bought them that one time? Did you ask her if they are her favorite?"

I shake my head, already annoyed. "She's my wife, Yelena. You'd think I'd know a thing or two about her by now."

"Right."

I roll my eyes, more at myself than her. "That was sarcasm."

She clicks her tongue, the playful attitude still there. "I knew it. Are you delivering them yourself, or will you let your ego get in the way of showing up at your wife's office?"

"Yelena," I say, the impatience clear in my voice, "I'm hanging up now. I'll call you back in two hours."

"Wait, I—"

I hang up, tuck my phone in my pocket, and get out of

the car, grabbing my coat as I step out. The florist shop door swings open easily, and the warmth inside contrasts sharply with the cold gnawing at my skin.

"Hi," a man with an apron and a name tag that reads "Aaron" greets me immediately. "What can I help you with today? Would you like to order a custom bouquet or to select one from our collection?"

My instinct is to ask for a bouquet of white carnations, but I stop myself. I never actually asked Ana what her favorite flowers are. How many assumptions have I made about her?

"Can you suggest something for a lover?" I ask, my voice as cold as usual, adding quickly, "Not roses or carnations."

He strokes his chin thoughtfully. "Hmm. Maybe something that matches the color of her eyes, then? It could symbolize true love—mixing something personal with something meaningful."

True love?

The thought hits me hard. Do I love her? I'm not sure if that's what this is. But I can't deny that whatever I feel for Ana is stronger than anything I've felt for anyone else. I want her. I want her more each day.

"Her eyes are blue," I say, a bit softer this time.

"Forget-me-nots," he suggests, walking me over to a section of delicate blue flowers, petals soft like velvet, the color just like her eyes—deep and unforgettable.

They're perfect. Like she is.

"I'll take them," I say.

I watch as he carefully picks the bluest ones, their light veins almost transparent in the right light. He arranges them with precision, but as I watch, I decide not to take them to her myself. Maybe it's better this way. The flowers can speak for me. At least they won't betray my inner turmoil.

I hand over my business card with Ana's office address written on the back of it. "Have them delivered. Call me when she receives them."

As I leave, I can't help but wonder what she'll think. I hope she understands the gesture. I don't say the right things when it comes to her. Hell, I don't even know what the right things are.

I'm back in my office, my mind half on Bianchi and the unfinished business I have with him, and half on Ana. I haven't heard from her since last night, and though I should be focusing on Bratva matters, my mind drifts back to her.

Jakob knocks and enters, dropping an envelope on my desk.

"This came for you, sir."

I glance at it. A butcher shop logo. Not just any butcher shop—a front for one of the Bratva's more unsavory operations.

I smile, tearing it open and reading the note inside:
How would you like your meat handled?

I think of what I told Ana the other day and her agreement to stand by me.

I grab my pen, scribbling on the back of the note:
Home delivery. Make sure it's well received.

Once Jakob leaves to handle the message, I try to return my focus to work. But my phone rings, and I see an unknown number on the screen.

Probably Bianchi, I think, ready to listen to whatever pathetic offer he might have.

"Is this Mr. Orlov?" The voice on the other end is unfamiliar. "This is Aaron, from the florist shop. You asked me to send a bouquet to your wife?"

"Yes," I reply, already irritated.

"She wasn't in the office."

I stop, my gut twisting. "Did you leave it with someone?"

"No, sir. They said she hasn't been in today. No one would take the flowers on her behalf there, so I thought I'd call."

My stomach tightens, a gnawing sense of dread building in my chest. Something's wrong. I stand up abruptly, heading for the door. I need to tell Jakob to start looking for her. My pulse quickens, and it feels like I've just been hit in the gut.

"Sir? What would you like me to do?" the florist asks, his voice fading into the background of my thoughts.

"Are you still at her office?" I ask, striding through the lobby.

"Yes, sir."

"Who told you she wasn't there?"

"I spoke to a guy named Maxwell. Said she hadn't been in all day and that her car wasn't there either."

I hang up, bolt for my car, and start the engine. I speed out of the parking lot, my mind whirling. She wouldn't just disappear. Would she?

Ana's strong—tougher than most—but that doesn't stop the fear creeping in. I've pissed off enough people to know how vulnerable she could be if someone decided to use her against me.

I punch the accelerator, my mind stuck on the thought that Ana might be in danger.

She can't be gone.

Not the woman I've started to fall for, despite everything inside me telling me to stay cold, to stay ruthless.

Trying not to panic, I dial Ana's number, but as I feared, her phone's switched off.

The only other time her phone was off was when she went drinking, and it died on her after a full day. But it's not even noon; I saw her this morning.

Somebody must know where she is.

After hours of driving, calling my men and asking them to look into people of interest, I find myself in front of Nikolai Petrov's building. Ana said she hadn't spoken to him in months, but I know he must be plotting something—maybe he's finally decided to carry out his plan. Maybe he's taken her, blaming my enemies, forcing me into a war.

I stride into the building, fury driving my steps.

His secretary, the same woman I saw the day I demanded Nikolai give up his daughter, stands at the entrance. She frowns when she sees me.

"Mr. Orlov, to what do we owe this pleasure?"

"Is he in? And don't lie to me," I growl, the threat hanging between us. "My wife is missing. Anyone who makes it harder for me to find her will regret it."

She glances behind her, her voice less sure now. "Anastasia is missing? Why would you think that?"

"She hasn't been in her office today," I bite out. "Now, is he here, or do I have to find out for myself?"

Her eyes flicker with hesitation, but she steps aside. "You think he kidnapped his own daughter? He hasn't seen her since she moved in with you. Why would he take her now?"

I don't answer, pushing past her and striding straight into Nikolai's office.

He's mid-conversation, but I don't wait for an invitation.

"Dmitri," he snarls, glaring at me. "How dare you—"

"Where's Anastasia?" I demand, my voice like ice. "Where's my wife?"

He scoffs. "How should I know? *You* took her. Why ask me?"

His arrogant face shows no fear. No concern. Suspicion lodges itself firmly in my gut. Where's the father who begged me not to take his daughter? The one who supposedly loves her?

"Do you even care what happens to her?" My voice drips with disgust.

Nikolai shrugs. "She's your wife, isn't she? You gave her your name. Whatever happens, you'll be blamed for it. Throwing her to the wolves of your world was your decision."

My fists clench, rage boiling just beneath the surface. Every muscle in my body tenses, aching to tear him apart.

He sighs, sensing the danger. "I don't have her, Orlov. If you think I'd harm my daughter, then you know nothing about the love of a father, even a *pakhan*."

I sneer. "If I find out you're behind this, I'll be back to make you pay."

I storm out of his office, barely keeping my anger in check. The moment I'm in the hallway, my phone buzzes. I yank it from my pocket. It's a message from one of my men.

Bianchi has your wife.

I see red.

I dial Lucia without hesitation.

"If you're with your father, leave," I say, my voice hard and final. "This is my only act of mercy. There won't be a second one."

There's silence on the other end of the line, but I don't need her response to know the tip is real. Bianchi has her.

I hang up, fury consuming me.

She's in danger, and this isn't just business anymore.

Ana isn't just a pawn.

And if Bianchi touches her, he'll wish he'd never been born.

I drive like a man possessed, my hands gripping the wheel so hard it feels like I'll snap it in half. The thought of putting a bullet through Bianchi's head is the only thing keeping me from losing it completely. I want to burn that bastard's entire operation to the ground, but innocent people would get caught in the crossfire, and I won't have that.

I pull up to the meet point, barely killing the engine before I step out. Leonid, a hulking man covered in tattoos, approaches immediately, bowing slightly.

"Leonid." I nod. "Where are the others?"

He points to the building behind him. "They're ready, sir. I gathered them as you instructed. But word is Bianchi's fortified his place. At least ten men inside. We're only six."

I bare my teeth in a smile that doesn't reach my eyes. "Six is enough. I'll go in first, and you'll follow. The only order is to shoot on sight. No one walks out."

"Understood, boss."

I slide back into my car, reaching for the glove compartment. The cold metal of the gun feels familiar in my hand, comforting.

Ever since I was young, my father drilled one lesson into me: Don't kill unless it's personal.

Well, this *is* personal.

By the time I reach Bianchi's place, his men are already outside, their guns trained on my car. I step out, my hand resting on the butt of my gun, calm but coiled, ready to strike.

"Bianchi!" I yell, voice cutting through the tense air.

"You want your men to die like pigs? Or do you want to come out and face me like a man? Let my wife go, and we'll settle this between us."

No movement, just a dead-eyed thug guarding the door.

I hear the hum of engines behind me as my men pull up and exit their cars, weapons drawn.

Bianchi's men shuffle nervously, inching forward. Then gunfire erupts, and I duck just in time, shouting for Leonid to cover me as I make a run for the house. Bullets zip past me, one grazing my ear. I take down the guy to my right before I'm at the door, kicking it open.

Inside, the chaos quiets. A man leaps up from behind a chair, but he's too slow. I shoot him in the shoulder, then the hand as he tries again. He drops, screaming. Another one steps out around a pillar. I duck to the right, firing straight into his gut. He goes down with a groan, and just as I'm about to take another step, Leonid's booming shot echoes behind me.

"Go, boss," he calls. "I've got this."

I stride up the stairs, my blood pumping with one goal in mind: Bianchi. Every door I kick open reveals nothing until I reach the one that won't budge.

He's in there.

I press my ear to the wood, catching faint footsteps. Someone's about to ambush me. I pretend to pound on the door, feigning ignorance, and just as the knob turns, I drop low. The second the door swings open, I kick the guy's legs out from under him, disarming him in one move. His gun clatters away as I slam mine against the back of his head, knocking him out cold.

Then I see him—Bianchi.

He stands in the center of the room, holding a gun.

Behind him on the bed, Ana's tied up, her eyes wide with fear, though she hides it well.

Oh, you should have untied her before I got here. I might've let you live.

I step forward, my eyes locking on his.

"Did you like the present I sent?" I taunt, my voice low and mocking. "How did it taste?"

Bianchi snarls. "You think you can send me a corpse and call it a message? Well, message received. But here's one for you—your wife's mine now."

The bastard actually has the nerve to gloat.

"You sold me out," I growl, stepping closer. "You tried to stab me in the back after my father died. You teamed up with Igor and Alexey, and now you want to pull this shit again?"

He shrugs, his tone as smug as ever. "Why not? We aren't brothers, Dmitri. You're a *pakhan*, and I'm an Italian *capo*. I worked with your Bratva because I saw an opportunity. Now I see a bigger one."

I'm closing the distance between us, my gaze darting to Ana, who's struggling to free herself. She's terrified but trying to stay strong. My heart clenches for a moment—a feeling I'm not used to.

Bianchi waves his gun at Ana, his smile sinister. "Drop your gun, and I'll let her walk. Or I'll blow her brains out right here in front of you."

I smirk, dark and cold. "Go ahead. Do it."

Bianchi's eyes narrow in surprise, but he's not ready to back down. He points the gun at her, trying to call my bluff.

"Don't think I won't."

"I never said you wouldn't."

I pull my gun, aiming straight at his chest. "But if you want to die like a man, you face me. Man to man. Using women as bargaining chips? That makes you an even bigger coward."

"Fine." He grins, points the gun at me and pulls the trigger.

But I'm faster. My bullet tears into his chest, even as his grazes my shoulder, sending a sharp, searing pain through me. I stagger but stay on my feet. Bianchi crumples to the floor, gasping for air, the life draining from his eyes.

I don't spare him a second glance.

Rushing to Ana, I press my fingers to her neck, relief flooding through me when I feel her faint pulse. She's fainted but is alive.

Scooping her into my arms, I turn my back on Bianchi's dying form.

This was never his game to win.

TWENTY-SEVEN

ANA

Why does it feel like someone dropped a piano on my head?

I slowly open my eyes, only to be stabbed by the brightest, most sterile light. It's like my retinas have signed up for an all-out assault, and the pounding in my skull doubles. I blink, groaning as I try to gather my bearings.

Where the hell am I?

There's an obnoxious beeping sound, and somewhere nearby, I hear a voice—familiar, distant. It's muffled, like when you're dreaming and someone tries to talk to you in real life. But I'm too busy figuring out why I feel like I got steamrolled.

As my vision clears, I realize I'm in a hospital bed, hooked up to machines like some sci-fi experiment.

"Ana?"

Dmitri. The voice snaps into focus, and I turn my head toward him. Well, try to. My entire body revolts, screaming in protest as pain shoots through every muscle.

"*Kotyonok*," he says softly, taking my hand in his. "I'm here. I'm right here."

"What...?" My voice is barely a croak, and even that hurts. "What happened?"

"You're in the hospital," Dmitri explains, his voice as gentle as I've ever heard it. "You fainted. Covered in bruises, too." His Adam's apple bobs thickly as he swallows. "I'm sorry. I shouldn't have let this happen to you."

The memories hit me like a sledgehammer. Flashes of a car pulling up, something rough being shoved over my face, struggling to break free, darkness, voices I didn't recognize.

Bianchi.

I sit up—big mistake—and gasp as the pain punches me right in the skull. "Bianchi," I wheeze, clutching my head. "He . . . he kidnapped me. He said he was going to kill you."

Dmitri's face tightens, dark rage swirling behind his eyes. I can tell he's keeping it together, but just barely. "I found you," he says, his voice low. "That's all that matters now."

"You . . . found me." My brain catches up. "Bianchi?"

"He's dead." The words are cold, final. No emotion.

I blink, staring at him. "Did . . . did you kill him?"

"Yes." His answer is simple, but the weight behind it isn't. "And I'm going to find whoever helped him. They'll pay the same price."

The way he says it—no hesitation, no doubt—should terrify me. But right now, I'm too tired, too sore to care. And honestly, after what I went through, I'm willing to let him rain down some vengeance on whoever put me in this bed.

Dmitri leans forward, guilt written all over his face. His shoulders slump, and for the first time, I see regret clouding his usually unshakable demeanor. "I should've protected you better, Ana. If I hadn't called off my men who were tailing you—"

I cut him off, squeezing his hand. "It's not your fault," I

rasp, feeling a flicker of sympathy for him. The fact that he feels this guilty over something that clearly wasn't in his control hits me in ways I'm not prepared for.

A tiny smile tugs at my lips, despite the pain. "I told Bianchi you were coming for him. Told him he'd regret touching Dmitri Orlov's wife." I give a little snort, wincing as the movement hurts my head. "And look, I was right."

Dmitri chuckles, shaking his head. "Only you, *kotyonok*, would laugh in the face of this."

"Learned from the best," I tease. "You're the infamous Orlov, after all. I'm just channeling some of that energy."

He leans closer, his lips brushing my forehead softly. The warmth of his breath, the tenderness of his touch—God, it feels like a balm to the ache in my chest, and not just the physical one.

"Anastasia," he says quietly, brushing a strand of hair from my face, his fingers lingering on my skin. "You're my love, Ana. I never thought I could feel this much, or that I could change. But you . . . you're like a storm, breaking through every barrier I've built."

Wait. What?

Come again?

I blink. Twice. I think I must have just hallucinated. "What did you just say?"

He smirks. "You heard me."

"No, no." I shake my head, feeling my heart do this ridiculous somersault thing. "Say it again. Because there's no way you said—"

"I love you, Anastasia." His voice is low, sure, unwavering. "I love you, *kotyonok*."

Oh, wow. This is happening. Dmitri Orlov just said he loves me. Me.

The hospital monitor beeps wildly, probably catching on to the fact that my heart is about to explode.

"Relax, you're going to give yourself a heart attack." Dmitri grins, clearly enjoying my stunned silence. "Maybe I should wait until you're feeling better to drop life-changing confessions."

"Don't you dare." I narrow my eyes, half-laughing, half-panicking. "You said it. No taking it back."

His lips curl into a smirk. "You're impossible."

"You love me," I counter, my voice wobbling as I point a finger at him.

"Yeah, yeah, I do." His smirk softens into something warmer. He leans down, pressing his lips to mine, just a soft, quick kiss, but it short-circuits my entire brain.

Oh, I am so screwed.

"That's for staying strong until I found you," he murmurs against my lips before kissing my forehead again.

"If this is what it takes for you to—"

His finger presses gently against my lips. "Don't. I'm not letting this happen again. I'll make sure you're protected, always. Two men stationed at your door, security reinstated. You won't have to worry about a thing."

I roll my eyes. "There are worse things out there than kidnappers, Dmitri."

He nods, deadly serious. "Exactly. And I'll make sure none of them touch you."

I can't help but laugh, though it comes out weak. "You do realize I grew up in the Bratva, right? My father taught me how to handle a gun when I was ten. I'm not exactly a damsel in distress."

His smile is soft, but there's something in his eyes that says he'll never stop protecting me. "I know. But you're my wife, and I'll make sure nothing happens to you."

Well, there's no arguing with that. He always gets the last word, anyway. "Fine," I sigh. "I guess I could use a bodyguard or two."

Before either of us can say anything else, the phone rings.

And just like that, life barges back in. "I've got to take this," Dmitri says as he stands up. "I might need to leave the hospital for a while, but I'll be back. I promise."

As he walks away, I sigh and close my eyes. I just hope he's safe.

I OPEN MY EYES AGAIN, blinking against the hospital's harsh, white lights. The steady beeping of the machines, the smell of antiseptic—yep, I'm still here. My body protests as I shift slightly, everything feeling heavier than it should. But before I can fully process anything, there's a loud pop that nearly makes me jump out of my skin.

I whip my head around, almost giving myself whiplash, only to see Viktor standing there with a ridiculous bouquet and an army of balloons.

"Welcome to the land of the living." He grins, eyes sparkling with mischief. "Sorry about that. One of the balloons popped."

I sigh, trying not to laugh, and watch as he awkwardly ties the balloons to the bedpost, the roses unceremoniously dropped on the bedside table.

"Hey, sis," he says, pulling me into a tight hug, kissing the top of my head. "How do you feel?"

"Oh, you know," I groan dramatically. "Like death warmed over. How did you know I was here?"

Viktor's expression darkens instantly, his usual lighthearted demeanor clouded with irritation. "It's not hard to find out which hospital your sister was admitted to when you hear that her husband let her get kidnapped by some Italian lunatic." His gaze darts around the room. "Where's Dmitri?"

Oh no. I can already sense the storm brewing.

"It wasn't his fault," I blurt, grabbing his wrist before he can fully channel his rage. The last thing I need right now is my overprotective brother going head-to-head with my husband.

Viktor sneers. "Not his fault? Like hell, it wasn't. He created the mess, and you're the one who got caught in it. You could have been killed!"

I sigh, my patience wearing thin. "Dmitri saved me."

But Viktor's not having it. "Saved you? He could've prevented it in the first place. Anastasia," he says, softening slightly as he cups my face, "Orlov is bad news. I told Father when you married him that his enemies would become yours. And now look where you are. In a hospital bed."

I mentally send a quick prayer to Dmitri: *Please, wherever you are, do not walk in right now.*

Because if Viktor sees him, there will be a brawl. No doubt about it.

Viktor takes a deep breath, gripping my hand. "That's why I came back," he says, his voice softer now, more earnest. "I came for you, Ana. I'm willing to pay whatever price Nikolai Petrov put on your head to free you from that brute."

I blink. "Price? Viktor, you're talking about going to war." My stomach drops as the weight of his words settles in.

He shrugs, like we're talking about a minor inconvenience. "It might not come to that. I'm working with Father again, and I'm pretty sure I can convince him to let a few things slide in exchange for your divorce."

Oh. Hell. No.

I shake my head vehemently. "You left this world for a reason, Viktor. Don't you dare come crawling back into it because of me. I don't need you getting tangled up in this mess."

But his expression is as stubborn as ever, his jaw set in that infuriating way that tells me I'm not getting through to him. "Don't worry about me. I'm my father's son, just like you're his daughter. But promise me something. Promise you'll leave Dmitri. Get away from all this."

And here it is. The moment I never thought I'd say aloud. I close my eyes for a second, steadying myself before the words tumble out. "I'm in love with him, Viktor. I love Dmitri."

The look on his face is priceless. Shock, disbelief, a touch of horror. He stares at me like I've just grown a second head. "Did . . . did he threaten you?"

I groan, throwing my hands up. "Even if he did, why would I use 'I love him' as the excuse? I'm telling you, Viktor, Dmitri *killed* the man who kidnapped me. He promised to make everyone who had a hand in it pay."

Viktor's face hardens again, arms folded across his chest. "Yeah, to save face. You don't think that's convenient?"

I rub my temples, wincing at the pain but more at his thick-headedness. "Viktor Petrov, if you don't stop acting like I don't have a brain, I swear I'll get out of this bed and smack you. I know what I'm saying. Dmitri loves me, and I love him. Period."

He stares at me for a long beat, then finally sighs, standing up from the bed. "Fine. If you're sure, I'll let it be.

But," he raises a finger in warning, "if the day comes when he doesn't save you, I'll be the one to end him."

I can't help but roll my eyes at the theatrics. My head is pounding, my body aching, and my brother is making grand threats.

Welcome to my life.

"Can I get some rest now, please?" I mutter, closing my eyes and sinking back into the pillow. "I just went through a life-or-death experience. I think I deserve a nap."

Viktor chuckles softly, leaning down to kiss my forehead. "Fine, fine. I'll be outside making some calls. And don't worry, nothing's getting past the two hulks your husband stationed outside the door."

Despite myself, a small smile tugs at my lips as I watch him leave. When the door finally closes, I fluff my pillow, sinking into the blessed quiet.

The men in my life are ridiculous—stubborn, hot-headed, and prone to making rash decisions—but I wouldn't trade them for the world.

TWENTY-EIGHT
DMITRI

One.

Two.

Three.

Boom.

Watching the warehouse go up in flames is satisfying. The kind of satisfaction that seeps deep into your bones. The crackling wood, the thick smoke curling up into the night sky—it all feels like a cleansing, a purge of anyone foolish enough to betray me. It's the kind of catharsis only fire can provide, a reminder to the world that Dmitri Orlov doesn't just make threats. I deliver.

"Is this the last one?" I ask, not tearing my eyes from the inferno as Leonid steps up beside me.

"Yes, boss," he says. "I just got word from the others. Two of the sites had some resistance, but it was handled."

Resistance. Pests. That's what a once-powerful *pakhan* syndicate and an Italian Mafia gang have been reduced to.

Handled.

Good. It's the beginning of the end for anyone who thinks they can move against the Orlov family. If this doesn't scare them, the fire will finish what my reputation started—reducing everything they built to ash. And if that still doesn't do the job? I'll burn them out, piece by piece. Down to the last brick.

I hear footsteps approaching, nervous ones, a familiar shuffle of someone who's spent too long lying to themselves and now finds themselves at the mercy of reality. I turn, catching Igor Pavlov making his way toward me. His face is tight, though he's trying to keep it together. I enjoy seeing him squirm.

"Pavlov," I greet him, my voice low, dangerous. "To what do I owe this pleasure?"

He stares at the flames, his expression a mixture of fear and curiosity, like a child watching a car crash but too scared to look away. "Bianchi?" he croaks.

"You sound concerned," I say, smirking. "I thought you said he wasn't one of us."

His eyes dart to mine, the fear evident before he quickly masks it, but I've already seen enough. He's rattled, and rightfully so.

"I was right, wasn't I?" he tries, his voice shaking. "The Italians can't be trusted. I heard rumors, but I didn't have proof, so I didn't—"

"You didn't tell me," I finish for him, enjoying the way he flinches at the edge in my tone. "You thought it'd be fun to see me fall."

He opens his mouth, no doubt to deny it, but I cut him off with a lazy wave of my hand. "I don't need you to be my eyes and ears, Igor. I already know who my enemies are."

I let the silence hang between us for a beat too long. My words are a warning, subtle but deadly, and I can tell it registers when he shifts his gaze, looking away.

"Well," he mutters, gesturing weakly with his hands, "you're Dmitri. You always know everything."

I smile, a cold, calculated gesture that holds no warmth. He's a coward—always has been. Useful, but a coward nonetheless.

As I walk back toward my car, I hear his footsteps trailing behind me, his pace quickening to match mine. "Did you come here to talk business? Because if it's about the casino deal, it's not ready yet." I spare him a glance. "I gave you a month, but these things take time. Unless you want to take over—"

"No, no!" he cuts in, his voice rising in a panic. "I trust you. I didn't come for that. I . . . I heard what happened, and I wanted to show my support. We're brothers in arms, after all."

I stop, turning to face him fully, my expression deadly calm. "Thieves in arms," I correct, the smile on my lips tight. "Thank you for the support, Igor. But I've got things under control."

I start to walk again, but his voice follows, laced with desperation. "Dmitri, I owe you for helping me with the deal. I couldn't have done it without you. I owe you."

I pause, turning slightly, just enough to let him see the cruel smile tugging at my lips. "Oh, you owe me more than you think, Pavlov."

He doesn't know yet, but his time is coming. His parting words are nothing but a weak attempt to pledge loyalty, to put himself in my good graces before I decide to turn my sights on him. But I'm not interested in false loyalty. I don't need someone who hides behind words when their actions say otherwise.

He thinks gratitude will save him. But in my world,

pretending to be loyal while you wait for an opportunity to betray only earns you one thing—a bullet. Or worse.

As I get into the car, my fingers drum on the wheel, my thoughts already moving from Pavlov's pathetic attempt at survival to the only thing that matters.

Ana.

She's different from all of this, different from the fire and the blood. She makes me feel things I've long buried—feelings that threaten the icy walls I've built around myself. She's the only person who can make me question whether the monster I've become is worth it.

But I know better than to think love makes you weak. It makes you sharper, hungrier, more dangerous. If anyone dares touch her again, I won't just burn them.

I'll tear them apart with my bare hands.

WHEN I GET HOME, Janet tells me Ana's resting. My pulse quickens, the need to see her pushing away the rest of the day's chaos. I take the stairs two at a time, eager to feel her in my arms, to bury everything else in the warmth of her skin.

But when I step into the room, it's empty. The faint sound of water catches my attention, and I turn toward the bathroom. The door is slightly ajar, steam curling out in tendrils, and I push it open, stepping inside.

There she is. My wife. Naked. Gorgeous. Partially concealed by the misty heat, her body glistens in the low light. She's humming softly to herself, completely unaware of my presence.

I let myself savor the moment. The curve of her back, the

delicate slope of her neck as she leans into the spray. She's a vision, something I could never have imagined would belong to me. *Me*—a man who's built a life on blood, betrayal, and fire.

I slip in quietly, the sound of the shower masking my footsteps. I place my hand gently on her shoulder. She jumps, gasping, her wide eyes locking onto mine as she shakes her head.

"You scared me to death, you brute."

"I would've brought you back to life," I murmur, my voice low, possessive, as my fingers trail up to cup her chin. I tilt her head back, making her meet my gaze, my mouth hovering just inches from hers.

Her lips part slightly, and my tongue flicks out to trace the seam of her mouth, teasing, a soft, needy sigh escaping her.

There's nothing gentle in the way I look at her—nothing soft. I've been cold, ruthless, dangerous all my life. But with Ana, there's something else. Something more.

My control frays at the edges every time she's close, and tonight, I don't intend to hold back.

I deepen the kiss, cradling her face with a hand and pulling her close with the other. Her body is soft, as usual, and warm from the water cascading down.

"You'll get wet," Ana whispers.

"Mm," I murmur against her lips, running my hand over her back and caressing her spine with my finger. I feel her shiver. "It's too late for that, *kotyonok*. Besides, I don't mind."

My hand on her back inches lower, grabbing her ass and kneading lightly. She moans, and her tongue slips into my mouth when I kiss her again, setting off a spark that travels through my body and turns into a wildfire along the way.

Her breasts spill out as I try to cup them with one hand, and she arches her back, pushing them against my chest.

"How has your day been?" I ask as I lower my head, licking the water droplets off one nipple. "Mine's getting better by the minute."

Ana's hands dive into my hair, panting softly when my mouth closes around her peaked bead, sucking on it. I scrape my teeth against it, making her gasp, and then I move to the other one, flicking with my tongue before sucking. With my head nestled against her chest, my other hand parts her thighs, and teasingly, knowing where she wants me to touch, I trail my fingers up her thighs.

She makes a sound of protest, reaching for my hand, but I pull back, biting her nipple as a small warning. It only makes her more aroused, and when my thumb flicks against her slit, she's *wet*.

Hell.

"*Kotyonok*," I growl. "You must have been thinking about me while you were showering, craving my finger inside you," I slide it in, "wanting me to fuck you, pounding hard as you come apart on my dick."

Ana whimpers when I curl my finger and rub the pad against her most sensitive spot. Her legs jerk, and her arms reach around my neck, holding on tight. My dick twitches too, eager to replace my fingers.

"I want you like this," I rasp as I withdraw my hand, turning her around.

Her ass grinds against my crotch as the warm water pours down on both of us. Her whimpers push me close to the edge of a primal need, the overwhelming desire to own and pleasure her.

With one hand around her neck, I spread Ana's legs again and find her clit with my thumb, circling it. She cries out as I apply a little more pressure, and my other hand cups her breast, gently tugging on her nipple.

When I slide my finger into her warmth again, she clenches tight and comes soon after, breathing heavily.

I hold her in my arms, then lift her, carrying her to the bed. Setting Ana down on it, with her eager eyes on me, I strip off my wet clothes.

Her eyes widen as I take my dick into my hand, stroking it while looking at her. *Beautiful eyes. Gorgeous woman.*

I climb the bed, kissing her softly on the mouth and then pulling her onto my body to straddle me.

"You want me here?" she asks, biting her bottom lip and looking naughty.

I brush a lock of hair from her face. "Yes, *kotyonok*. I want you on me, taking my dick into you, riding hard. I want to watch your eyes roll back and see you unravel. I *need* to hear my name on your lips while I fuck you."

She grows bolder with each word, and I bite back an oath when she places my hands on her hips, guiding my tip to her entrance. I thrust in slowly, watching her pupils widen as she takes me in.

"Fuck, Ana," I groan. "You feel so fucking good. I'll never get enough of you."

When she doesn't respond, I increase the pace of my thrusts, tilting my hips higher and pounding faster. My thumb finds her clit again, and I watch her eyes as they roll back, her chest heaving and her breasts bouncing.

I pour myself into her, giving back as much as I take. Her keen sounds of pleasure turn into loud moans that echo in the room, and she braces her hands on my chest, pushing down and rubbing her ass against my thighs.

The sound of her ass slapping against my body is nothing short of dizzying and unapologetically primal. It's like the other times, but also as if it is the first time I'm discovering what it feels like to touch her body, learn her curves, and get a taste of heaven.

Her walls squeeze my dick as she falls over the edge, her body tensing, then relaxing. I find climax seconds later, letting go with my eyes tightly closed and the world shattering.

TWENTY-NINE
ANA

Well, here I am, standing outside the house where I grew up, feeling like I'm about to walk into a minefield.

The door swings open before I can chicken out, and suddenly, I'm surrounded by Papa's minions—I mean, *associates*. God, I'd forgotten how creepy it is when they all stare at you.

Maria, our housekeeper—and let's be real, probably the only sane person in this place—gives me a sympathetic smile. "He's in his study, Miss Ana."

Great. Papa's lair. Where dreams go to die and organized crime goes to thrive.

I take a deep breath, straighten my shoulders, and march toward certain doom. Okay, maybe I'm being dramatic, but after months of radio silence, what else am I supposed to think? If it weren't for Viktor practically begging me to come, I'd be home binging Netflix and pretending I don't have a family.

I knock twice, push open the door, and there he is—Nikolai Petrov, criminal mastermind and emotionally unavailable father extraordinaire, typing away on his laptop like he's just another CEO and not the boogeyman of the underworld.

"*Dochka*," he says, arms open wide like we're in some Hallmark movie. "How are you?"

How am I? Oh, you know, just peachy. Got married off like a prized cow, haven't heard from you in months, but hey, who's keeping track?

Instead of saying any of that, I plant myself in the chair across from him and cross my arms. "Why did you send for me, Papa? After all this time?"

Damn it, my voice cracks. So much for my ice queen routine.

He has the decency to look ashamed, at least. "I'm sorry," he says, and for a second, he actually sounds sincere. "I needed to make some things right before we could meet again."

I can't help it, I scoff. "Make things right? I don't see that anything's changed since you pawned me off to Dmitri like a bad poker debt. So, what's your grand plan?"

He comes around the desk, perching on the edge like he's about to deliver a pep talk. "Petrov men have always been proud, Ana," he starts, and I resist the urge to roll my eyes. Here we go.

"I let that pride get the better of me. I couldn't see that I was hurting you, my own child, even when Daria and Viktor pointed it out. I have no excuse. I'm just hoping you can forgive this old man for putting his ego before the only thing that truly matters."

And just like that, the dam breaks. Tears start flowing, and I hate myself for it. I hate that even after everything, his words still have this effect on me.

"What changed?" I manage to choke out.

He takes my hand, and it's so achingly familiar that, for a moment, I'm that little girl again, looking up at her dad like he hung the moon. "Would you believe me if I said there was nothing behind it? That I woke up one day and realized I might lose my child forever?"

I want to believe him. God, I want to so badly. "I guess," I mumble. "But on mom's anniversary, you never showed."

He shakes his head, looking pained. "I did come. I saw you there, at her grave. I couldn't face you then. I'm so sorry, *dochka*. Your father failed you, and I'm regretting it every minute of every day."

And just like that, my resolve crumbles. I might have Dmitri, Yelena, and Viktor now, but this man in front of me? He's been my rock for most of my life. How can I shut him out completely?

"It's okay," I sigh, feeling the weight of months of anger start to lift. "I don't . . . I can't hate you. You're my father, after all. I was hurt, and I still don't like this whole lifestyle, but . . . I love you."

Next thing I know, I'm wrapped in a bear hug, sobbing into his shoulder like I'm five years old again.

"There, there," he murmurs, patting my back awkwardly. Always the emotional genius, my Papa. "What can I do to make it better? Shopping, perhaps? I'll pay for whatever you want."

I almost say no, but then I think of Yelena. If anyone deserves a shopping spree, it's the two of us. "Alright," I agree. "It's a start."

An hour later, I'm watching Yelena's eyes nearly pop out of her head as I wave Papa's credit card in her face. "This is the best day of my life!" she squeals, dragging me into Christian Dior like she's on a mission.

. . .

AS WE BROWSE through outrageously priced dresses, Yelena gives me a sidelong glance. "So, you made up with your dad? No more freezing you out?"

I snort. "I'm still pissed. Months of silence aren't fixed by one teary conversation and a blank check. But it's something."

She squeezes my hand. "Well, let's focus on the now. We're here for therapy. Retail therapy!"

We spend the next hour trying on ridiculous gowns, giggling like schoolgirls, and generally making nuisances of ourselves. By the time we're done, I've swiped Papa's card for an amount that makes me wince, but hey, he offered, right?

As we're settling in at Palomar for a post-shopping feast, Yelena brings it up again. "You know, it's a little weird that your dad bribed you with a shopping spree. I mean, shouldn't it be more like, I don't know, a family dinner or something?"

And just like that, the doubts come creeping back in. She's right. Papa didn't even ask when I'd visit again. So why did he really call me over?

I push the thought away. "Maybe that's just what happens when your daughter gets married? You forget how to be normal?"

Yelena laughs. "I guess. The men in our lives are a special breed." Then she claps a hand over her mouth, giggling. "Oh God, I forgot for a second that my brother is your husband. You're like a sister to me, and sometimes I have to remind myself that this sister has an 'in-law' attached to it."

We stare at each other for a moment before bursting into hysterical laughter, drawing stares from nearby diners.

"They might kick us out," Yelena whispers conspiratorially.

I grin. "Good thing we are rich, beautiful and don't give a damn."

As we dig into our obscenely expensive steaks, I can't help but notice how Yelena's eyes light up whenever Viktor's name comes up in conversation.

Oh boy. Looks like Cupid's been busy.

I EYE Yelena over the rim of my wine glass. She's got that look, the one that screams "I'm hiding something juicy." Time to poke the bear.

"Alright, spill it," I say, setting down my glass with a dramatic clink. "What's going on in that pretty head of yours?"

She hesitates, chewing her lip. "I don't want to hurt Viktor, Ana."

Here it comes.

"He's just so hot!" she blurts out, and I almost choke on my drink. When I collect myself, I nod, smirking. I've never looked at Viktor that way, but it's hard to argue with Yelena's assessment.

"But," she sighs, and I brace myself, "I don't think I can commit again. I've been there, done that, got the emotional scars to prove it."

I wave my hand, trying to keep things light. "Hey, no pressure. I'm sure Viktor will be fine."

Yelena's face falls faster than a soufflé in an earthquake, and I mentally kick myself. Way to go, Ana. Real smooth.

"I didn't mean that," I backpedal. "But you can't force

feelings, right? That's like . . . Relationship 101 or something."

She nods, but her eyes are a million miles away. "The truth is, your brother is exactly the kind of person I'd love to be with. But I'm just not ready. My ex and I were supposed to get married."

Oh. Oh no.

"Sounds like he was important," I say, stating the obvious because, apparently, that's my superpower today.

Yelena's voice cracks as she continues, "I thought I could handle what he put me through. That his excuses were valid reasons for the things he did. But he broke me, Ana. It took months of therapy to even start putting myself back together."

And just like that, I'm around the table, wrapping her in a hug tight enough to make a boa constrictor jealous. When Yelena came into my life, I found a sister and a friend. Now it's my turn to be her rock.

After a while, she clears her throat. "It's all in the past, though. Maybe I'll be ready to take a chance in the future. But for now, I'm good where I am. And I don't want to break your brother's heart like I've done to others."

I raise an eyebrow, and she adds quickly, "They had it coming."

I can't help but laugh. "Oh, I bet they did. Don't worry, I'm not about to judge you for being yourself. That's kind of the whole point of friendship, isn't it?"

Yelena grins, then swiftly changes gears. "So, back to you. What's the game plan with Daddy Dearest?"

I shrug, suddenly fascinated by the pattern on my napkin. "Honestly? No clue. Something's broken there, but fixing it isn't my job. Ball's in his court now."

She gives me a thumbs up. "That's the spirit! Now, how

about we order dessert? I think we've earned it after all this emotional heavy lifting."

And just like that, we're back to giggling over the menu like two teenagers on a sugar high. Family drama, romance woes—they can wait. Right now, there's tiramisu calling our names.

THIRTY

DMITRI

The door to my office swings open, and I can't help but chuckle mirthlessly at the sight of my unexpected visitor. Nikolai Petrov, in the flesh. How quaint.

"I never would've expected Nikolai Petrov to grace my humble abode," I drawl, sarcasm dripping from every word. "What brings you to my office?"

He approaches my desk with the caution of a man who knows he's walking into the lion's den. "May I sit?"

"Sure." I shrug, feigning nonchalance. "You came all this way. It would be rude for me not to offer you a seat."

As he settles in, I fold my arms, giving him rope to hang himself with. I have a hunch this has something to do with Ana and their so-called reconciliation, but I trust Nikolai about as far as I can throw him. Once a traitor, always a traitor.

"I came to apologize," he finally says.

A scoff escapes me before I can stop it. "For what? Stealing from my father? Threatening to usurp me from a position that was rightfully mine? How about for neglecting your daughter? Pick one."

For a split second, I think I see a flicker of remorse cross his face. But I've been around snakes like him long enough to know better. It's all part of the act.

He launches into some sob story about a conversation with my father before he died, about promises to look after the legacy and me. It takes every ounce of my self-control not to laugh in his face.

"My father," I emphasize, my voice dripping with cynicism, "told you that he was worried about his legacy when he spent the entirety of my life, up until he died, training me?"

When he tries to deflect by bringing up Ana, I cut him off. "You know that's not true. Ana told me you never wanted her to be a part of the Bratva, and she even had to fight you on allowing her to study law."

He presses his lips together, clearly caught in his own lie. "That was before I knew she had what it took to follow in my footsteps."

I say nothing for a long moment, studying him like the specimen he is. If he were anyone else, his tells would be obvious—darting eyes, crossed arms, flushed face. But Nikolai Petrov isn't just anyone. He's a respected *pakhan*, feared and connected. Which makes this whole charade all the more suspicious.

"I'm sure you know that Ana told me about the visit to your house," I finally say, deciding to lay my cards on the table. "Now, if you want to reconcile with your daughter, that's one thing. But the man who took her from you? We both know there is no love lost between us, Petrov."

He chuckles, rubbing his chin. "You're your father's son, after all."

I shrug, unmoved by the comparison. "Forgive me if I'm unwilling to accept things without scrutiny."

The conversation dances around the real issue, with Nikolai spouting more platitudes about protecting what he loves. As if I'd believe for a second that he sees Ana as anything more than a chess piece.

"And you think mending fences will ensure her safety?" I finish for him, my tone making it clear I'm not buying what he's selling.

I stand, pacing behind my desk. The truth is, I do love Ana. But our marriage was meant to be Nikolai's punishment, and I can't let him see any weakness.

"I might have taken Ana from you," I say, turning to face him, "but you're the one at fault. Why would I continue to punish her?"

Something flashes behind his eyes, something cold and unforgiving. It's gone in an instant, replaced by a smile that doesn't reach his eyes. "I should thank you, then. Someone else would've made her pay the price."

"I'm not anybody else," I say curtly. "And you should know that. I spared you a fate that would've sent you into hiding."

The mask slips for just a moment, revealing the disdain beneath. But Nikolai recovers quickly, smoothing his expression back to neutrality.

As he prepares to leave, he has the audacity to suggest we might work together in the future. I give him a noncommittal "We'll see," though we both know it's never going to happen.

I watch Nikolai's retreating back as he leaves my office, my mind already dissecting every word, every gesture from our little chat. The old fox thinks he's clever, coming here with his paper-thin apologies and talk of reconciliation.

I settle back into my chair, a humorless smirk playing on

my lips. "Fucking Petrov," I mutter, the words tasting bitter on my tongue.

This wasn't about making amends. No, this was reconnaissance. The bastard's still sore about losing Ana, still can't stomach the fact that I outplayed him at his own game. And now he's fishing, trying to gauge how much influence he might still have over his daughter.

Over my wife.

My fingers drum a steady rhythm on the armrest as I replay our conversation. Nikolai's tells were subtle, I'll give him that. But I didn't climb to the top of this bloody heap by missing details. The way his eyes tightened when I mentioned Ana, the slight twitch in his jaw when I brought up his past mistakes. Oh yes, the great Nikolai Petrov is planning something.

"You want to dance, old man?" I murmur to the empty room. "Let's dance."

I reach for my phone, speed-dialing Jakob. "Increase surveillance on Petrov," I order without preamble. "I want to know every move he makes, every breath he takes. If he so much as sneezes, I want to know what brand of tissue he uses."

As I hang up, my gaze drifts to the photo on my desk, Ana's smiling face looking back at me. For a moment, my expression softens. She's the wild card in all this, the one variable I can't fully predict or control. And God help me, I love her for it.

But love is a luxury in our world, and Nikolai just proved he's still a threat. I won't let him use Ana as a pawn again, even if it means shielding her from the ugly truth about her father.

"You're out of your league, Petrov," I say to the empty chair across from me. "You just don't know it yet."

I turn back to my laptop, fingers flying over the keys as I set new plans in motion. Nikolai wants to play? Fine. But this time, I'm changing the rules of the game.

And I always play to win.

"YOUR FATHER CAME to see me today," I tell Ana after kissing her while we stand by the door of our walk-in closet.

She helps me remove my tie, tossing it across the room to the chair in the corner. I shake my head, smiling softly.

"What did he say?"

"Not much. He might have apologized for what happened, asked me to treat you well, and then hinted at a partnership." I shrug.

"Huh." She presses her body close, rubbing her hand on my chest and bringing her lips to my ear. "You already treat me well."

My hands encircle her waist. Through the loose-fitting chiffon gown she has on, her skin feels like silk. I cup her ass with both hands, squeezing and making her whimper.

"How was your day, *kotyonok*?" I ask in an even voice while I pull the gown up her thighs, dragging it slowly so the material caresses her skin.

"Mm," she murmurs. "It was okay. I had a client who said one of your *pakhan* friends referred him."

I pull away slightly to look at her face. "Did he give you a name?"

"Roman," Ana responds. "The dude made a deal with the Italian Mafia, and now they're coming for him."

I know Roman, and I know he's smart enough to know where his business starts and ends.

But—

I tilt Ana's chin, staring into her eyes. "I hope it's nothing that'll get you in trouble?"

She pokes out her bottom lip. "I'll make sure of it. Also," her hand trails down, fingers gliding across my erection, "I can count on you to watch my back, right?"

The things she does to me.

"Damn right," I grunt as I capture her lips in an intimate, deep kiss, sliding my tongue in, nipping her lower lip, and kneading her ass while I tilt my hips against her stomach.

I'm about to take her to bed when we hear a knock on the door.

"I hope I'm not interrupting." Yelena's voice comes through the door. "But it's time for dinner. I didn't want to bother you two, but Viktor is here, and I thought we could all eat together."

"We'll be down in a minute," I call out.

Hearing Yelena's retreating footsteps, I turn to Ana again, pulling her snug against my body. She mutters a surprised "oh" and ends up laughing. I tilt my hips forward, and a needy sigh slips past her lips.

"We can have dessert later," I say.

"Mm," she murmurs.

"I'll even be civil to your father," I throw in, mostly because I would do anything to see her happy.

Her eyes widen and then narrow a fraction. "Really? After everything?"

The astonishment written on her face makes me laugh. "I'll think about it," I amend, ending the conversation with a kiss against the hollow of her temple and my lips tracing the line of her cheekbone.

Her fists knot in my shirt, and my lips are on hers feverishly, coaxing moans and heavy breathing while I take it deeper, feeling my pulse race in my chest.

There's nothing like needing Ana. It consumes the mind and replenishes the soul.

"Now or later?" I ask, even though I know the answer.

"Now," she whispers.

I lift her in my arms, bridal style. "Your wish is my command, my love."

THIRTY-ONE
ANA

Seeing my father twice in one week? It feels strange after months of radio silence. We're suddenly doing the whole father-daughter bonding thing.

Color me surprised.

"*Dochka*," Papa says, arms open wide. I hug him back, but it feels about as natural as a fish riding a bicycle. How exactly does one hug the father who's been MIA for months?

He plants a kiss on my cheek, all misty-eyed. "I didn't know how much I missed you until you left that day."

I resist the urge to roll my eyes. "Why didn't you call then?" I ask, channeling my inner Yelena. "You could've asked me over for dinner, you know."

Papa sighs like he's auditioning for a soap opera. "I wasn't sure if you'd forgiven me. I wanted to give you time. Be less overbearing."

Right, because ghosting your daughter is the epitome of being overbearing. "I see," I say, biting my tongue. "So why the summons now? And please stop using Viktor as your messenger pigeon. I have a phone, remember?"

He offers an apologetic smile that doesn't quite reach his eyes. "I'm sorry. I won't lie, I use Viktor because it's the only time he'll come around to see me."

Well, that's news to me. "I thought Viktor started working for you?" I prod. "He told me a few weeks ago he was joining the family business."

Papa strokes his cheeks, looking every bit the troubled Bratva boss. "He is, but we only talk about work. I've tried inviting him for dinner, but he always declines. You'll help me talk to him, won't you?"

Great, now I'm the family therapist. But I can't help wondering why Viktor's keeping Papa at arm's length. If it's because of me, well, that's a whole other can of worms.

Time to change the subject. "I heard you met with Dmitri the other day," I say, trying to sound casual. "Something about uniting our families?"

I don't mention forgiveness. Papa's pride is as fragile as a house of cards, and I'm not in the mood to deal with it.

But instead of elaborating on this supposed deal, Papa's face darkens faster than a storm cloud.

"What's wrong?" I ask, my stomach doing somersaults.

He pushes back from his desk, chair scraping across the floor like nails on a chalkboard. His shoulders are so tense, I'm half expecting them to snap.

"Papa," I say, worry creeping into my voice, "what's going on?"

He fixes me with a look that could freeze hell over. "He told you about it? Do you think he bought the idea of a partnership? Did he look like he believed it when I asked for forgiveness?"

I blink, feeling like I've missed a crucial page in the script. "Uh, I guess? He seemed fine. We didn't really discuss it much. We were kind of busy having dinner, you know?"

Papa exhales, settling back into his seat. He leans forward, hands on the desk, and I mirror his posture, bracing myself for whatever bomb he's about to drop.

"Everything I said to him was a lie."

Well, there it is. The other shoe, dropped with all the subtlety of a piano in a cartoon.

He smiles, and it's the most chilling thing I've ever seen. "To make Dmitri Orlov think I'm weak. A *pakhan* like me, apologizing? I might as well hand over my tough guy card. But I did it because I have a plan."

Alarm bells are going off in my head like it's New Year's Eve in Times Square. "What kind of plan?" I ask, dreading the answer.

"I never forgave him for taking you from me," Papa hisses, his voice cold as ice. "You were the one person who mattered most to me, Anastasia, and he knew it. I would've let it go if he took some territory or seized my business, but you?" He laughs, and it's not a pleasant sound. "I'm going for revenge."

Oh, God. This is not happening. "Please don't tell me you're about to start a war," I plead. "You know how the last one ended. You know how these Bratva wars turn out."

He shrugs like we're discussing the weather, not potential bloodshed. "This isn't some hasty plan, Anastasia. It's why I haven't contacted you for months. I've been planning, gathering my people, waiting for the right moment. And I've found it. You," he reaches for my hands, but I pull away, "only need to ensure he's at the right place at the agreed upon time."

I stand up so fast my chair nearly topples over. "You aren't going to use me as a pawn anymore. I did that once, paying for your mistake by marrying a man I didn't love." I fold my arms, trying to look braver than I feel. "You need to fight your own battles."

Papa approaches me, but I hold up a hand to stop him. I'm the only one who knows what I went through, and I won't do it again.

"I'm sorry, *dochka*," he says, not sounding sorry at all. "But I promise you, this time, I'm putting that bastard down for good."

The realization hits me like a freight train. "You're planning to kill my husband?" I ask, my voice barely above a whisper.

"That's the only way to make sure he doesn't torment our family again," he replies, like he's suggesting we try a new restaurant. "You know it, Ana. I wouldn't do this if I had other options."

I grit my teeth, anger bubbling up inside me. "Dmitri will end you. You don't know what he's done to people who've tried to stab him in the back. Plus, you're planning to kill the man I fell in love with."

"You don't love him," Papa snaps. "At best, you have Stockholm syndrome, and that's my fault. Let me make things right, darling. I'll even give you what you've always been asking for," his voice softens, "a real position in the family business."

But I can see that Papa's rage has blinded him. It's doubtful Dmitri will fall for his ruse, whether I play a part or not. If Papa tries to kill him, Dmitri won't spare his life. And if there's even a small chance Papa succeeds, I could lose the man I love. I'll lose Papa too because Dmitri's people will come after him.

Either way, I'm caught in the middle of a war I never wanted to fight. A war that will never end.

Some days, I really wish I'd just become a librarian or something. At least then, the only thing I'd have to worry about is late fees.

I take a deep breath, trying to appeal to whatever shred of fatherly love might be left in him. "I'm happy," I plead, feeling like I'm talking to a brick wall. "Can't you see that I'm happy with how things have turned out? Why can't you just let sleeping dogs lie?"

But the look in his eyes is pure venom. If hatred could be bottled, his would be top shelf. "I was insulted," he spits. "My dignity and self-esteem were stripped from me. I'm not going to take that lying down."

I gulp hard, feeling like I'm trying to swallow a golf ball. "It's me asking you to back off. What if you had me back? Wouldn't that make everything whole again?"

He scoffs. "He's never going to give you up."

"I'll run away," I blurt out, grasping at straws.

His brows furrow like I've just suggested we all become circus clowns. "What good will that do?"

I throw my hands in the air, feeling like I'm in some twisted version of a negotiation show. I don't know what running away will actually accomplish, but I'm desperate for a solution that doesn't end with either of them six feet under.

If only Papa could let go of his pride, we could all move on. But no, his ego's in the driver's seat, just like before.

An idea pops into my head. It's not great, but it's all I've got. "I want you to know that I'm not doing this because of you," I say, my voice firm. "I don't think I can summon any love for you right now. Or anytime soon, for that matter."

"You'll thank me one day," he says.

Yeah, I'll thank him the same day pigs fly and hell freezes over. "When Dmitri and I married, he used it to gain respect and expand his territory. People thought our families were working together. It benefited him."

Papa sniggers. "Well, that makes one of us."

I take a deep breath. Here goes nothing. "As you've said, he won't let me go. But if I run away, you can blame him for it. Act like he's committed some unforgivable sin. Spread rumors that a rival kidnapped me. But for heaven's sake, let it end there."

He purses his lips, considering. My heart's pounding so hard, I'm surprised it hasn't burst out of my chest. The thought of life without Dmitri—the man I've grown to love, who'd set the world on fire to keep me safe—it's almost unbearable.

"Fine," he says finally, reluctantly. "It'll keep him distracted. While he's occupied, I'll take what I want."

I feel sick to my stomach. This isn't my father anymore. This is a stranger wearing his face. "I'm not doing this so you can finish what you started months ago," I say, my voice hard. "If you go back on your word, I'll go straight back to Dmitri."

His eyes darken. "Never. I won't see you married to that bastard."

"Then stop going after him," I counter. "My disappearance and the enemies he'll make looking for me, that's enough to weaken him."

The grin that spreads across his face makes me want to shower for a week. I can barely stand to be in the same room with him anymore.

"We have a deal?" I hiss through gritted teeth.

"When are you leaving?"

"One week," I say, already feeling the weight of what I'm about to do. "I need time to act normal so he doesn't suspect anything."

"You've got one week," he agrees.

As I walk out of his office, my legs feel like lead. One week. Seven days to dismantle the life I've pieced together, to say goodbye to the man who's become my world. All to save two stubborn men hell-bent on destroying each other. If this were a soap opera, I'd be the tragic heroine, sacrificing everything for love. But this is real life, and I'm just me, caught in a tug-of-war between the family I was born into and the one I've chosen.

But hey, who needs a boring nine-to-five when you can play human shield in the world's most dysfunctional game of Bratva chess?

AS SOON AS I close the door, I let the tears flow. They rain down my cheeks, carrying my grief and spreading it to other parts of my body.

"Anastasia?" Daria hurries over when she notices me, pulling my trembling body into her arms. "What's going on?"

I can't tell her. The words stick in my throat like I've swallowed a fistful of sand.

Instead, I crumble into Daria's arms, sobbing. The deal I made with Papa already feels like a noose around my neck. The thought of life without Dmitri—his stubble scratching my chin when he kisses me, his warm hands making me feel safe—it's like someone's taken a cheese grater to my soul.

And Yelena. Oh God, Yelena. My partner in retail crime, my unexpected bestie. What am I supposed to do without our therapy sessions at Bloomingdale's? She was the first person in forever to make me feel like I belonged somewhere.

What's she going to think when I leave?

"I don't know what else to do, Daria," I choke out, trying to muffle a sob that threatens to shake the whole building. "I can't . . . I can't think of any other way to stop my father from going full Rambo."

"Oh, Anastasia," Daria croons, probably wishing she'd called in sick today. "You don't have to be Atlas, carrying the weight of the world on your shoulders. You can let go. It's not going to be your fault."

But it will be, won't it? If I call Papa's bluff, he'll go after Dmitri, guns blazing. I'll have to live knowing I could've prevented a bloodbath.

Some choice, huh? It's like being asked if I'd rather lose an arm or a leg.

I cry for what feels like centuries. Daria, bless her heart, lets me turn her shirt into a Kleenex. When I finally pull myself together, I feel like I've been through a human car wash.

"Thank you, Daria," I manage to croak out.

She nods, clearly holding back from saying more. "If you ever need help, you can come to me, okay? I promise I'll be here."

I try to smile, but it probably looks more like a grimace. "Thanks."

I shuffle out of the building, feeling about as lively as a deflated balloon. The waterworks start up again as soon as I'm in my car. I sit there for an hour, crying until I'm pretty sure I've single-handedly solved California's drought problem.

But I can't go home yet. Dmitri will take one look at me and know something's up. He's like a human lie detector, and right now, I'm a walking, talking fib.

So, I do what any sensible person would do when their

life is falling apart—I head to a bar. Tucked away in a corner, nursing a glass of Chardonnay, I try to figure out how the hell I'm going to pull this off.

By the time I crawl back to my car, I feel like I've aged a decade. Is this what it feels like to be caught between a rock and a hard place? Because if so, I'd like to file a complaint with whoever's in charge of metaphors.

"ANA?"

Dmitri's voice catches me off guard. He's awake, sitting on the sofa in our room when I walk in.

"Hey," I say, trying to smile. It's forced, and I pray he doesn't see right through me.

His brows furrow, and I can feel my facade crumbling. "What's wrong?" he asks, taking my hands and gently pulling me to the bed. We sit on the edge, his arm around me, holding me close. "What happened?"

Tears well up in my eyes again, and I blink rapidly, willing them away. I can't fall apart. Not now.

"Make love to me," I whisper.

It's the only thing I can think of to ease the ache in my heart, to distract myself from the weight of what I'm about to do.

Dmitri looks confused, but he nods. His lips meet mine in the gentlest, sweetest kiss he's ever given me. He lays me down on the bed as if I might shatter at any moment.

"Are you sure you're okay?" he asks, concern evident in his voice.

I wrap my arms around him and kiss him firmly. I try to memorize every touch, every sensation, knowing that soon, it will all be just a memory.

But even as I lose myself in Dmitri's embrace, a single tear escapes, rolling down to my ear. It's a quiet reminder of the countdown that's begun, of the heartbreak that's waiting just around the corner.

I hold onto Dmitri tighter, wishing I could freeze time and stay in this moment forever. But I know I can't.

So, I close my eyes, willing every second of this night to imprint in my memory.

THIRTY-TWO
DMITRI

"What're you doing here?" I ask, unable to suppress the smile that spreads across my face as Ana appears in the doorway. It's a reaction I'm still getting used to, this involuntary warmth that floods through me at the mere sight of her.

She approaches my desk with a secretive smile, one hand hidden behind her back. "Is it weird for me to come see my husband?" she says, but I can see right through her attempt at nonchalance. Something's definitely up.

I've noticed she's been off for the past four days, ever since she came home late that night. I didn't push then, it was clear she didn't want to talk about it. But now...

"It's not weird at all," I say, rising to meet her. I take her in my arms, kissing her tenderly. We've been gentler with each other lately, mostly at Ana's initiation. I find myself craving these soft moments more and more.

She's been coming home early, making dinner, insisting we all eat together. It feels almost like courtship. The thought both thrills and unnerves me.

"I brought this for you," Ana says, presenting a box. "I hope you like it."

As I open it, I'm momentarily stunned by the timepiece inside. It's a Rolex Daytona, its platinum case gleaming under the office lights. The ice blue dial catches my eye immediately, a color as captivating and unique as Ana herself. The chronograph subdials add a layer of sophistication that speaks to both form and function.

"A man like you should have a watch that matches your power and influence," Ana says softly, a hint of pride in her voice. "Something that commands respect the moment people see it."

Her words stir something deep within me, not just pride, but a profound appreciation for how she sees me. As I slip the watch onto my wrist, feeling its comfortable weight, I pull her close again. Her lips part under my touch, and I can't resist nipping at her bottom lip. She whimpers, and the sound sends a shiver through me. My hands roam her back, cupping her ass gently.

Ana purrs, her palm warm against my chest. It takes all my willpower to pull away.

"What's the special occasion?" I ask, searching her eyes.

She shrugs, biting her lip in that way that drives me wild. "No occasion. I just thought you deserved something special. And . . . I thought we could go for a picnic after work. Watch the sunset together."

The combination of her thoughtful gift and the suggestion of spending time together makes my heart swell in a way I'm still getting used to. It's a feeling that only Ana can evoke in me. But I can't hold back a sigh. Something's not right, and I can't ignore it anymore.

"Is there anything going on, *kotyonok*?" I ask gently.

"No," she says quickly. "Why would you think that?"

I move back to my seat, needing some distance to think clearly. When she's close, it's too easy to get lost in her.

"You've been acting differently since that night you came home late," I say cautiously. "I didn't want to pry then, but I'm getting worried, Ana. What's going on?"

Her smile is too bright, too forced. "Nothing. I just . . . I went to see my mom's grave. I got emotional. Then I stopped for a drink. That's all."

My heart clenches. "I'm sorry," I say softly. "I didn't know."

"I didn't tell you," she admits, perching on the edge of my desk. "I didn't want you to worry."

I pull her close again, kissing her gently. "I want you to tell me everything, Ana. The good and the bad. You're my wife. Okay?"

She nods, lips pressed tight. "Okay."

I glance at the clock, an idea forming. "You know what? Let's go now. We can have some fun while we wait for the sunset."

Her smile—genuine this time—is all the answer I need. As I lift her into my arms, I'm struck by how much she's changed me. The old Dmitri would never have dropped everything for an impromptu picnic. But for Ana, I'd move mountains.

Her fingers fist my collar and she tilts her hips, grinding against my crotch.

"You naughty woman." I chuckle, cupping her ass and rubbing it. "It looks like you want an appetizer first?"

"You know what I want," she murmurs.

I grab her chin lightly, looking into her eyes. "Say it."

Her eyes hold a challenge and a fire that fuels desire inside me, increasing the urge to fuck her against the wall, on the desk, until everyone can hear us.

"I'm waiting," I prompt.

She pulls a corner of her lip between her teeth and rubs

her palm across my chest. I spank her ass, and she gasps, her pupils widening.

"*Kotyonok?*"

"You."

"What do you want from me?" My palm swats across her behind again, and she almost loses the grip of her other hand around my neck.

"I want you. Inside me," she murmurs.

I grunt in satisfaction. "Good girl."

Setting her down, I lead Ana to the wall, gesturing for her to put her hands against it. Slowly, I pull down her pants and underwear, kissing her thighs as I slide down.

She moans quietly as I spread her legs, making my way up again with more kisses, and her back arches when my tongue glides over her pussy, licking from her clit and down her slit.

I push my tongue in, lapping and feeling her wetness coat me as she pushes back, riding my face with reckless abandon. Her moans get louder the faster I get, and when I feel her pulsing, I pull away.

"I want to feel you clench around my dick when you come," I say, unbuckling my pants. "I want you begging me to make you come."

With my hands firmly on her hips, I slide in.

My thrusts are deep and slow at first, and she takes me eagerly, gasping when I spank her. Her legs tremble, and I bring her close with my hands around her waist before hoisting her high and going to the chair.

Leaning back, I watch Ana as she bounces on my dick, her hands cupping her breasts and her head thrown back.

"*Kotyonok*," I groan, nearing the edge. "Fucking gorgeous," I say hoarsely, replacing her hands with mine. "I could look at you every day for the rest of my life and never get used to how beautiful you are."

When her head falls on my chest, I take over—pounding hard this time and angling my hips to hit every spot.

She exhales heavily in my ear as her climax hits, shuddering for a minute before she goes limp. I grunt as I come.

"I love you," Ana says as my fingers lazily comb through her hair, her head resting on my chest.

She lifts her head, and in her shining eyes, I see the truth, bright as day.

Have I ever felt this happy before?

"I love you, Anastasia Orlov," I respond with every iota of love and the promises I've made to myself—to love and cherish her.

She sighs contentedly. "I'm happy."

"Me too," I caress her cheek.

We bask in rich silence for a while before she gets off my lap. "Are we still going on the picnic?"

"I've got a more beautiful sunset in front of me, but yeah." I nod.

I watch as she puts her clothes back on, exhaling repeatedly. If anyone had suggested that I might fall in love with Ana when we got married, I would've swiftly judged them to be a fool.

But this, to me, is what life should be like.

I just hope I can hold onto it forever.

THIRTY-THREE
ANA

I clear my throat, trying to get Viktor and Yelena's attention over the clinking of cutlery in the museum's restaurant. I've dragged them here under false pretenses because, let's face it, if I'd told them the truth, at least one of them would've run for the hills faster than you can say "family drama."

This is it. My last hurrah with the two people who matter most to me, besides Dmitri. God, just thinking about him makes my heart do a little tap dance of misery.

"I'll cut to the chase," I say, taking a sip of liquid courage. "Viktor, you like Yelena, don't you?"

My brother's poker face is about as convincing as a kid with chocolate all over their fingers swearing they didn't touch the cake.

"You're a meddler if there ever was one," he grumbles.

I shrug, aiming for nonchalance. "What can I say? I'm just trying to spread a little happiness before—" I catch myself. "I mean, you two deserve it."

I hold up my hands, trying to look innocent. "Look, I'm not trying to play Cupid here. I'm just saying what we're all thinking."

Yelena shifts uncomfortably in her seat. "Ana, I don't think—"

"No, no," I cut her off, standing up abruptly. "You two clearly have some things to discuss. I'll leave you to it."

Viktor raises an eyebrow. "And where are you off to in such a hurry?"

I force a laugh, hoping it doesn't sound as hollow as it feels. "Oh, you know me. Can't resist the allure of some dusty old bones. There's a fascinating exhibit on extinct mammals I've been dying to see."

Yelena looks skeptical. "Since when are you interested in paleontology?"

"Hey, people change," I say, backing away from the table. "Maybe I'll discover a hidden passion for fossils. Who knows? Life's full of surprises."

As I turn to leave, I catch a glimpse of their confused expressions. I throw them a wink over my shoulder, trying to keep up the charade.

"Don't do anything I wouldn't do," I call back, my voice only wavering slightly.

As soon as I'm out of their sight, I lean against a wall, taking a deep, shaky breath. "Pull it together, Ana," I mutter to myself. "You've got this."

But even as I say it, I'm not sure I believe it.

As I wander through the museum, I think about the last few days. The picnic with Dmitri, shopping with Yelena, wine tasting with Viktor. My little bucket list of memories to hold onto when...

No. Don't think about it.

I blink back tears, nearly colliding with a display case. A nearby tourist gives me a concerned look, and I force a smile. I promised myself I wouldn't cry, dammit. This is my duty.

When I return to the restaurant, Viktor and Yelena are sitting closer, a tentative hand on an arm. Progress. My heart clenches, knowing that soon Yelena won't want to confide in me about this.

I end up in a butterfly garden, staring at a case full of delicate creatures. A man nearby starts spieling facts about how butterflies need to warm up in the sun before they can fly.

"Sometimes," he says, "you meet the most cold-blooded soul, but when you get to know them better, you see that all they needed was a little sun to bring out their beauty."

My mind immediately goes to Dmitri. My terrifying, ruthless, surprisingly soft-hearted husband. The man I thought I'd hate forever, until I fell head over heels for him.

I focus on a butterfly with dark wings, wishing I could take it with me. A little reminder of the man who'd burn the world down to keep me safe. The man I'm about to leave behind.

As I stand there, surrounded by fragile beauty, the weight of what I'm about to do hits me all over again. I'm not just leaving; I'm shattering the life we've built. But if it keeps the people I love safe . . . well, that's just the price of being an Orlov, isn't it?

God, I could really use a drink right now. Or ten.

I STUMBLE INTO OUR BEDROOM, feeling like I'm walking to the gallows instead of coming home. Dmitri's there, his face lighting up. Before I can even manage a "hello," he's swept me into his arms.

"Have I ever told you I never get tired of kissing you?"

he murmurs, his fingers finding the zipper of my dress. "That I won't ever stop?"

His lips brush against my back as the dress falls away, and I shiver. It's not just the chill of the air, it's the bittersweet realization that this might be one of our last moments together.

No, Ana. Don't go there. Today is just another day, remember?

"Want me to run you a bath?" Dmitri asks, all thoughtful and perfect, making my heart ache in ways I didn't know it could.

I shake my head, mustering up a smile that feels more like a grimace. "I've got it, thanks."

As soon as the bathroom door closes behind me, my facade crumbles like a sandcastle at high tide. I lean against the cool tile, trying to steady my breathing. This is it. The moment of truth.

I open the medicine cabinet, my hand hovering over the usual suspects—aspirin, face cream, that weird herbal thing Yelena swears by. But that's not what I'm after. My fingers tremble as they push past the everyday items, searching for the one thing that could change everything.

There, hidden behind a bottle of multivitamins like some dirty little secret, is the pregnancy test. I bought it on a whim—or maybe out of fear—the day I visited Dmitri's office. It's been lurking there ever since, a ticking time bomb of potential.

I pull it out, the box feeling impossibly heavy in my hand. For a moment, I just stare at it, this innocent-looking stick that holds the power to rewrite my future.

"No chickening out now," I mutter, trying to summon some of my usual bravado. "You're running out of time, Ana."

I tear open the box, fumbling with the wrapper. It's just a piece of plastic, for crying out loud. So why does it feel like I'm disarming a bomb?

As I sit on the toilet, test in hand, I can't help but think about how absurd this all is. Here I am, wife of the most feared man in the Bratva, about to pee on a stick like some teenager in a high school bathroom. Life has a sick sense of humor sometimes.

I set the test on the counter, refusing to look at it. Now comes the hard part, waiting. Two minutes have never felt so long. I pace the small space, my bare feet slapping against the tile. I bite my nails, a habit I thought I'd kicked years ago.

Finally, when I can't stand it anymore, I force myself to look. My hand shakes as I pick up the test, squeezing my eyes shut before I can see the result.

Come on, Ana. You've faced down mafia bosses. You can handle a little plastic stick.

I open my eyes, and just like that, my world tilts on its axis.

"Fuck," I whisper, my voice cracking. "Fuck, fuck, fucking hell!"

Two lines. Clear as day.

I'm pregnant. With Dmitri's child.

And I'm supposed to leave tomorrow.

Dmitri's voice through the door nearly gives me a heart attack. "Ana? You okay in there, my love?"

"Peachy keen!" I call back, my voice only an octave higher than normal. Totally not suspicious at all.

I splash some cold water on my face, trying to erase the evidence of my mini-meltdown. Taking a deep breath, I open the door, ready to win an Oscar for "Most Convincing Everything's-Fine Performance."

But the moment I see Dmitri's face, full of love and concern, my carefully constructed mask shatters. He doesn't say anything, just cups my face in his hands and kisses me so tenderly, it breaks my heart all over again.

How am I supposed to leave now? How can I tell him he's going to be a father, only to disappear? It's like the universe is playing a cosmic joke, and I'm the punchline.

I bury my face in his chest, breathing in his familiar scent. How am I going to say goodbye?

THIRTY-FOUR
DMITRI

The bouquet of carnations feels heavy in my hand as I stride down the hallway toward Ana's office. This impromptu visit isn't my usual style, but being near her workplace, I couldn't resist. Her smile has become a temptation I find increasingly difficult to deny.

I knock on her door, anticipation building in my chest. Silence. I knock again, harder this time. Still nothing. Strange. I try the handle—locked.

Unease settles in my gut. I call her phone, then send a text when she doesn't pick up. No response.

"What's going on?" I mutter, sending another text. Perhaps I should have called beforehand. I'm trying to match Ana's romantic gestures of the past few days. After her melancholy mood last night, I thought she could use some cheering up.

"Hi." A voice interrupts my thoughts. Some suit is approaching me, all smiles and familiarity. "Are you looking for Anatasia?"

"Yes," I nod curtly. "I'm her husband, Dmitri Orlov." The words come out more possessive than I intend.

His eyes widen with recognition. "You're the man who swooped in and took Ana from the rest of us. It's nice to meet you finally. I'm Steve."

I shake his hand firmly, making sure he feels the strength behind it. A warning.

"Do you know if she's in a meeting?" I ask, trying to keep my voice level.

Steve shakes his head. "Nope."

"Nope, as in you don't know?"

He sucks his teeth. "I meant that I haven't seen her today. I stopped by her office hours ago for a document, but it was locked. I tried calling her phone, but she didn't answer. I assumed she was taking the day off."

My jaw clenches. "Thank you," I say curtly, turning to leave.

I storm out of the building onto the bustling Manhattan street, my rage barely contained. The cacophony of car horns and pedestrian chatter fades into white noise as I pull out my phone, dialing Ana's bodyguards with shaky fingers.

"Where is she?" I snarl as soon as the line connects, not bothering with pleasantries.

There's a pause, then a confused voice. "Mr. Orlov? We don't understand. Mrs. Orlov should be in her office."

My blood boils. "Should be? You fucking idiots! I was just there. She's not!"

"That's impossible, sir," the other guard chimes in, sounding bewildered. "We've been monitoring the building entrance all day. She hasn't left."

I rake my fingers through my hair, fighting the urge to put my fist through the nearest wall. "Well, she's not there now, is she? So, tell me, you incompetent fucks, how did my wife vanish from under your noses?"

The guards stammer, clearly at a loss. My mind races, considering the possibilities. Did someone grab her again?

"Sir, we—"

"Shut up," I cut them off, my voice low and dangerous. "If anything's happened to her, I swear I'll end you both. Slowly. Painfully. Do you understand me?"

Their silence is answer enough.

"Now listen carefully," I continue, forcing my voice to steady, "I want you to check on every rival we have. Every fucking one. Someone must have seen something. And if you come back empty-handed, don't bother coming back at all."

I end the call, resisting the urge to hurl my phone across the street. My mind whirls with possibilities, each more terrifying than the last. Who could have taken her? Bianchi's people seeking revenge? One of the other Bratva groups testing my resolve?

As I stand there, surrounded by the oblivious masses of Manhattan, I've never felt more helpless.

I dial Yelena.

"What's up, brother? Did you miss me? I'm free tomorrow by—"

"Is Ana with you?" I cut her off, my patience wearing thin.

Her pause speaks volumes. "I haven't seen her since we parted ways yesterday. What's wrong? Have you tried calling her? Checking her office?"

I bite back a sarcastic response. "I'll try Viktor," I say instead, my voice tight with worry.

Yelena's attempt at reassurance falls flat. "I'll try her too. I'm sure nothing happened to her. Probably just an out-of-office meeting or something."

I hang up and call Viktor, going straight to the point.

"Hey, have you heard from Ana today? She's not in her office. A colleague of hers says he hasn't seen her all day. She's not responding to my calls or texts either."

He sounds puzzled. "No." It does nothing to ease my growing anxiety.

I sit in my car, mind racing through possibilities. Maybe Yelena is right. Ana might be safe, with a good reason for being unreachable. But in our world, when something can go wrong, it usually does.

After the incident with Bianchi, Igor's sneaky attempt to switch sides, and Nikolai's blatant attack disguised as an apology, I know I have many enemies waiting for the right moment to strike.

Thirty minutes of silence feels like an eternity. I keep trying Ana's number, but now it just switches off immediately. This isn't right. There might be a reason for her not returning my calls, but not for her phone to be completely off.

Trusting my instincts, I call Igor.

"Dmitri," he greets, too cheerful. "I was just about to reach out. How are the plans with the casinos? It's been a while since you said we would open, and we haven't talked. I know things are going slower than planned, but you could use my help, right? Anything at all, ask."

"Where are you?" I ask curtly, cutting through his babble.

"Ah," he pauses, clearly caught off guard. "Do you need me to meet up with you? I could come to your office."

"Where are you, Pavlov?" I repeat, my tone leaving no room for evasion.

He clears his throat. "I came to . . . um . . . it's a place where you find entertainment," he whispers, and I hear a flirty giggle in the background.

I roll my eyes. He doesn't have the guts to take my wife and use her against me. Igor Pavlov is a weakling who survives by siding with whoever has the upper hand. The only reason he's stayed alive this long is that he knows not to get too deeply involved.

"Do I come over?" he asks, but I end the call without responding.

I toss my phone onto the passenger seat in frustration, running my fingers through my hair. Where could Ana be? She only goes to a few places—home, work, shopping, and lately, her father's house.

My blood runs cold at the last thought. Nikolai. The first time she went missing, I went there. Would he know her whereabouts now?

I start the car, tires screeching as I pull out. I'll tear this city apart if I have to, but I will find Ana. And God help anyone who's laid a finger on her.

I STRIDE into Nikolai's office, tension coiling in every muscle. His first words catch me off guard.

"What happened to Ana?"

I keep my voice level, eyes scanning for any tell. "Why do you think something happened to her?"

He smiles grimly, adjusting his cufflinks. The fact that he remains seated isn't lost on me. A subtle power play—this is his territory, not mine.

"There's no other reason for you to be in my office, Orlov. You know we can never agree on anything because you'll always see me as the man who betrayed your father."

I chuckle darkly. "That is what you are, Nikolai. Why should I take away a title that's rightfully yours? But yes, you're right. I fear Ana might be in trouble. She's visited you frequently lately. Do you know where she might be?"

Nikolai shrugs, his nonchalance grating on my nerves. "My daughter and I have only begun working through months of hurt. She wouldn't tell me anything about her life, and I don't think I've earned the right to ask."

His next words are calculated to wound. "I heard about Bianchi. You let my daughter get taken by that barbarian because you were careless. I'm sure one of them has taken her again. You claim to be smarter than your enemies, but they hurt the woman you vowed to protect."

Despite the heavy accusation, I sense detachment in Nikolai. It's as if he rehearsed this speech, like he knew about Ana's disappearance before I arrived.

Time to show my hand. I sit down uninvited, a mean smile curling my lips as I drum my fingers on his desk. "What's your game here? To paint me as a weak man?"

He shrugs. "If that's what you are, that's what it is. After all, what can be said for a man who takes a woman as his wife and then throws her to the wolves? We might be thieves, Dmitri, but we still value our reputations."

"And a hypocrite?" I spit back. "A man who sells his daughter instead of begging for his own head to be on the gallows, what would you call him?"

He grins, leaning back. "Touché. If you must know, I don't know where she is. We're supposed to have dinner tomorrow. If she shows, I'll tell her you came looking. If not, I'll assume you threw her out."

"I would never," I growl, my eyes boring into him.

"Then go find her," he says, his tone darkening. "Don't come to me. You took my only child. And mind you, don't think that because I'm sitting here calmly, I won't come after you if anything happens to her. I will, with everything I've got."

His words hang in the air, a thinly veiled threat that makes my blood boil. For a moment, I consider ending him on the spot. It would be so easy to reach across the desk and snap his neck.

I rise slowly, my eyes never leaving his. "Be careful, Nikolai," I say, my voice low and dangerous. "You're playing a game you can't win. If I find out you're involved in this..."

I let the threat linger, unspoken but clear as day. He might think he has power, but he has no idea what I'm capable of when it comes to Ana.

I storm out of his office, fury pulsing through my veins with every heartbeat. My mind is already racing, formulating plans, considering every possibility. I bark orders into my phone as I stride to my car, mobilizing my network.

"I want every Bratva hideout, every safe house, every goddamn hole in the wall searched," I growl to my second-in-command. "No stone unturned, you understand? Use whatever means necessary. Just find her."

THIRTY-FIVE
ANA

The sharp knock on the door nearly gives me a heart attack. I drop the spoon I'm holding, and it clatters to the floor like a mini cymbal crash.

Real smooth, Ana.

Who could that be? I've been holed up in this suburban Dmitri protection program for two weeks now, where the neighbors are about as social as hermit crabs. The only visitor I've had was dear old Dad, and I made it crystal clear he wasn't welcome for a repeat performance.

"Maybe it's just a really persistent Girl Scout?" I mutter, trying to calm my racing heart. But let's be real, I'm on edge because I'm waiting for the other shoe to drop. For Dmitri to show up and demand answers I'm not sure I'm ready to give.

The knocking gets louder, more insistent. Guess Girl Scouts are really upping their cookie game. I creep to the door, feeling like I'm in some low-budget horror movie. Peering through the peephole, I gasp.

"Ana?" Viktor's voice carries through the door, strong

and reassuring. "I know you're in there. Please open up. We need to talk."

I shake my head, even though he can't see me. This wasn't part of the plan.

"Anastasia?" he tries again, and this time I can hear the concern in his voice. "It's Viktor. I need to see you. Please."

Guilt sucker-punches me in the gut. How can I ignore him? I left without saying goodbye, and here he is, probably worried sick.

Taking a deep breath, I open the door. Viktor's there, looking like he's seen a ghost. Which, considering how I probably look right now, isn't far off.

"You're here," he breathes, relief washing over his face. Before I can say anything, he pulls me into a bear hug.

It's almost too much—the human contact, the familiar smell of his cologne, the safety I feel in my big brother's arms. The dam breaks, and suddenly, I'm sobbing like a baby, all over his probably very expensive shirt.

Viktor, bless him, doesn't say a word. He just guides me to the couch, holding me tight as years of pent-up emotion come pouring out. I cling to him like he's a life raft in this stormy sea I've found myself in.

When I finally calm down enough to form coherent sentences, Viktor asks the million-dollar question, "Why did you leave?"

I sigh, suddenly feeling very small. "I'm sure you know."

But Viktor, ever the lawyer, isn't letting me off that easy. His frown is a mix of concern and determination. "I only know what he told me. I want to hear it from you, Ana. Why'd you disappear without a word? Do you have any idea what it's been like? Dmitri's gone off the deep end, starting wars with other Bratva groups. He's a man possessed."

My heart sinks. I knew there'd be fallout, but this? "Viktor, I—"

"Tell me everything," he says, his voice gentle but firm. It's the same tone he used when we were kids, and he was helping me through a problem. It makes me feel safe, like maybe everything isn't completely ruined.

So, I spill. I tell him about Papa's threats, the impossible choice I was faced with. Viktor listens, his jaw clenching tighter with every word.

"You should have let him start that war," he says, anger flashing in his eyes. Not at me, but at our father. "You can't keep offering yourself up as a sacrifice, Ana."

"I couldn't," I choke out. "I couldn't live with myself if either of them got hurt because of me."

Viktor's expression softens, and he pulls me close again. "Oh, Ana. You've got the biggest heart of anyone I know. It's not your fault our father decided to use you like this."

As he holds me, I can't help but think how lucky I am to have him. Viktor's always been my rock, my protector. Even now, when I've messed everything up, he's here, strong and steady.

"How did you find me?" I ask, my voice still shaky.

Viktor's eyes darken, and I can see the barely contained rage as he recounts his confrontation with our father. "I went to his office, ready to tear him a new one. I couldn't believe he could be so callous about his own daughter."

HE PACES AS HE TALKS, all coiled energy and righteous anger. "He tried lying at first, but I saw right through him. It didn't take long before he cracked and told me where you were."

I nod, fresh tears threatening to spill. "Do you think Dmitri knows?"

Viktor pauses, considering. "Hard to say. Nikolai's probably still playing the concerned father act. But Dmitri's no fool. He might be biding his time, waiting for the right moment to strike."

As I watch my brother, so strong and protective, I'm hit with a wave of gratitude. No matter how messed up things are, at least I have Viktor in my corner. And for the first time in weeks, I feel a tiny flicker of hope. Maybe, just maybe, we can figure this out together.

I can't help but notice how Viktor now refers to our father only as "Nikolai," his voice as cold as a Siberian winter. It's like he's mentally disowned the man. I wonder if their relationship is as irreparably broken as mine is with dear old Papa.

"You have to come back," Viktor insists, his eyes a mix of determination and concern.

"I can't," I sob, shaking my head. "Papa swore he'd kill Dmitri if I went back!"

Viktor snorts, looking at me like I've just told him the earth is flat. "Come on, Ana. You really think that man has any power over Dmitri? Your husband would end him without breaking a sweat."

I clutch at Viktor's arm, desperation making my voice shrill. "But what about you? Papa thinks you're still on his side. Dmitri will think you've betrayed him too!"

Gently, he pries my fingers loose, his gaze steady and reassuring. "Not if I tell him everything. Dmitri's not unreasonable. He'll understand once he knows the truth."

Viktor's face darkens as he continues, "Nikolai blames everyone but himself. I've never seen him like that before. He's... he's not the man we thought he was, Ana. When he realized I could expose him, he actually tried to threaten me."

I sit back, feeling like I've been sucker-punched. I thought I couldn't hate our father more than I already did, but apparently, I was wrong. God, I wish I'd never tried to save him in the first place.

"Please, don't tell Dmitri," I beg, my voice barely above a whisper. "Even if he kills Papa, the Bratva will retaliate. It'll be a bloodbath. Let me try to fix this mess."

Viktor runs his fingers through his hair, a gesture so familiar it makes my heart ache. "It's killing me, but . . . okay. I'll keep quiet for now. But Ana, Dmitri's tearing the city apart looking for you."

"Thank you," I murmur, relief and guilt warring inside me.

He sits beside me again, and I lean my head on his shoulder, suddenly exhausted. As I sigh deeply, my hand unconsciously brushes over my stomach. Oh, Dmitri, if only you knew...

I must have dozed off because the next thing I know, Viktor's gently shaking me awake. The sun's setting, painting the room in shades of orange and pink. He's draped a blanket over me, and for a moment, I feel like a kid again, safe under my big brother's protection.

"I should go," he says softly, and I nod, not trusting my voice.

We walk to the door in silence. I'm blinking back tears, determined not to break down again. Not yet.

Viktor pauses in the doorway, his eyes searching mine. "See you later, sis," he says, squeezing my arm gently. I manage a nod, and then he's gone.

The moment the door clicks shut, it's like a dam bursts. My legs give out, and I crumple to the floor, sobbing uncontrollably. All the pain, the fear, the loss—it all comes pouring out in great, heaving waves.

By the time the tears finally stop, night has fallen. I drag myself to bed, curling up into a tight ball, willing sleep to come and take me away from all of this.

As I drift off, my last coherent thought is of Dmitri. I hope wherever he is, whatever he's doing, he's okay.

THIRTY-SIX
DMITRI

My fist connects with the table, the impact reverberating through the wood. Another dent to add to the collection. Fitting, given the state of my patience.

"Why the fuck would you fail? I gave you a simple task!" I snarl at Kirill, my voice dripping with barely contained rage.

"I'm sorry," Kirill mumbles, his head bowed like a scolded dog. "I'll send them again. I promise I'll find her this time around."

I let out a dark chuckle, the sound devoid of any humor. "Oh, if you don't, your head will hang above my door for everyone to see. Get out."

He scurries away like the incompetent rat he is. I run my fingers through my hair, frustration coursing through every fiber of my being. I'm beyond my wits' end. I passed that point weeks ago.

Three weeks. Three fucking weeks since Ana vanished, and I'm no closer to finding her. I've turned over every stone, searched every Bratva house, every company, every goddamn hideout. Now I'm reduced to scrutinizing anyone who's so much as breathed the same air as me in recent years.

Yesterday, I met with a few *pakhans*. One fool had the audacity to suggest Ana might have run away. My fist nearly rearranged his face for him. Let them think I've gone insane. I don't give a fuck. I'll burn this entire world to the ground if that's what it takes to find her.

A sharp knock at the door reignites my anger. It better not be Jakob. I gave him explicit instructions to walk in, not waste my time with pleasantries.

"Come in!" I bark.

To my surprise, it's Viktor, Ana's half-brother. I've been so consumed by my search, I'd almost forgotten about him.

"I'm sorry," I say, the words tasting unfamiliar on my tongue. "I should have been more vigilant. I promise you, I'll find her. And they'll pay. Whoever they are."

Viktor shakes his head, his expression grave. "That's not why I came. There's something I need to tell you, Dmitri. I should have told you a week ago, but I made a promise to Ana."

The mention of her name sends a jolt through me. My eyes darken, fury bubbling up inside me like molten lava. "Ana?" I practically spit the name. I'm across the room in an instant, my hand fisting in Viktor's shirt. "Where is she? Tell me now!"

To his credit, Viktor doesn't flinch. He meets my gaze steadily, his voice calm. "You may need to sit down for this, Dmitri."

I laugh, a harsh, grating sound. "Sit down? You come here with information about my wife, and you want me to sit down? Start talking, or I swear to God—"

"It's not that simple," Viktor cuts in, gently but firmly

removing my hand from his shirt. "Ana's safe, but there's more to this than you know. A lot more."

I take a step back, my mind reeling. Ana's safe. The relief that floods through me is quickly replaced by a fresh wave of anger. "If she's safe, then why the hell isn't she here? What game are you playing?"

Viktor sighs, running a hand through his hair. "No game, Dmitri. Just a very complicated, very fucked up situation. Ana left to protect you. To protect all of us."

"Protect me?" I scoff. "I don't need protection. I need my wife back."

"You do need protection," Viktor insists, his voice growing stronger. "From Nikolai. From the war he was planning to start."

The mention of Nikolai's name makes my blood boil. "What does that backstabbing bastard have to do with this?"

Viktor takes a deep breath. "Everything. He threatened to kill you if Ana didn't leave. She thought by disappearing, she could keep you safe and prevent a war."

For a moment, I'm stunned into silence. Then the rage comes, white-hot and all-consuming. "And you've known this? You've let me tear this city apart, start wars with other Bratvas, and you said nothing?"

"I made a promise to my sister," Viktor says, standing his ground despite the murderous look in my eyes. "But I can't keep silent anymore. Not when I see what this is doing to both of you." He pauses, his jaw clenching. "Besides, I needed time to secure my position."

That catches my attention. "Your position?"

Viktor nods, his eyes hard. "I'm taking over. Nikolai's lost his mind, and he's lost the respect of our people. I've been gathering support, making sure I have the backing I need to step in without causing a civil war within our ranks."

I study him, reassessing. This isn't just Ana's protective older brother anymore. This is a man making calculated moves in a dangerous game.

"And now?" I ask, my voice low.

"Now, I'm ready," Viktor says, his tone leaving no room for doubt. "I have the support I need. Once Ana is safe and you're done with Nikolai, I'll step in. We can end this war before it begins, Dmitri. But first, we need to get my sister."

Rage burns in my chest. That bastard. I knew he was hiding something. As Viktor speaks, my fingernails dig into my palms, drawing blood. In my mind, I'm already wrapping my hands around Nikolai's neck, watching the life drain from his eyes as he begs for mercy.

He won't get it. Not after what he's done.

"Do you need my help?" Viktor asks as we stride down the hallway. "He'll be expecting you. He'll have men waiting."

I turn, a grim smile on my face. "The more, the merrier. I should have ended him months ago when he first crossed me. When he betrayed my father's memory. This time, I'll make an example of him. One that no one in our world will ever forget."

I storm out of my office, Viktor's revelation fueling my rage. On the way to Nikolai's office, I alert my men, ordering them to scope out the place for traps. As much as I'd like to put a bullet through Petrov's head myself, I won't risk any casualties.

The drive is a blur of adrenaline and fury. I race down the highway, weaving through traffic, my knuckles white on the steering wheel. Every second feels like an eternity, but finally, I screech to a halt outside Nikolai's building.

As I stride toward the entrance, I spot a cop, his gun visible in his waistband. He doesn't approach.

Smart man.

"Cocky bastard," I mutter. If Nikolai thinks being in a public place will save him, he's sorely mistaken. My influence reaches far beyond his petty attempts at protection.

I BURST into the outer office, making his secretary jump. "H-hi," she stutters.

"Leave," I bark. She doesn't need to be told twice.

Without hesitation, I kick open Nikolai's door. He looks up, a false calm on his face. "Dmitri." He nods, as if we were meeting for afternoon tea.

I refuse to return the courtesy. "You bastard," I snarl, advancing on his desk. "You knew where she was all along. You sent me on a wild goose chase."

Nikolai leans back, unfazed. "I merely reclaimed what was mine. If you disapprove of my methods, well . . . you would have done the same."

His casual demeanor only fuels my rage. I slam my fist on his desk. "How long have you been playing this game? How long have you been treating Ana like a pawn instead of your daughter?"

A flicker of . . . something crosses his face, but it's gone in an instant. "And who's going to believe you, the tyrant? Even if Ana speaks on your behalf, who would listen?"

I'm about to retort when he delivers the killing blow. "You're finished, Dmitri. I'll happily sell you to your enemies, just like I did your father."

The world stops. My ears ring as if a bomb has gone off. "What did you just say?"

Nikolai's smirk widens. "You heard me. Your father's death? That was my handiwork."

Something inside me snaps. With a roar of liquid fury, I vault over the desk, grabbing Nikolai by his shirt and slamming him against the wall. "You son of a bitch! He trusted you!"

For the first time, fear flickers in Nikolai's eyes. Good. He should be terrified.

"He would've done the same," Nikolai gasps. "We're all thieves!"

I shake him violently, years of pain and grief surging to the surface. "He was your best friend!"

My fist draws back, every fiber of my being screaming for vengeance. But a small voice in the back of my mind stops me. This isn't what Ana would want. This isn't who I am anymore.

With monumental effort, I release Nikolai, shoving him away. "I planned to kill you myself," I growl. "But death would be too merciful for you."

Nikolai straightens his shirt, his composure returning. "Then you're a bigger fool than I thought, Dmitri."

A soft click echoes through the room. I turn to see a hidden door sliding open, revealing a man with a gun trained on my head.

Nikolai's laugh is cold and triumphant. "Did you really think I'd face you without insurance? It's over, Dmitri. You've lost."

But as I stare down the barrel of the gun, a calm settles over me. Nikolai thinks he's won, but he's forgotten one crucial detail.

I'm Dmitri Orlov.

I always have a plan B.

Nikolai steps forward, his lips spreading into a smug

grin that makes my blood boil. "Why do you think I didn't order you killed on sight, Orlov? This moment, right here, is what I've been waiting for."

He circles me like a shark, his confidence palpable. "I'm going to end you myself. And thanks to your dramatic entrance, I can claim self-defense. Poetic, isn't it?"

My hand instinctively moves to the gun tucked in my waistband. Nikolai notices, wagging his finger like he's scolding a child.

"Ah, ah, ah. The second that gun comes out, my friend here will put a bullet through your skull. Let's keep things civil, shall we?"

"Civil?" I spit the word. "You want to gloat first, is that it?"

He shrugs, spreading his arms wide. "Why not? It's not every day you get to end a bloodline. Especially one as... troublesome as yours."

As I stare at Nikolai, all I see is a man drunk on his own power, bloated with overconfidence. Even with his gunman and his secret doors, he should know better than to think everything will go according to plan.

I take a careful step to the right. The gunman mirrors my movement, his weapon now inches from my head.

"Any last words, Nikolai?" I ask, injecting as much boredom into my voice as I can muster. "A message for your daughter, perhaps? I'd be happy to pass it along."

He laughs, the sound grating on my nerves. "Look at you, still so cocky. You think because you outsmarted that Italian fool and manipulated Pavlov, I'll be an easy mark? You've got a lot to learn, boy."

I shrug, mildly impressed that he knows about my plans for Igor. "You've clearly been busy. But humor me. Why wait all this time? You've had plenty of chances to take me out. Hell, you could've had one of your goons run me off the road any day of the week. Why the elaborate setup?"

Nikolai's eyes gleam with malice. "Because I wanted to savor this moment. I wanted to see the realization in your eyes when you finally understood that you've lost. That everything you've built is about to crumble."

As he rambles on, something catches my eye. There's a building nearby, tall enough to have a clear shot into this office. And on its roof, I spot a figure.

I get the signal and cut Nikolai off mid-gloat. "Hey, Nikolai. Quick question—what kind of animal can both swim and fly?"

He blinks, thrown off by the non sequitur. "What?"

I smirk, raising my hand with four fingers extended. "Let me spell it out for you. D-U-C-K."

The last letter is punctuated by the sound of shattering glass as a sniper's bullet finds its mark in Nikolai's chest. I drop to the floor, but I'm a split second too late. Nikolai's gunman manages to get off a shot that grazes my shoulder, sending a bolt of white-hot pain through my body.

Gritting my teeth against the pain, I draw my weapon and fire in one fluid motion. My bullet tears through the gunman's hand, sending his weapon flying across the room. Not taking any chances, I empty my clip into him, each shot echoing in the suddenly silent office.

The gunman crumples to the floor, no longer a threat. I struggle to my feet, my injured shoulder protesting every movement, and survey the scene. Nikolai lies motionless, taken out by my sniper's precision. His henchman is a bloody heap by the hidden door.

When the echo of gunfire fades, I make my way to Nikolai's body, staring down at the man who caused so much pain.

"Too bad," I mutter, a mix of emotions swirling inside me. "I would've loved to see the light leave your eyes."

I glance around the office, wondering if there are security cameras. If so, the footage will make for interesting viewing later.

But that's a concern for my team. Right now, there's only one person on my mind. One woman I need to see more than anything.

It's time to bring Ana home.

THIRTY-SEVEN
ANA

The knock on my door jolts me awake. For a moment, I'm disoriented, unsure how long I've been napping. These days, exhaustion is my constant companion.

It must be Viktor, I think, my stomach knotting with dread. He's probably here to tell me my time's up, that I need to make a decision. I've been dreading this moment, putting it off as long as I can.

I sigh heavily, my feet dragging as I make my way to the door. What am I supposed to tell him? That I still don't have an answer? That I'm torn between protecting everyone and following my heart? That I miss Dmitri so much it feels like a physical ache, a constant hollowness in my chest that nothing can fill?

My hand hesitates on the doorknob. Maybe if I'm quiet, Viktor will think I'm not home. But no, that's just delaying the inevitable. I take a deep breath, steeling myself for the conversation to come.

"Viktor, I—" The words die in my throat as I open the door.

It's not Viktor.

It's Dmitri.

Standing right there, in the flesh, looking at me with those intense eyes I've dreamed about every night since I left.

I blink hard, certain I must be hallucinating. This morning, I could have sworn I saw him sleeping beside me, but when I reached out, the bed was empty.

Just another cruel trick of my desperate mind.

But this... this feels different. More solid. More real.

I shake my head, trying to clear it. "This can't be real," I whisper, more to myself than to him. "You can't be here."

"Anastasia," he says, so softly it brings tears to my eyes.

Then he's holding me, and I'm engulfed in his warmth, his strength. My hands roam his body, needing to make sure I'm not dreaming.

"Oh my God," I choke out, touching his face. "It's you. It's really you, Dmitri."

"*Kotyonok*," he whispers, and then we're kissing. I pour everything into it—my fear, my longing, my love.

As I break down in his arms, he covers my face with kisses, wiping away my tears. He doesn't need to say anything. Him being here is enough.

"My love," he murmurs, "I thought I was a dead man without you."

I want to tell him how sorry I am, how I wasn't really living either, but suddenly, panic grips me. "Dmitri, you can't be here. My father threatened to kill you if I came back. He'll start a war. I can't let that happen. I can't lose you."

My mind races. How did Dmitri find me? Did Viktor crack under pressure and tell him? Or worse, did my father somehow set this up as a trap?

"We have to leave," I insist, pushing away from him

even as every fiber of my being screams to hold on tighter. "It's not safe. My father—"

The room starts to spin, black spots dancing in my vision. The stress, the lack of sleep, the shock of seeing Dmitri—it's all too much. My knees buckle, and I feel myself falling.

"Ana!" Dmitri's voice sounds far away as everything fades to black.

When I come to, I'm in an unfamiliar bed. For a moment, panic sets in. Where am I? Did my father's men find us? Then I hear Dmitri's voice, low and soothing, guiding me back to reality.

I blink awake, disoriented and panicked. "Dmitri, we have to go! My father—"

"Shh, *kotyonok*," Dmitri soothes, his hand warm on mine. "Everything's alright now."

I shake my head frantically. "No, you don't understand. He'll hurt you. How did you even find me?"

Dmitri's eyes darken. "Viktor told me everything."

"Everything?" I whisper.

He nods, jaw clenching. "About your father's threats. The ultimatum he gave you."

I close my eyes, shame washing over me. "I'm so sorry, Dmitri. I thought I was protecting you, but—"

"Hey," he cuts me off gently, cupping my face. "You have nothing to apologize for."

As I lean into his touch, I notice a bandage peeking out from his shirt. "You're hurt," I gasp. "What happened?"

Dmitri hesitates, conflict clear in his eyes. "Ana, there's something you need to know."

My heart races as he recounts his confrontation with my father. The threats, the hidden gunman, the sniper. By the time he finishes, I'm numb with shock.

"Papa's . . . dead?" I whisper.

Dmitri nods solemnly. "I'm sorry, Ana. I never wanted it to come to this."

I don't know how to feel. The man who raised me, who I once adored, who then used me as a pawn, is gone. Part of me wants to grieve, while another part feels relief.

"I don't know what to say," I admit, my voice small.

Dmitri pulls me close, his warmth anchoring me. "You don't have to say anything. Just know that I'm here, and I love you. We'll get through this together."

As I bury my face in his chest, letting his steady heartbeat calm me, I realize that for the first time in weeks, I feel safe. The war I feared has been averted, but at what cost?

I don't have the answers, but wrapped in Dmitri's arms, I know we'll face whatever comes next together.

Dmitri holds me close, murmuring comforting words. I let him, even as I try to push down the complicated mess of emotions threatening to overwhelm me.

I won't mourn the man who put us through all this. Nikolai Petrov might have been my father, but in the end, he only cared about himself.

Still, a small part of me, the little girl who once thought her daddy hung the moon, weeps silently.

I sigh deeply, feeling the weight of everything bearing down on my shoulders. It's been a wild ride, from our tumultuous wedding to those first confusing months, wondering if Dmitri hated or liked me, all while fighting that undeniable chemistry between us.

And then, finding out—

Wait.

My heart starts racing, panic rising in my chest like a tidal wave. How could I have forgotten, even for a moment?

"The baby," I gasp, my hands flying to my stomach protectively. "Oh my God, Dmitri, the baby!"

His eyes widen, and I realize with a jolt that I never told him. Guilt crashes over me, mixing with the fear and panic already churning inside.

"I—" I swallow hard, trying to find the right words. "I found out I was pregnant the night before I left. I'm three months along now." My voice breaks as tears well up in my eyes. "I'm so sorry I kept this from you. I wanted to tell you, but then everything happened, and—"

To my surprise, Dmitri gathers me close, his strong arms enveloping me in a comforting embrace. "I know, my love," he murmurs, his voice thick with emotion. "The doctors did a blood test when you were brought in and then checked the baby. They are just fine."

Relief washes over me in waves so powerful I start to tremble. "You knew? And . . . and the baby's okay?"

He nods, pressing a kiss to my hair. "Our baby is perfect, *kotyonok*. Strong and healthy, just like its mother."

I break down then, all the fear and worry of the past months pouring out of me. "I'm so sorry," I hiccup against his chest. "I should have told you sooner. I was so scared, and I didn't know what to do, and—"

"Shh," Dmitri soothes, his big hand rubbing circles on my back. "It's okay. I'm here now. We're all going to be okay."

I pull back slightly, searching his face. "You're not... angry? About the baby, about me not telling you?"

His eyes soften, a smile tugging at his lips. "Angry? Ana, finding out about our child is the most incredible news. I just wish I could have been there for you from the start."

Fresh tears spill down my cheeks, but this time, they're

tears of joy. "We're really doing this?" I whisper. "We're going to be parents?"

Dmitri's hand joins mine on my stomach, and the tenderness in his touch nearly undoes me. "We are," he says, his voice full of wonder. "And I promise you, Anastasia, I will love and protect both of you with everything I have."

For the first time in close to a month, after repeating empty reassurances to myself night after night, I finally believe that everything will be okay. Here, in Dmitri's arms, with our baby growing inside me, I feel safe. I feel loved.

I feel like I'm finally home.

EPILOGUE
DMITRI

Two months later

"You know," Ana says as she picks a slice of watermelon from the fruit plate beside her, both of us lying on the deck of my yacht, watching the ocean as the vessel drifts, "I think I should go ahead and buy myself a jet."

Not knowing where the sudden desire is coming from but used to her saying random things out of the blue—*I think it's a pregnancy thing*—I go with the safest response.

"Of course. Which and when?"

She turns to me, a smile blossoming on her lips and her face positively radiant. It's hard to believe she's the same Ana I saw when she opened the door two months ago.

The doctor said rest, exercise, and sleep would bring the color back to her cheeks.

And I might be biased, but I think she's more gorgeous too. Lying down on the deck chair with the small bump, her body gleaming from oil and sunscreen, and the little sun hat over her head, Anastasia Orlov looks like a dream come true.

"You are a sweet man, Dmitri, and you spoil me silly. I might run out of space for my bags pretty soon."

I shrug, popping a cherry into my mouth. "Then we'll just make more room. I'll have Idrina do more shopping for you if you'd like."

"I'm good," she says, waving her hand around. "If you indulge me further, I might get too greedy."

"*Kotyonok,*" I drawl, getting up from my reclining chair and kissing her cheek, "there's nothing like greed when it comes to you and me. You ask, I give."

She grins, and her hands pull me lower. I smile as I kiss her softly, caressing her cheek with my thumb and rubbing the baby bump with the other. When her hand goes to my shorts, tugging on the ties, I pull away.

"You heard what the doctor said," I admonish.

"He said that I should get enough rest."

"And avoid stress," I point out.

Ana pouts. "Are you saying that making love to your wife and the mother of your baby is stressful? Am I stressing you?"

I chuckle, shaking my head in amusement at how she decided to turn the tables. "You are one crafty woman."

She shrugs with a twinkle in her eyes. "I try. So," her hand finds its way to my cock again, "are you going to indulge me, or do I have to drag myself off this chair and put the moves on you?"

My guilty pleasure? I like it when she gets mouthy.

But I also like to show her who's in charge, which is what I do when I kiss her again. I gently brush against her mouth first, coaxing and teasing, pulling away when she gets too impatient, and then going back in with a nip to her bottom lip.

"You have a smart mouth, *kotyonok,*" I murmur, "and I

love when you moan my name with it, my dick inside you and your pussy clenching tight."

My hands cradle her head, providing a touch of delicacy, but my lips devour, sinking into her. I thrust my tongue past her lips, and she moans, grabbing fistfuls of my hair.

In seconds, I have the straps of her bikini top undone, and I drag my lips down her throat, pouring kisses and tiny bites, soothed with my mouth sucking on her skin.

She rolls her hips, running her fingernails over my back. When my mouth closes over her nipple, she gasps and sinks her fingers back into my hair, pushing my head low.

"Fuck me," Ana purrs, trembling from my touch.

"Soon, *kotyonok*," I whisper as I make my way down her body, kissing every inch of her skin and lingering on her stomach.

Sometimes, I can't believe that there's a life there, a baby that's a product of *us*. It's unbelievable and humbling at the same time.

Her bottoms come off easily, and I guide myself between her thighs, touching her with my middle finger. She rocks her hips against my hand as I glide across her pussy, gently rubbing her clit.

"Dmitri," she moans, and I slide my finger in. Then another.

"*Fuck*," she pants as my fingers rub against her spot, thrusting in fast and hard while pleasuring her thoroughly.

My dick jerks in my shorts, straining against the inelastic fabric, begging to be buried inside her warmth and covered in her wetness.

"Fuck me," she begs. "Please. I need you."

I yank down my shorts, positioning myself with my tip at her entrance. I pause just before, though, leaning down and kissing her again. "Let me know if you feel uncomfortable," I say. "I don't want to hurt you."

"You won't," Ana replies.

Fucking hell.

I grunt harshly as I thrust in, and she gasps loudly, clinging to the edges of the chair. My hands sit possessively on Ana's hips as I slide in and out, slowly at first, watching her body's response.

"It's fine," she whispers, taking my hand and placing it on her stomach. "I want you, Dmitri."

I give in to her, pounding in hard and deep, the sound of my thighs against her ass fading with the seagulls' cries. It doesn't matter, though—it's just us, two people obsessed with each other, and maybe with an unhealthy number of cravings.

"You feel so good," I groan as need overwhelms me, and her heat makes me almost explode. "So fucking good."

I need to see her, the look on her face when she falls apart. And I want to feel her squeeze me until I'm lost in nothing but total bliss.

"I'm close," Ana cries, and I reach down, interlocking our fingers and still fucking her deep and hard as she climaxes, a soft scream slipping through her lips and echoing around us.

I grunt as I come, shutting my eyes as it overtakes me for a moment, stretching into infinity, then bliss.

Afterward, I hold Ana in my arms, relaxing on the plush couch in the cabin, stroking her hair. We sit in silence for a while until she tilts her head and looks at me.

"Now that my father is dead and Viktor has taken over, will you work with him? He's a good man."

I know she's put much thought into this question because I've also been thinking about the same thing. "My grudge wasn't with your family, Ana. It was with your father. If Viktor proves he's not another Nikolai, then I see no reason we can't be allies."

"Really?"

I nod, kissing her forehead. "I'll meet him when he returns from his trip."

She sighs and moves to lay on the couch with her head on my lap. I comb through her hair, working on the roots the way she likes. Marriage to Ana has made me a well-adjusted man—I know when to be soft and when not.

I'm mostly soft toward her, though. I keep thinking about how Nikolai made her believe that he loved her when he was just playing her, and I don't want Ana to ever feel that way again.

I need her to know that I would do anything—massage her swollen feet after a day at the office, and also burn the world—for her sake.

"Our wedding anniversary is coming up soon," she says as she touches my cheek fondly. "What are we going to do about it?"

I make a humming noise in my throat. "Mm. How about we get married again, and we'll go on a honeymoon this time?"

She sits up abruptly, her eyes wide like pretty saucers. "Another wedding?"

Linking my fingers with hers, I bring her hand to my lips and place a kiss. "The first time, I could tell that you weren't happy. I want the memory of our wedding to be something you'll look back on without regrets. And," I shrug, "I need an excuse to steal you from work for six months while I take you around the world."

She laughs and swats my chest playfully. "You're not stealing me from anything. I'd go anywhere with you. But," she purses her lips, "if we're going to be on a honeymoon for six months, it means the baby is going to be born somewhere else."

"Pick a country, then," I say. "Or an island. I could buy the place, and we'll name it after the baby."

Ana's eyes sparkle as she laughs some more, subconsciously touching her stomach. I smile, too, infected by the happiness radiating from her. "We're not buying an island," she says. "That's too expensive."

"You don't understand, *lyubov moya*. Nothing is too expensive when it comes to your happiness." I brush my thumbs gently over her fingers. "If you wanted the moon, I'd find a way to give it to you."

Her laughter fades as she sees the serious intent in my eyes. "Dmitri, I . . . you don't have to do that. As long as we're together, that's all that matters."

Cupping her cheek, I lean in till our foreheads touch. "You and our baby are my entire world. I want to give you everything your heart desires."

Our noses brush in a gentle kiss. Ana's breath hitches, and I take the chance to capture her lips again. She melts against me with a sigh of contentment.

"You've already given me more than I ever dreamed possible," she whispers. "I'm a lucky woman."

I'd argue that, but I know she'll have a ready comeback.

It's the truth, though. I'm the one who's lucky to have married a stunning, amazing woman like Anastasia Orlov, and no matter what it takes or what I have to do, I'll make sure the smile on her face never fades away.

THE END

ALSO BY A J SUMMERS

Did you like this book?

Then you'll love Ruthless Mafia King, an age gap brother's best friend romance.

Life as a mafia princess is full of unexpected plot twists.

One day, I'm scouting for new bands in downtown clubs, living the life of the rich and the beautiful.

The next, I'm sold to a Russian mobster to pay for my brother's screw-up.

It's just another Tuesday with Mercury in retrograde.

Cue Nikolai Volkov. A devil in Armani with a body built for sin.

Protective. Ruthless. Magnetic.

Oh, and did I mention he's hot enough to melt Siberia?

I should despise him for stealing my freedom. Instead, I'm playing house with the beast and melting every time he growls 'mine'.

But as it turns out, this good girl has a knack for taming monsters.

Only that now, it looks like I'll be trading club-hopping for baby-shopping.

I'm pregnant.

START READING RUTHLESS MAFIA KING

RUTHLESS MAFIA KING
CHAPTER 1

My fingers fumble with the knot on my tie as I make sure that I'm presentable for the unexpected visit. It's not every day that the powerful and feared *pakhan* comes to my office. In fact, it has only happened once before when he signed a contract agreeing to buy oil and weapons exclusively from my company. Since then, I continued expanding the scope of my business. My firm supplies goods to various groups around the globe, but this man is my biggest client, and his business counts for more than half of what my company sells.

My secretary discreetly knocks on the door. I drop my hands and lift my chin.

"Come in," I call out.

The door swings open, and Dimitri Sokolov struts in, flanked by two of his sons, who also serve as his bodyguards.

I stand up behind my desk and run my palm over the dark fabric covering my chest, smoothing out invisible wrinkles. A small smile sneaks onto the corner of my mouth as I make brief eye contact with Igor, the middleman in charge of making sure our partnership runs smoothly. A womanizer in his late twenties, Igor resents seeing me enjoying a degree of power that he won't achieve while his father is alive.

"Mr. Sokolov," I greet, stretching out my hand to shake his. "To what do I owe this pleasure?"

"Come on, Nik. Why do you have to be so damn formal?" He laughs, grabbing my hand.

"Because people wouldn't respect me if I behaved any other way," I reply, waving to the seats around my desk. "Let's make it easy for everyone." I push a button, and the door behind him opens.

My secretary peeps inside. "Sir?"

"Coffee and a bottle of vodka," I order.

"Right away, Mr. Volkov."

Dimitri sits in the middle chair while his sons take one on each side. I wait for him to speak. Dimitri's mind always works at high speed. His eyes trail over the small details, taking in everything from the large windows to the black executive desk and my six monitors displaying multiple live feeds.

"We've been working together for years," he starts, examining his black and gold cufflinks with an engraved letter S. They undoubtedly cost more than my secretary's weekly salary. "And my respect for you has only grown. That's why I decided to share with you a piece of information that has been kept a secret."

I squint slightly, and my hands pull into tight fists, wondering what his true motive might be.

"Consider it a display of trust," he adds.

My eyes move back and forth across his face, anticipating his next words.

Dimitri takes a deep breath before he speaks, the only

indication of his nerves. "We've found ourselves in a bit of a pickle, out of which we could use your help."

An internal sigh of relief escapes my lungs, but still, my hands stay fisted under my chin.

I expect Dimitri's following words to be a warning. He doesn't know that nothing coming out of his mouth holds the power to scare me.

"Igor here," Dimitri continues, glancing at his son, who wisely avoids his father's gaze, "couldn't keep his worthless dick in his pants. He somehow managed to wiggle his way into Gargarin's daughter's bed."

A knot tightens in my throat as my jaw slacks, eyes snapping to meet with Igor's before shooting to Dimitri, then to his other son, Aleksander, and back to Igor.

My brows are shooting up at the same time as I ask with utter shock, "You slept with your rival's daughter?"

"Well," Igor drawls, giving me a cheeky grin and a cocky shrug, "I didn't know she belonged to that pig. She's much prettier than him."

No matter how idiotic his son has acted, it isn't exactly out of the ordinary. Scandal-free families are a rarity in a business as demanding as ours. Despite their money, they can't live on a far-away island and never see anyone but close relatives. It's basically an impossible dream, and although annoying and dangerous, these kinds of affairs are accepted by the Bratva community.

"Obviously, Gargarin wants him dead now," Dimitri continues. I brace myself, expecting that he'll finally reveal to me the reason for his visit. "We need more guns. To protect ourselves."

"And because I control the weapons in this town, you've decided to come see me," I conclude out loud.

Dimitri draws closer and lays his arms on the table, shrugging. "You've said so yourself."

Of course, I wouldn't outright accept, but as his words sink into my mind, I shift my weight to the back of my chair, folding my arms across my chest. "I'll offer you a deal."

This takes him by surprise if the slight shift in his posture and the frown on his forehead are anything to go by.

"I have to warn you, though," I say in a low voice. "It's going to cost you."

Dimitri straightens his back and waves a dismissive hand. "Name it. It won't be an issue."

"Very well," I declare in a short voice, a small smile slowly sneaking onto the corners of my lips. "I'll give you access to all the weapons you need, and in return, you'll give me your daughter's hand in marriage."

Pure shock flickers in his eyes, and I can almost hear Igor and Aleksander's brains spinning, desperately searching for a way out.

Not receiving an answer, I continue, "No one can protect her like I can. Hell, if you reject my offer, you'll all be dead within a week. Once she agrees to become my wife, our union will guarantee the cooperation of both parties."

"Volkov," Dimitri starts, searching for the proper words. The man's got it all, but whether his fortune will last depends on his answer.

Still, his eagerness to buy so many weapons is an indication that his reign as the *pakhan* is not as safe as he'd like it to be.

My hands drop to my thighs and my legs spread under the desk as I lean closer to him. "Let's be honest for a moment. No one wants to fight you. You've worked hard to conquer New York City, but to survive, sometimes compromises have to be made."

He gives me a long stare, one in which I catch a glimpse of the uncertainty that gnaws at him.

I nod toward his son. "You shouldn't have to die for him."

"This isn't right," Igor challenges me, his voice barely above a whisper, but Dimitri throws him a warning glance, and he immediately clamps his mouth shut.

Aleksander reaches for his brother's shoulder, trying to calm him, but Igor's reaction makes perfect sense. Never before has someone dared to make such a brazen demand from the Sokolov family.

"What will it be, Mr. Sokolov?" I provoke, twisting my lips into a forced smile.

He places both his arms back on the table and leans closer. "Do you think you've impressed me with the way you've built your life, son?" He shakes his head dismissively.

"Like everyone before you, I've worked hard and made sacrifices."

His voice drops lower as he points one of his thick fingers at my face. "No one lives forever."

"And you'll be the first one to attest to that," I grumble as my fist aches to slam against my desk. But I hold back. He still hasn't declined my offer. I decide to push and put another nail in his coffin.

"Or, perhaps, I should contact Gargarin and see what he's willing to offer me for a shipment of guns." I smirk, forcing his hand.

I've had my eye on his daughter for a while now, biding my time ever since I first saw her. And now is finally the time to get what I want.

Dimitri's eyes burn with anger, but he's realizing he has no other options. I don't need him to say the words to know that I've won. I get to my feet and put my hand out for him to take. Dimitri's deep blue orbs watch mine warily as he pushes himself to his feet and, with a stiff posture, grabs my hand.

"We have a deal then," I conclude as we shake. "Will you tell her, or should I?"

CONTINUE READING NIKOLAI AND KATARINA'S STORY

Printed in Great Britain
by Amazon